Bloodchild

OTHER BOOKS BY Tim Bowler

Tim Bowler
Bloodchild

OXFORD
UNIVERSITY PRESS

OXFORD
UNIVERSITY PRESS

Great Clarendon Street, Oxford OX2 6DP

Oxford University Press is a department of the University of Oxford.
It furthers the University's objective of excellence in research, scholarship,
and education by publishing worldwide in

Oxford   New York

Auckland   Cape Town   Dar es Salaam   Hong Kong   Karachi
Kuala Lumpur   Madrid   Melbourne   Mexico City   Nairobi
New Delhi   Shanghai   Taipei   Toronto

With offices in

Argentina   Austria   Brazil   Chile   Czech Republic   France   Greece
Guatemala   Hungary   Italy   Japan   Poland   Portugal   Singapore
South Korea   Switzerland   Thailand   Turkey   Ukraine   Vietnam

Oxford is a registered trade mark of Oxford University Press
in the UK and in certain other countries

British Library Cataloguing in Publication Data

Data available

ISBN: 978-0-19-271980-5

1 3 5 7 9 10 8 6 4 2

Printed in Great Britain by Mackays of Chatham plc, Chatham, Kent
Paper used in the production of this book is a natural,
recyclable product made from wood grown in sustainable forests.
The manufacturing process conforms to the environmental
regulations of the country of origin.

For Liz

Sleep, sleep, happy child,
All creation slept and smil'd;
Sleep, sleep, happy sleep,
While o'er thee thy mother weep.

WILLIAM BLAKE

1

His first impression was a grey light, the absence of pain, and a certainty that he was dead. A pause; a shift from grey to gold, from the absence of pain to the presence of something else; and with that . . . doubt.

This was not death. Yet nor was it life. It was something he didn't recognize, and the presence he'd sensed was now a form, a clearly solid form in this most unsolid place.

Another pause. Who or what it was that paused, he didn't know—himself or this form, perhaps both. He had a feeling it was aware of him. More light, a deeper gold: not pleasant or unpleasant, just gold.

Then a voice.

'It's a boy about fifteen.'

He felt a flicker of recollection, not of the voice—he had no idea who this was, except that it was a girl— but of himself. A boy about fifteen. Somehow he'd forgotten that. But he had no time to ponder this. The girl was speaking again.

'I can't find a pulse.'

There was something in her voice that he liked: a musical quality. It took him a moment to realize that he was more struck with this than with the sudden realization that his first conviction was right: he must be dead after all.

Another pause, and now he understood. She was speaking on a phone. The pauses were when she listened to the other person.

'Yes,' she said. 'I've turned him on his side.'

Still the musical voice. He wondered who she was, what she looked like, how old she was. Maybe she was a female equivalent of him: a girl about fifteen. She sounded about that age. Not that it mattered. He was dead anyway.

She was saying something about a tree.

'The sycamore tree. You can't miss it. It's by the turning to Havensmouth.' Silence, then, 'No, I didn't manage it.'

Manage what? he wondered, but she quickly answered this.

'I tried. I did mouth to mouth and pumped his chest but nothing worked.'

Silence again. He listened to it, aware of the girl close by, though all he saw in this golden sea was her shadow floating upon it. There was nothing human about it at all, just the trace of her voice, which hung strangely over it. Then he caught a new sound, somewhere above him.

Birdsong.

One bird, as far as he could tell, but a virtuoso singer. It rippled through its song and he listened, confusion cascading through him. Somewhere he sensed memories flooding, too, but they were memories without definition: words and pictures that moved too fast. He clung to the song of the bird.

Bird, he told himself. The girl spoke.

'Can you hear it?'

He wished she'd stop talking on that wretched phone.

2

'Can you hear it?'

A change in the voice, a new direction. She was speaking to him.

'You said, "Bird". Can you hear it?'

He listened to the song, aware of the movement of gold, the clearing of the haze, the sudden heaviness within himself. He peered through the shifting light, searching for the strange form, and there it was—something of a paradox: dark and bright at the same time, more a ghost than a girl.

'Can you see me?' she said.

But he'd lost her. She was enveloped in gold once more. She spoke again.

'He's alive. I heard him say something.'

The phone again.

'I definitely heard him,' she said.

A long silence this time. Even the bird was quiet. He tried to think, tried to understand, but there was nothing in his mind that made sense. A girl about fifteen, he told himself. A girl about fifteen.

'He's doing it again,' she said suddenly. 'I heard him. He said something about a girl. Like he's talking to someone.'

But this only filled him with more confusion. He hadn't heard himself speak, hadn't felt his mouth move, hadn't felt—couldn't feel—any part of him move. As far as he was concerned, he was a thought, nothing more. A memory of a boy. The only human voice he'd heard so far was the girl's, and here it was again.

'He definitely said something about a girl.' Another pause, then, 'No, still no pulse. I've been checking all the time I've been on the phone.'

No, you haven't, he thought. I'd have felt you.

'There!' said the girl. 'He just spoke again. I heard him. He said, "No, you haven't". He's trying to communicate.' Another change in the direction of the voice and he knew she was speaking to him again. 'Can you hear me?'

Yes, yes, he thought, and this time he heard his own words, 'Yes, yes.'

'I knew you could.' Still the musical voice. 'Can you feel this?'

Something warm, something soft.

'Hand,' he muttered.

'Yes. My hand round your wrist. Try and open your eyes.'

He'd thought they were open, but no, she was right. He must have closed them without remembering it. He opened them again. Gold broke upon him still, shadows merging on shadows, and here was the girl's form again, or some part of it. He still couldn't make out her face or features, just the spectral shape of her as she leaned over him.

But now his other senses were starting to work. He could feel warm air brushing his skin, dusk falling over him. He could see the outline of a tree, hear the sound of the bird high up. He felt a rush of excitement. He was going to live. He was going to pull through.

Then everything changed.

First the pain. It tore through him like a racing tide, scattering thought, hope, feeling; then the darkness, snuffing out what was left. He heard the girl screaming into the phone.

'Quick! I'm losing him again!'

More pain, more darkness, more screams from the girl.

4

'What do I do? What do I do?'

But there was nothing she could do. He knew that. More pain—harsh, relentless spasms that seemed to reach every part of him—then suddenly they ceased, and he felt a new sensation: a queasy tremor deep inside him.

He resisted, sensing what was coming, but it was no good. He had no power left to fight. Another tremor. Some part of him was moving and it wasn't his body. He hated this feeling. It was almost worse than the pain. He tried again to resist.

It made no difference. The movement continued, quickened. He was slipping through darkness now, aware only of sounds: the weeping of the girl, the song of the bird, the roar of an engine somewhere far away, but growing louder, louder; then the girl's voice again. It was urgent and close, and he knew she was speaking to him.

'I'm sorry.' She was almost whimpering. 'I'm sorry, I'm sorry.'

He wanted to answer, say something, anything, but no words would come and there were no more from her. All he heard now was the bird, and the engine, and then . . . men's voices.

'Christ, he's got no pulse.'

'Where's the girl?'

'No idea. Must have legged it.'

'I'll get the gear.'

Again he tried to speak; again nothing would come. The voices were fading already. He heard them a few moments longer, then they were gone. So too was the sound of the bird, the engine, everything. He was floating through a world he could neither hear nor see.

Then something appeared in the darkness.

A flicker of light, as though a curtain had been drawn back, and suddenly there was the lane below him, the tree, the bird up at the top—a dumpy song-thrush—and far down at the base of the tree an ambulance, and two men bending over a body.

His.

But already he was moving from them, up, up, up, and darkness was closing round again, not the darkness he'd felt before but a deep, ocean blue. He stared into it. For all its beauty, he knew he had to resist. But as before, it was no good. The ocean sucked him in.

This time he did not try to fight. He knew there was no point. All he could do was cling to what memory of himself was left—a boy about fifteen, a boy about fifteen—and for a while the image swam with him. Then that faded, and the colours changed again.

A darker blue, then black, then a misty redness, and with that the disappearance of everything except fear. Cumbrous forms squeezed through the murk. He had no idea what they were. He tried to scream at them but no sound came. The forms stiffened into shapes, the shapes into shadows, the shadows into faces.

Too many to count. They pressed close: hideous, distorted things, staring at him through hollow eyes. He flailed about him, tried to thrust them away. They pushed forward, smothering, then again everything changed.

A turbulence of pain, a tug, a shake, and he was streaming backwards, colours racing over him, red mixed with black, and then blue again—and suddenly he found himself staring into the face of a girl.

A girl about fifteen, black hair and blue eyes that seemed so wide they felt like the ocean itself. He gazed at her, trying to understand who she was. Some part of his mind told him this was not the girl who had phoned the ambulance.

'Who are you?' he felt himself say.

She did not answer. She simply watched, her eyes widening all the time. He hoped she was a friend. She was beautiful but she was scary. He was losing sight of her now. He tried to hold her image but it was no good. She was slipping away, or he was.

Something touched him: something firm, light, insistent. He sensed it came from her, but there was no time to think. He was moving fast now, away from her, and the ocean was swallowing him once more.

Another touch, another, and suddenly he understood. She was fighting for him, trying to pull him back. This time he fought too. He knew where the ocean led and he didn't want to go back.

But he had no power left. He was tearing from her against his will, through the blue, through the black, into the red murk. It closed over him again, suffocating the light. A tunnel opened before him. The shadowfaces pressed round once more.

'Go away,' he muttered. 'Go away.'

They clung to him, gaping.

'Go away,' he begged.

He saw the mouths widen, widen, then heard a scream. It seemed to come from somewhere inside him—yet he knew it was from the girl with blue eyes. But it was not a scream of fear. It was a command.

'Come back!' it said.

He felt a surge of pain that ripped through him and scattered into nothing. The shadowfaces vanished and the tunnel with them, but the murk remained, only now it was a void, a vast, red void, and he was floating in it. Nothing else was left but the sound of a bird singing somewhere far off.

Then that slipped away too.

2

'Will,' said a voice.

The word hung before him. He had no idea what it meant. The darkness closed round it like breath. Another voice spoke.

'Is it my imagination or has his right eye opened a fraction?'

A third voice.

'Black hair, blue eyes.'

'Did you hear that?' The first voice again, louder, closer. 'He said something.'

'I heard it,' came the second voice. 'Will? Can you see us? Can you hear us?'

He tried to think. The voices sounded pleasant but he didn't know them at all. The first was a man, the second a woman. The third voice seemed to have been his own, though he didn't remember speaking. He didn't remember anything . . . except . . .

'Black hair, blue eyes,' he heard himself say.

'Will?' said the man.

What did they keep calling him Will for?

'Black hair, blue eyes,' said the woman. 'That's what he said.'

'He must be talking about one of the nurses,' said the man. 'Pippa probably. He must have opened his eyes and seen her.'

'Pippa?' called the woman.

9

Footsteps, then another woman's voice.

'Has something happened?'

'He spoke,' said the man. 'And he must have opened his eyes at some point. He just described you. Look at his right eye. It's more open than it was, isn't it?'

'I'm not sure about that, Mr Bly.'

'But he did describe you.'

'You definitely heard him?'

'Yes. He said "Black hair, blue eyes". Julie heard him too, didn't you?'

'Yes,' said the other woman. A pause, then, 'Will, can you hear me? It's Mum. And Dad's here too. If you can somehow open your eyes, you'll see us.'

He tried to say something, do something, but nothing seemed to work. All was darkness.

Will.

The name meant nothing to him, just as the name Bly meant nothing to him, and these people. They were obviously friendly, but they weren't Mum and Dad. Mum and Dad were nothing like these two. Mum and Dad were . . .

He felt his mind waver.

Mum and Dad were . . .

But it was no use. Whatever Mum and Dad were, he no longer remembered. He sensed that they existed. But what they were like he did not know. He searched his mind for their faces.

Nothing came.

'We're here, Will,' said the man. 'We're right here beside you. You've had an accident and you've been in a coma, but you're going to be all right. You're going to come through this. And Mum and I are going to help you.'

10

The image came back, the one image he remembered.

Black hair, blue eyes—and now a pale light spreading like a tide.

'He's opening his eyes,' said the man.

And suddenly there they were: the man, the woman, the nurse with black hair and blue eyes. Three faces. Three strangers. They smiled at him.

He didn't know if he smiled back. He wasn't sure of anything right now. He stared at them for a moment, then slowly took in the rest of his surroundings: the walls and ceiling of the hospital ward, the bed, the chairs, the gadgets beeping and winking close by.

The woman called Julie took his hand.

'Will,' she murmured. Her eyes were filling with tears. 'I can't believe you've come back to us.'

The man leaned forward.

'Don't feel you've got to talk, Will. You must be very confused.'

'Just lie quiet if you want,' said the woman.

He stared at them both. They seemed to assume he was called Will, that he knew who he was and who they were. He saw the nurse watching him closely.

'Will,' she said suddenly, 'do you know who this lady and gentleman are?'

'Of course he does,' said the man.

The nurse leaned closer.

'Do you remember your mum and dad? Do you remember who you are? Or anything at all?'

'Black hair, blue eyes,' he said.

The words fell from him without effort. He heard them clearly. The nurse frowned.

'And is that me you're describing? My hair and eyes? Or is it someone else?'

It wasn't the nurse. That much he knew. She glanced round at the other two.

'I don't think it's me, not judging from his expression. Maybe it's someone from the accident, the driver perhaps. Or the girl who rang the ambulance and ran away.'

Girl.

A new image dropped into his mind. There was a girl—no, two girls. There were definitely two girls: the one he'd heard but hadn't seen, the one they must be talking about, and then the other . . .

The beautiful one, the scary one, the girl with black hair and blue eyes.

He looked back at the three faces. The woman called Julie was still crying. He felt a sudden desire to give her something. He squeezed her hand.

'Will,' she said.

She kissed him on the cheek, rested hers against it.

'Easy, Julie,' said the man. 'Don't overwhelm him.'

The woman drew back a little.

'I'll get Doctor Paige,' said the nurse, and left.

'Will,' said the man, 'I know you must be feeling really strange, but . . . can you give us some sign to show us if . . . ' He hesitated. 'If you know who we are?'

'Chris,' said the woman, 'don't ask him that.'

'We've got to know.' The man glanced at her, then back. 'Will? Can you . . . can you show us somehow?'

He felt his head move. The woman gave a gasp.

'Chris!'

'Easy, Julie.'

'He doesn't know us!'

'Julie—'

'He shook his head. He doesn't know who we are.'

12

'Easy, easy.' The man's voice was calm but he seemed unsure what to do. The woman looked away, biting her thumb. The man put a hand on her shoulder but she shrugged it off. He turned back to the bed.

'Will, listen, it's going to be all right, OK? Everything'll come back. It's just a matter of time.'

'Yes!' The woman turned sharply back. 'That's right. It's just . . . ' Her breath was coming in jerky inhalations. 'It's just a matter of time, OK? You'll soon be right again.'

He stared up at them, unsure what to feel. Part of him wanted them to go so that he could think, but another part wanted them to stay. He liked them. They were kind people. He just didn't know them. The woman calmed down a little and stroked his hair.

'It'll come back,' she whispered.

He slanted his gaze from her.

'Black hair, blue eyes,' he murmured.

'Maybe he's talking about the driver,' said the man.

The woman said nothing.

'Will,' said the man, 'don't tire yourself, but when you're ready, when you're feeling strong enough, try to remember anything you can.' He paused. 'Someone ran you over or knocked you down. At least, that's what the police think. No one's quite sure. You've got bruising to the head and back. It seems like it was hit-and-run but we don't know who did it or what happened. So if there's anything you remember . . . you know . . . about the driver maybe. Could that be the person with the black hair and blue eyes?'

'Or was it the girl?' said the woman.

He looked from one to the other, his thoughts as frozen as his words. The man spoke again.

13

'There was a girl, Will, and she probably saved your life. You were lying close to a tree at the junction of the lane to Havensmouth. She used your mobile phone and called the ambulance but she wouldn't give her name, wouldn't say anything about herself. And when the medics got there, she'd vanished. That's why the police want to find her. She might know something about what happened.'

'Chris,' said the woman. 'We're tiring him.'

'Sorry, Will,' said the man. 'I'm not thinking.'

The woman leaned over the bed again.

'You're not ready for all this, are you, sweetheart?'

No, he agreed, he wasn't. Yet even so, their words had forced new images into his mind: lane, phone, tree . . .

There was a tree, yes, a sycamore, and there was something else, something he couldn't place. He tried to conjure pictures from the recent past: the lane, the tree—and then it came. There was a bird, too, and it was singing, and he'd glimpsed it up in the tree, and then everything had gone dark, and he'd seen the girl.

And the shadowfaces.

He heard footsteps down the corridor. The man and the woman looked nervously at each other, then, as if by a shared impulse, leaned quickly forward.

'Will,' said the woman. Her voice was low, almost confidential. 'I know you're confused but . . . we are your mum and dad, and you're Will, and when we get you home, we'll prove it to you. Who you are and who we are.'

'We'll be here for you,' said the man. 'We'll help you trust us again.'

'Because we know you don't,' said the woman.

They were wrong, he thought. He did trust them. He could even imagine loving them one day. He just didn't know who they were. The footsteps grew louder.

'Will?' said the woman. 'Will you do something for us? Will you . . . I mean . . . even if you don't think we're your mum and dad . . . ' She hesitated. 'Will you pretend that we are?'

He looked into their faces and saw the fear there.

'Yes,' he answered.

3

Long days, longer nights. Visits from Mum, Dad, medical staff, police: names and faces that came and went. Conversations of a sort, meandering exchanges without sense or conclusions and mostly silent on his part. Words had flooded back into his mind, but now that they were here again, he found he didn't much care to use them.

Without memory, they seemed pointless.

Not that all memory was gone. He seemed to know plenty of things. He knew what a chair was and a table and a bed. He knew how to wash and eat and tie his laces. But the history of himself was gone. He searched his mind for it—who he was, where he'd come from, what he'd done, who the people in his life were—and found an empty space.

The lack of sleep made things worse. Two or three hours a night seemed the most he could manage and even that was no refuge, as the shadowfaces that had haunted him before now came to him in dreams. His head pounded where the bruising had taken place.

Five days struggled past; six, seven, eight.

'Will?'

He saw Mum's eyes upon him. They seemed pale in spite of the morning sun that caught her face as it broke into the ward.

'It's time, darling,' she said.

He stared at her, then realized with a start that he was dressed and standing by the bed. Somehow he'd forgotten he was going home today. Dad was watching nearby, with three of the nurses just behind him.

'Did your mind drift off again, Will?' he said.

'Yes.'

'Are you sure you're up to this?'

He nodded. He was a thousand times sure. Another night in the hospital would drive him mad. He'd just forgotten himself for a moment—again.

'I'm ready,' he said. He turned to the nurses. 'Thank you.'

Pippa smiled.

'Good luck, Will.'

Awkward goodbyes, then the shuffle down the corridor, out of the hospital and into the car park.

'Here's our car,' said Mum. 'Do you recognize it?'

He shook his head.

'Never mind,' she said. She opened the front passenger door. 'You sit here. I'll go in the back.'

He climbed in, closed the door and sat there, mute. Mum and Dad climbed in too. He looked round at them, aware that they wanted him to talk.

'Thank you,' he said.

His voice sounded as stilted to him as it had done when he'd thanked the nurses, and he knew it wasn't what Mum and Dad wanted; but it was all he could manage right now. Dad clipped on the seat belt and turned to him.

'Will?'

Will looked back at him.

'The belt,' said Mum from behind.

He looked down at it. Another misshapen memory. There were so many now, too many to count, and each day brought new ones: opening things, closing things, switching things on and off.

Processes.

Why did he remember processes but not people, places, the story of who he was? He stared at the seat belt, hating it suddenly. He knew exactly how the thing worked and its familiarity felt obscene when Mum and Dad were still strangers.

Yet they were indeed Mum and Dad. They'd proved that to him. The photos and records and other things they'd brought to the hospital filled a suitcase. They were his parents. Dad was a tutor in Maths, Mum a tutor in English. Both worked from home.

And he was Will.

Or rather William Edward Patrick Bly, as the passport had it. He lived in a house called The Four Winds in a small seaside town called Havensmouth, neither of which he remembered. Perhaps he'd recognize both when he saw them. But he doubted it.

He clipped on the seat belt without a word.

'Well done,' said Dad, and started the engine.

They drove out of the hospital car park and away towards the town. Will stared out of the window at the streets slipping by. This was not Havensmouth, Mum had said. This was another town, a bigger town with a hospital better equipped to deal with coma victims.

But nothing here seemed familiar either. The old Will must have known the place and if that missing person ever came back, no doubt the town would too. But for now it was a foreign country.

A pleasant-looking place, though. Cobbled streets, weathered stone, a church, a market, a sense of relaxed busyness. He tried to remember what the

18

town was called—Mum had told him only yesterday, or was it the day before? But the name would not come. He looked round, searching for a signpost.

'All right, Will?' said Mum from the back.

'Yes,' he said, then, 'Town . . . '

'What's that, darling?'

'What's . . . the name of . . . the town?'

'Newton Barnet,' she said. 'Remember? I told you the other day.'

'Yes.'

'They brought you to Newton Barnet because of the hospital facilities.'

He said nothing. Mum touched him on the shoulder.

'Give it time, Will.'

They drove through the town and out the other side. He looked about him again, anxious to find something he recognized. But still it felt like a foreign country: no buildings now but a long hill rising, the road narrowing, conifers on either side, and then gradually the ground flattened out, the trees thinned and a plain opened before them.

He gazed at it as they hummed along: a vast stretch of open ground, green and grassy, rolling vistas to the left and far away to the right a sense of blue rising from the land and merging with the sky. Dad nodded towards it.

'The sea's that way,' he said.

Will stared.

The sea. He tried to picture it in his mind. The word 'sea' was clear but their sea, his sea, he could not envisage. Other sea was easy to imagine, though whenever he thought of it now, he thought of the girl's face.

Perhaps it was the blue of her eyes. He didn't know. She seemed so close sometimes, though he couldn't see her. Even when the shadowfaces came in dreams, he felt her there; and there was another thing he now remembered.

She had called him back from death.

The countryside was still rushing past: fields, meadows, walls, fences, farms here and there but otherwise an ocean of green. A junction appeared with a sign pointing right and the words: 'Havensmouth 7 miles'.

Dad glanced at him as he turned down it.

'It wasn't this junction, Will. Where you had your accident, I mean.'

'I know.'

'You do?'

'Yes.'

'Is that because you've got a picture in your head of the place where it happened? I thought you didn't. I thought everything was blank.'

Will frowned. It was hard to know what to say. He hadn't tried to describe the place to anyone. Firstly he hadn't felt like talking and secondly he wasn't sure of very much. He didn't know why he was so certain that the junction they'd just left behind wasn't the place.

'Will?' said Dad. 'You haven't answered my question.'

'Don't push him, Chris,' said Mum. 'Don't make him talk if he doesn't want to.'

Will twisted round in his seat and caught Mum's eye. She smiled.

'You don't need to talk, Will,' she said. 'Not if you don't want to. Just take things slowly. All the things you've forgotten, they'll . . . you know . . . '

'Come back,' said Dad.

Will looked away. He knew there was no guarantee of that. Doctor Paige had been refreshingly blunt: sometimes it all comes back, sometimes some of it comes back, sometimes none of it comes back. You deal with it as best you can. Your loved ones do the same.

End of story.

Or a beginning, he thought: the beginning of a new life he hadn't chosen and didn't want. But if he couldn't have his old one back, he supposed he'd have to make do with this one.

They drove on, the road narrowing and twisting with the miles, woodland to the left, higher, more open ground to the right with farms and fields, and again the blue haze climbing beyond the rim. Dad pointed towards it.

'You'll see the sea over there shortly. Do you recognize any of this?'

He didn't. He'd hoped he would but it was still foreign ground. He stared out of the window.

'Did I . . . come here a lot?' he said.

'We weren't always sure where you went,' said Mum. 'You were always a bit on the independent side. But we're close to home now and you used to wander off a lot, so I suppose you may well have come this way. We've certainly driven you down this road a few times since we moved to Havensmouth.'

'A few times?' Will looked round at her again. 'Just a few times?'

'Well, we only moved here five months ago.'

'Oh.'

Mum coloured.

21

'I'm sorry, Will. I thought we'd told you and I keep forgetting you can't remember things.'

He said nothing.

'Will,' said Dad, 'I want you to look straight ahead. There's something round the next bend you might recognize. And if you do, I want you to tell us.'

He stared ahead. The farms and open landscape to the right had vanished and there was now woodland on both sides of the road. Dad was slowing down as they approached the bend. Again Will felt Mum's hand on his shoulder. He stiffened slightly and felt it go. Dad changed down to third gear, then to second.

'Get ready, Will,' he said.

They eased round the bend and there, a short way down, was a lane leading off through the woodland to the right. A small signpost pointed down it with the words 'Havensmouth 2 miles'. Close to the signpost was a tree.

Dad pulled over to the side of the road just up from the turning and switched off the engine. Silence fell over them. Will stared hard at the lane.

'Do you recognize anything?' said Mum.

He recognized the tree. Nothing else.

'Tree,' he murmured.

'The sycamore?'

'Yes, and . . . '

He broke off. There was something else. There was . . . something else. He started to fumble with the door.

'You want to get out?' said Dad.

'Yes.'

'Pull that lever thing. Here, I'll show you.'

But he'd worked it out now. He thrust open the car door, climbed out and started to run down towards the tree. From behind came the sound of Mum and Dad hurrying after him.

'What is it, Will?' called Mum.

He stopped by the sycamore and listened. Mum and Dad joined him, both breathing hard.

'What is it?' said Dad.

'Bird,' he answered. 'I can . . . I can hear it. Same song.'

The sound was clear, the same rippling melody as before, but distant, not in this tree but somewhere deep in the woodland. Mum and Dad listened.

'It's a song-thrush,' said Dad eventually.

'Are you sure?' said Mum.

Will barely heard them. He was still listening to the bird. It went on singing for several minutes, then fell silent. He shivered suddenly.

'Maybe it's an omen,' said Mum. 'A blessing for Will.'

He looked up at the tree and shivered again.

'Maybe,' he said, and turned back to the car.

4

The slow drive, the narrow lane, trees on either side. He did not know them. He could name them—sycamore, horse chestnut, oak, beech—but they were strangers to him, like the people now appearing along the lane.

Faces turned towards them as the car approached: an old man with white hair, a group of women, a couple holding hands, two teenage boys on bikes. All stared. None smiled.

'Don't worry, Will,' said Dad. 'People are bound to be a bit awkward seeing you. Everyone's heard about the hit-and-run. And it's probably got round about . . . you know . . . you losing your memory.'

He said nothing. He was watching more faces on the lane ahead: teenagers again, two boys and a girl, about his age. They were sauntering in this direction but they veered off the lane at the last minute and waited for the car to pass.

The taller of the two boys was wearing a bandana and had the air of the leader. The second boy had short, reddish hair and a somewhat bovine expression. The girl was bent over, lighting a cigarette, but Will caught a glimpse of mousy-grey hair as the car cruised by. Both boys stared at him.

'Don't let it upset you, Will,' said Dad. 'People can be a bit funny when they don't know how to react.'

Will turned in his seat and peered out through the rear window. The three figures were walking on, their backs to him, but then, as if he'd felt Will's gaze, the boy with the bandana glanced over his shoulder, and their eyes met again.

'Will?' said Mum.

He looked at her.

'We're coming into the town,' she said. 'And it's a special view.'

He studied her face. Something in it told him she wasn't saying what she meant. He glanced at the boy again. He'd turned back to his companions and the three were now walking purposefully away.

'Don't miss it, Will,' said Mum.

He looked at her again. She wasn't interested in the view. He could tell that. It was something else. He had the impression she was trying to distract him from something—the figures presumably.

'Who are they?' he said. 'Those three.'

'Just kids from Havensmouth.'

'Get ready, Will,' said Dad. 'I want to know if there's anything you recognize ahead.'

Will twisted back in his seat and saw that Dad had pulled over to the side of the lane but had left the engine ticking over. Something about Mum and Dad felt wrong but it was hard to work out what it was. He gazed about him.

The woodland had thinned and they were close to what looked like the brow of the hill they'd been climbing since they'd turned off into the lane. He looked back at Mum and Dad. There was still something wrong. They seemed to have become wary of him since these people from the town started showing up.

25

'What are we stopping for?' he said.

Dad gave an unnaturally cheery smile.

'Didn't want you to miss the view as we hit the town,' he said. 'You were facing the other way. I want you to be looking forward. Like your mum said, it's a special view.'

Will frowned. Dad was lying too; it was so obvious. His father's face was as edgy as Mum's. Maybe they did want him to enjoy the view, but he had the much stronger impression that the car was stuck here because they didn't really want to take him into town at all; and it was something to do with the reaction of all these people.

'Ready?' said Dad.

He didn't answer. He was watching the lane ahead as it rose towards the top of the hill. He could imagine something of what lay on the other side, but he could not picture it. Whatever Havensmouth the old Will had known, this one would be different.

'Let's go,' said Mum.

Dad drove on and the car climbed the last part of the rise. Will waited. Still he could see nothing but sky beyond the rim, that curiously hazy blue he had noticed from afar, but then suddenly they reached the top of the hill and the vista opened below. Dad stopped the car again.

'See what I mean about the view?'

The over-cheery smile again and now the over-cheery voice to go with it. Will stared down the other side of the hill. Below him was the sea stretching away to the horizon and close in a beach that sprawled a mile or more to a rocky headland, with a further beach beyond. Behind both beaches hillocky dunes retreated to the woodland they'd been passing through.

Round to the left was a small harbour with fishing boats and pleasure craft; inland from that a pub, a church, shops and other buildings clustered around the centre of the town. Further to the left was a huge hill with houses and cottages dotted about the slopes, and at the top a large white building with what looked like gardens.

Close to the nearer of the two beaches was a second—much smaller—hill that rose almost to the level of the dunes. It too had a building on top with a garden. Will stared about him, trying to remember.

It was all unfamiliar—picturesque but unfamiliar—and there was something else about this place that wasn't right. It was unsettling in some way. He didn't know why. He stared at the sea, the beaches, the dunes, the headland, the town buildings, the sea again.

'Beautiful, isn't it?' said Mum.

He looked at her, still unsure what was wrong.

'Can we drive on?' he said.

They drove on down the hill, more faces appearing on the road, staring just as the others had done. He studied these new people: a group of men with fishing gear, boys playing football on a patch of grass, a girl with a skipping rope, an old man walking a dog; faces watching him as if he were a ghost.

They weren't scary, not like the shadowfaces, but they were unsettling and he didn't like them. He thought of the girl with black hair and blue eyes. She was scary too but in a different kind of way. He wished he could see her now instead of these watching corpses.

They reached the road that ran towards the centre of the town, then, to Will's surprise, Dad turned right

27

and drove up the little hill that climbed in the direction of the dunes.

'Recognize this, Will?' he said.

Will shook his head. But he remembered the house he'd just seen on top of the hill and he could guess now what it was.

'We're coming to The Four Winds,' he said.

'Right,' said Dad.

They climbed on, the lane twisting as it rose, then suddenly they were at the gate of the house. He stared through it at a large, untidy building with a long garden to the right. Beyond it, the dunes stretched away towards the headland at the far end of the beach. Mum jumped out of the car and opened the gate.

'Here we go,' said Dad, and he drove in.

Will looked at him. The voice was still forced and Mum seemed just as nervous as she leaned down to open the passenger door for him. He wanted to tell her he could manage it himself but she pulled it open before he could speak.

'The Four Winds,' she said.

He was feeling worse than ever now. Lack of sleep, lack of memory, and now Mum and Dad talking to him as though he were a guest. He scowled. Maybe that's what he'd become: a guest in his own house, a guest in his own life.

He climbed out of the car and stood there, looking round. The wind was strong up here but it was warm too and he was glad of it. He'd started shivering again. Mum touched him on the arm.

'Try and pretend it's home, Will.' She smiled at him. 'Even if it doesn't feel like home.'

Somehow he managed a smile back.

'Come on,' she said. 'Let's go in.'

He followed her into the house while Dad put the car in the garage. The hall opened before him, another unknown place. To his relief, Mum didn't ask him if he recognized anything. She simply showed him the kitchen, the lounge, the study, the conservatory, then led him upstairs.

'Here's your room,' she said.

He heard the tension in her voice. She pushed open the door and he stared in. A large room, airy and bright, bed to the left, desk to the right, a glass-panelled door at the far end leading to a balcony overlooking the beach.

Papers everywhere.

On the floor, the desk, the bed, some in piles, some scattered about; and even from here he could see they were covered with drawings. But that was not all. The walls too were covered with drawings, and not just any drawings. It was all one drawing, obsessively repeated.

The girl's face.

She stared back at him from every wall and every sheet of paper visible to him. There was no mistaking who it was. Even without colour he could see it was the girl with black hair and blue eyes—and it was the eyes that gave her away. They had been exaggerated in size.

He remembered how they'd seemed to widen, to fill the face with blue. These drawn eyes had no blue—they were just pencil sketches—but even without the blue, he felt he was staring into an ocean. It was her. There was no doubt about it: the girl who had called him back from death, as beautiful and scary as she had ever been.

He looked round at Mum.

'We left everything exactly as it was,' she said, somewhat apologetically. 'You used to get so upset if we tried to tidy things up. You've always been like that with your drawings. We just . . . didn't feel we should move anything, even when you were in hospital.'

She paused, watching his face, then went on.

'They're your pictures, Will, if that's what you're wondering. You drew them. Did you know that?'

'I guessed.'

'But did you know?'

He said nothing. He didn't remember drawing them. He didn't remember drawing anything.

'We tried to stop you sketching on the walls,' she said, 'but you've always done it, since you were very little, and we gave up in the end. You've just always seemed to need to draw things that are in your head. And since we came to Havensmouth, it's this girl who's been in your head. You wouldn't ever tell us who she is and I don't suppose you remember now, do you?'

Again he said nothing. He was desperate to be alone now. He needed to think. He saw Mum watching him closely.

'Will?' she said. 'Do you want a bit of time to yourself?'

He nodded gratefully.

'I thought so,' she said. 'I know the signs. I'll leave you for a bit. You just get your bearings again. Only, listen . . . ' She glanced towards the balcony door. 'Can you—'

'I'll be careful on the balcony.'

She smiled.

30

'It's a bit of a drop, that's all. You've probably forgotten, but we're pretty high up here. Just be careful
if you go out there, all right?'

'OK.'

She kissed him and left. He waited till he heard her
talking to Dad downstairs, then closed the door, sat
on the bed, and squeezed his hands into fists.
Everything felt crazy now. Somehow it hadn't
occurred to him that he'd known or seen this girl
before the accident. Now it was clear she'd been part
of his life before, or part of the old Will's life.

But not part of Mum's life, or Dad's, except in the
form of these drawings. They clearly had no idea who
she was. He stared round at the face on the walls and
on the papers scattered about him. Who was this girl?
How had she come to him at the moment of death?
And why? He stood up and walked over to the balcony door.

Through the glass panel he could see the balcony
itself and beyond that the beach below with the headland at the far end. He twisted the handle and pushed
at the door. It was locked. He turned the key and tried
again. The door opened and he stepped out onto the
balcony.

As usual, nothing looked familiar. He walked up to
the rail and leaned on it. Immediately below him was
a sheer drop to the beach path at the base of the hill.
Beyond that the sand stretched away, the sea driving
hard upon the shore. He stared over the beach,
searching for figures, but there was no one to be seen.

Then he stiffened. Just above the tide-line was a
set of markings in the sand. He studied them, tracing
with his eyes the shape they made; and as he did so,
he felt his hands tighten round the balcony rail.

For here was another drawing, a drawing in the sand, not a very good one and already the sea was licking some of it away; but the image was clear enough. As with his own pictures, it was the exaggeration of the eyes that gave everything away.

This too was the girl's face.

5

'Who are you?' he murmured, staring down; and an hour later, long after the lines in the sand had been washed away, he was still gazing from the balcony. The sea washed up the beach, smooth and strong.

He eased his fingers from the rail, stepped back into his room and closed the door. The house felt quiet after the song of the wind. He stared round at his own drawings of the girl. She was so beautiful, even sketched like this.

'Maybe you're an angel,' he said. 'A slightly scary angel.'

He frowned. Whatever she was, someone else knew about her too, unless he'd completely misread the picture in the sand. He looked down at the mess of papers on the floor, kicked some aside to create a space, then sat down and sifted through a few.

Faces, faces, faces, always the girl in some form or other, sometimes looking towards him, sometimes to the side, sometimes down. He stared at the images, trying to understand, but nothing made sense.

This was ridiculous. He stood up and strode to the door. It was time for words now, time to find things out. He hurried downstairs and looked for Mum and Dad. They were in the kitchen.

'Just making some coffee,' said Dad. He reached for the kettle. 'Do you want some? You used to like it.'

Will stared back.

'Will?' said Mum. 'Are you all right?'

'Tell me,' he said to her.

'Tell you what?'

'Everything.'

She walked up to him, her eyes softening.

'About you?' she said.

'Yes.'

'Are you sure? You got really stressed when we tried to tell you things at the hospital.'

'I couldn't cope with it then. And you were trying to tell me too much too soon. But now I . . . '

'Sit down,' she said quietly.

He sat down with her at the table. From far below came the sound of surf crashing on the shore.

'What do you want to know first?' she said.

He swallowed hard. There was so much and he didn't know where to begin. He just wanted it all at once. It might not turn him back into the old Will but it was a start: a way of glimpsing the person he once was, if only from the outside.

'Just . . . everything,' he said.

Mum glanced up at Dad.

'Can you make that coffee?'

'Sure.'

She looked back at Will.

'We'll tell you everything we can think of,' she said, 'just as it comes. But if there's anything you want to know, just ask, OK?'

He looked down. He didn't want to ask questions. He didn't want coffee. He wanted words. He wanted his past back.

'Just . . . tell me stuff.'

'You're fifteen,' she said. 'Your birthday's the four-teenth of November. You're a Scorpio.'

'But you don't believe in Astrology,' put in Dad, looking round from the kettle.

'You don't like crowds,' said Mum. 'Or people who try to make you think something or believe something against your will. You don't like organized religions. Though you do sometimes come with Dad and me to the church in Havensmouth. You did anyway. A few times.'

'You go to church?'

'Yes.'

'Both of you?'

'Yes. But you don't. Except those few times. And that was just to keep me happy.'

'Will?' said Dad. 'Do you remember any of these things?'

Will shook his head.

'Go on,' he said. 'Keep telling me stuff.'

'You're an only child,' said Mum. 'You had a com-plicated birth and very nearly died. You had further complications during your early years. Lots of ill health and some strange . . . well . . . behaviour. People started to tell us you had . . . '

She hesitated.

'Special needs,' said Dad.

'For want of a better term.'

Will saw them watching him uneasily, as though wary of how he might react.

'Go on,' he said.

The kettle boiled and switched itself off. Dad glanced at it, but went on.

'You sleep badly. Three hours a night, four if you're lucky. Some nights no sleep at all.'

35

'You don't like gadgets,' said Mum. 'You're hopeless with them. You press all the wrong buttons. You don't like watching television. It gives you migraines. You don't like computers or radios or other electronic equipment for the same reason. The microwave sends you into the next room if I put it on. You've got a mobile but you never use it. Never used to anyway. Even after we got you clued up on what buttons to press, you never used it. You only carried it because we made you.'

'Why?' he said.

'Why what?'

'Why did you make me carry it?'

'Because we were worried about you,' said Dad. He filled the cafetière and put it on the table. 'As usual.'

'As usual?'

'Yes, as usual.'

Dad looked at Will in silence for a few moments.

'Will, listen,' he went on, 'we're not criticizing you here, OK? We're just doing what you asked—telling you stuff. We love you to bits. We always have done and we always will. Loving you is our default position. But the point is, not everyone feels quite so fond of you as we do.'

'Meaning what?'

'Well, that you've not always been great at making friends.' Dad paused. 'Or to put it bluntly, you're quite good at doing the opposite.'

Will thought of the faces he'd seen staring at him from the road.

'So nobody likes me,' he said. 'Apart from you two.'

'That's not what I said.'

'It's what you meant.'

Mum put an arm round him.

'It's not what he meant, Will. He just put it badly.' She shot a glance at Dad, then looked back. 'Lots of people like you. It's not just Dad and me. But sometimes you unsettle people. Certain kinds of people anyway. And that's why we gave you the mobile. In case you ever got into trouble.'

'And just as well,' said Dad. 'You might not be alive if your rescuer hadn't used it to phone the ambulance.'

Will thought of the unknown girl: the second unknown girl. Strange that there were two. One with the voice, one with the face. Both a mystery.

'She probably had her own mobile,' said Mum, 'and just used Will's because she didn't want to be traced. For whatever reason.'

'Coffee,' said Dad.

He put the mugs, milk, and sugar on the table and sat down with them. Will breathed in the aroma from the cafetière. It was rich and strong and pleasant. Mum pressed down the plunger and started to pour.

'Milk and sugar, Will? Like you used to?'

'Black, no sugar.'

She glanced at him.

'I was just testing you,' she said.

'I know.'

'You do?'

'I guessed.' He looked at her. 'You're a lousy liar.'

She shrugged.

'Anyway, you did use to like coffee that way. Black, no sugar. And you've just remembered, so that's a good sign, isn't it? Or were you just guessing about black, no sugar?'

He looked away, unsure of the answer, and not really caring.

'Tell me more things,' he said eventually.

'You don't like milk or sugar,' said Dad. 'Or meat or fish. Or cheese or eggs. You don't like people getting hurt. You're scared of animals. You get upset by stories of violence.'

'You don't like loud noises,' said Mum. 'Or aggressive music. You don't like sport. You don't like rowdy people. You don't like fights.'

'Fights?' said Will.

'Yes.'

'Have I had any fights?'

'A few,' said Mum.

'How come?' Will looked from one to the other. 'I mean . . . if I don't like them.'

'It's not that you start them,' said Dad. 'But like your mum said, sometimes you unsettle people. And they go for you. And because you don't really fight back, you get . . . well, you've been knocked about a few times.'

Will stared down at his coffee cup.

'So there's lots of things I don't like.'

'Yes,' said Mum.

'What do I like?'

'Drawing.'

'What else?'

'Walking,' said Dad. 'Thinking. Being by yourself.'

'That's it?'

'That's it. You walk and think and draw.'

'By myself.'

'Yes.'

Silence. He felt the weight of what they were telling him; and what they weren't.

'Go on,' he said quietly.

38

Dad's eyes flickered in Mum's direction, then returned to Will.

'You don't go to school. Haven't been for years.'

Another silence.

'Why not?' said Will.

'Didn't seem much point once we saw what was happening.'

Again Will heard the sound of the surf below. Dad took a sip of coffee.

'Schools weren't right for you,' he said. 'And you weren't right for schools. Nobody's fault.'

It was obvious Dad was lying; and he was as bad at it as Mum.

'Why not?' said Will.

'Just wasn't the best environment for you,' said Dad. 'Like I say, nobody's fault.'

'Tell me, will you?'

Dad and Mum exchanged glances.

'I need to know,' said Will.

'It started at nursery school,' said Mum. 'Carried on at infants school, and every other school we tried. And it got worse as you grew older. Complaints from every place we took you to. Teachers, parents, other kids.'

'Me unsettling people?'

'Yes.'

'But how?' Will stared at them. 'How do I unsettle people?'

Again Mum and Dad exchanged glances.

'How?' said Will.

Dad took a slow breath.

'Have you seen any strange things since the accident? Faces, shadows, anything weird?'

'Yes.'

'OK.' Dad's eyes darkened and he said no more. Will stared at him.

'OK what?'

Dad didn't answer.

'OK what?' said Will. 'I don't get what OK's supposed to mean.'

'It means your memory might be gone but it's business as usual on the other front,' said Dad. He looked quickly away. 'Sorry, I didn't put that very well.'

'No, you didn't,' said Mum.

Will turned to her.

'What's he talking about?'

'He's just . . . ' She leaned closer. 'We're just . . . '

'Don't mess about with me,' said Will. 'I've got to know all this.'

'You used to see strange things,' she said. 'Or claim you did. Sort of . . . visions, I suppose you'd call them. No one really knows because obviously . . . I mean . . . no one else sees these things except you. So it's hard to know what you're experiencing.'

If anything.

He heard the words in her mind, though she didn't speak them. He looked at her, then at Dad's averted face. It was obvious they didn't believe him. He sensed they never had done. They loved him but they didn't believe him. Perhaps no one did.

He thought of the angel girl, and the shadowfaces.

'I've seen things,' he murmured. 'And I'm not lying.'

Dad turned back to look at him.

'No one's saying you are, Will. It's just that . . . well, the things you used to claim to see were pretty hard to believe, and for some people . . . slightly offensive.'

40

'Not us,' said Mum. 'Not offensive to us.'

Will looked into her face again.

'I don't mean to hurt you,' he said.

'You're not hurting us, Will. Like Dad said, we love you, OK? That's our default position. That's non-negotiable.'

But you don't understand me, he thought, and now after the accident I don't understand myself either. Yet again he searched his mind for some memory of all this: what he'd done, what he'd said, what he'd felt. But all he found was the echo of his own questions.

'So what do people say about me?' he said. 'Do they say I'm mad?'

'People say all kinds of things,' said Mum. 'But that doesn't make them right.'

'I'm funny in the head, is that it? Mentally ill?'

'We don't know what causes your experiences,' said Dad. 'No one's been able to make sense of the things you do and say.' He paused. 'All your life you've just . . . been a bit different. You come out with strange, supernatural kind of stuff you claim to see or feel or hear or whatever. And you get these . . . trances.'

'Trances?'

'Yes,' said Dad. 'If we're lucky, you have them when we're around but sometimes you'll go missing and we'll find you in some other place, and when we ask you what's happened, you'll say you don't know how you got there. That's the main reason why we moved to Havensmouth.'

'What do you mean?'

'Did you see that big white building on top of the hill? Right up above the town?'

41

'The one with the gardens?'

'Yes. That's Acacia Court. I don't suppose you remember the name?'

'No,' said Will.

'It's a private care home,' said Mum. 'With special facilities for—'

'Head cases.'

'No,' she said firmly. 'For people with particular . . . disorders. They've got specialists there. It's a lovely place, very supportive. We moved to Havensmouth because we wanted you to have access to Acacia Court if you needed to go. It was recommended to us. We've only had to take you there once, when you got a little . . . out of hand.'

'What did I do?'

'It doesn't matter.'

'Tell me.'

Mum hesitated.

'It was an incident at the church. You got a bit upset and had to be taken away.'

'What does that mean?'

'Never mind,' said Dad. 'The point is, like I say, you're a bit different from most other people, OK? We've tried over the years to find out what's behind it. We've taken you to doctors and psychiatrists and God knows who, but no one's got to the bottom of it. Most of the time, you don't need any treatment. But some-times, when you get these trances, you lose control and there's medication they can give you that calms you down. Though it doesn't stop you having these hallu—'

Dad broke off.

'Hallucinations,' said Will.

'Yes.' Dad shrugged. 'You remember the word, then?'

Will said nothing. Dad watched him for a moment, then went on.

'None of the specialists who've seen you over the years have come to a definite conclusion as to what's wrong. But the general view of the experts is that you're probably experiencing hallucinations. Some think these may have been exacerbated or possibly even caused by the chronic lack of sleep you've always suffered. But no one's really sure.'

Will stared out of the window. The sound of the surf seemed unpleasantly loud.

'Will,' said Mum, 'it doesn't mean the experts are right, and it doesn't mean that we don't realize you're experiencing something incredibly difficult to deal with.'

'But I'm still a freak.'

'You're not a freak, darling.'

Will thought of the picture in the sand, the angel girl. He squeezed his fists tight under the table. This conversation hadn't gone well. He'd wanted to know things, but not these things. He pushed the coffee away and stood up.

'Will?' said Mum. 'You're not going?'

'I don't know, I—'

'I thought you wanted to hear things about yourself.'

'I do. I did. But—'

'I know it must be distressing for you.' Mum caught his hand. 'But try to bear it if you can. Talking might help you remember.'

He shook his head. Remembering was too frightening now. Forgetting might have been better after all. Leaving the old Will to himself. He looked down at them.

'I'm not ready for any more. Not right now.'

He felt a pounding inside his skull.

'What is it, Will?' said Dad.

He didn't know. Mum squeezed his hand.

'Will?'

'I'm all right,' he said. 'It's just that . . . talking hurts. More than I thought it would.'

He let go of her hand and walked over to the window. Below him he could see the waves crashing on the beach. A quarter of a mile offshore three fishing boats were heading past the point; a fourth was just leaving the harbour over to the left.

He closed his eyes and saw a familiar face inside his brow. Yes, he thought, watching it, she was like an angel: a beautiful, scary angel. But was she really there? And if so, why? He opened his eyes and stared down at the beach again. Something was moving at the far end.

A figure with thick, black hair.

6

He stared at it. Too far away to see clearly and moving towards the headland at the other end of the beach. It might be coincidence, might mean nothing at all. There must be lots of people with thick, black hair.

And yet . . .

He closed his eyes again, searched for the face of the girl, saw nothing, opened them again. The figure was still moving away along the beach. He turned to Mum and Dad. There was no way they'd let him go out on his own. They were worried enough about him already.

'I'm going to my room,' he said.

'Will?' said Mum. 'Are you all right?'

'I'm really tired.'

'OK.' She smiled. 'Just come down again when you're ready. No rush.'

'Have a good rest,' said Dad. 'We can talk more later.'

'Thanks,' said Will, feeling guilty.

He closed the door behind him, hurried up to his room and stepped out onto the balcony. The figure was still visible on the beach but now well over by the headland. It was hard to tell whether it was a boy or a girl.

Someone small, certainly, perhaps too small to be the girl he was looking for, but the hair was so similar he had to check. He waited for a moment to make sure Mum and Dad weren't following up from below. No sound on the stairs, but a murmur of voices in the kitchen. They were still there, talking about him, no doubt.

He waited a moment longer, then tiptoed back out of his room and down the stairs. At the front door he stopped and listened again. Still the voices in the kitchen. He was right: they were talking about him.

'He's out on his feet,' Dad was saying. 'Best to let him rest.'

'If he could just get some decent sleep,' said Mum.

Will looked at the front door and changed his mind. It had made a loud click when they arrived. He remembered that distinctly. He crept to the back door instead, slipped out and closed it behind him, then waited again for sounds of Mum and Dad coming after him.

Nothing.

He hurried round the side of the house to the lane, then set off down it, trying to remember the way to the beach. It was no good. This place just didn't feel familiar. To his relief, he soon saw a path with a sign saying 'Beach'.

He ran down it. To his right he could now see The Four Winds perched above him on top of the hill, and even the underside of the balcony outside his bedroom. Ahead of him the path was starting to flatten out as it merged with the sand. He put on speed, anxious to get to the beach before the figure disappeared from view.

But it had already vanished.

He stopped and stared towards the headland. There was nobody in sight, just the beach stretching

46

away with sea to his left and dunes to his right. He started to walk, his feet plunging deep in the sand. As before, the surf felt unpleasantly loud. He remembered what Mum had said.

You don't like loud noises.

She was certainly right about that. The thunder of the waves felt so violent it seemed to reach right inside him; and there was something else he didn't like, something to do with the beach, or the sea, or both. But he couldn't work out what it was. He stopped and looked around him.

No sign of any obvious danger. Up on the hill the windows of The Four Winds blinked against the noonday sun. To the right of the house, half-hidden by the rise, he could see the roofs of the other houses that straggled down into Havensmouth, and further round, the buildings and shops of the town itself, the church spire rising among them; and over to the right, at the farthest extremity, the outer wall of the harbour.

Two more fishing boats were chugging out.

He turned the other way. Nothing moved among the dunes, nothing he could see anyway. He narrowed his eyes and stared across at the headland, scanning right to left from its innermost point to where the tip braced itself against the sea—and there, as he scanned back again, was the flash of black.

He stiffened. The figure must have run down to the water's edge and hurried along parallel to the surf, perhaps hidden by the spray, or even in the surf itself. But now more figures had appeared, moving fast along to the top of the dunes towards the headland. He recognized them at once. The three teenagers he'd seen on the lane: the tall boy with the bandana, the shorter lad with the bovine face, the girl with mousy-grey hair.

He watched them. As before, it was clear that the boy with the bandana was the leader. He had an air of confidence that was obvious even from here. The other boy seemed a little clumsy in his movements and was obviously deferring to the bigger lad. The girl was finding it hard to keep up with them and her hair kept blowing round her face.

Will stared back at the figure with black hair, now close to a cave at the base of the headland. Suddenly there was a shout from the top of the dunes. The small figure stopped and looked up. Will strained his eyes to catch a glimpse of the face, but it was too far to see. He gazed up at the top of the dunes again.

The two boys were now gesturing down towards the figure by the cave. There was no mistaking their hostility. Another shout, and another, then a volley of jeers from both boys. The black-haired figure darted into the cave and disappeared. Will hurried across the sand towards the headland.

He had no idea why he was doing this. There seemed nothing but trouble ahead and the teenagers on top of the dunes were clearly unfriendly. He kept his eye on them as he made his way across the sand. They hadn't started down the slope towards the cave but they hadn't moved away either. More of Mum's words filtered back to him.

You don't like fights.

She was right there too, he thought grimly. He hated the prospect of trouble with these three. They frightened him, especially the boy with the bandana. He clenched his fists. He couldn't go back. Whatever the danger, he had to find out more about the figure with black hair. It might lead to nothing, but it might be significant. It might even be the girl he'd seen.

The three on the dunes were facing him now. He wondered whether they'd seen him earlier. It was hard to tell. As he drew closer, he saw their attention shift from him to the cave, and back again. He walked stubbornly on, his mind on them, and on the figure hidden in the cave.

There were no further shouts from the boys. All he heard now was the sound of the surf, more deafening than ever. The headland drew closer, the entrance to the cave straight ahead. Again he glanced up at the dunes. Three faces looked coldly down at him. He looked back towards the entrance of the cave and saw another face watching him.

A girl.

He stopped. It wasn't *the* girl. That was clear at once. This girl had a thick head of hair but it flashed blonde as the sun caught it. Even so, she was striking in another way. Tall and slim with a full mouth and strong, defiant eyes. She ran them over him for a moment, then turned and squared up to the figures on the dunes.

No words passed between them, but after a few moments of staring, the boy with the bandana glanced at the others, then all three turned away and set off along the top of the dunes towards the town. Will watched them go, then looked back at the cave.

The girl had disappeared, but there was no mystery about where she was. The only mystery was who she was, and what she knew about the figure with black hair, who must also be inside the cave. He walked over to the entrance, paused for a moment, then stepped inside.

The place looked strangely familiar. Tall sides, almost vertical, and a ceiling so high it was hard to make out the features in the sparse light that crept in from the entrance. There was a smell of salty air and the sound of the sea felt loud and muffled at the same time. He looked for the girl but couldn't see her. Then he heard a voice.

'I knew you'd come back.'

She was sitting in the shadow among the far rocks.

'Back where?' he said. 'To this cave?'

'Just back.'

He glanced round for the small figure he'd seen earlier but there was no sign. The girl stood up, moved into the light and stopped. He studied her: about his age and either very confident or acting so.

'Remember me, Will?' she said.

He went on studying her, unsure what to think. With the light now on her he could see more clearly the features that had struck him before: the full mouth, the blonde hair, the strong eyes, watching him intently. Suddenly she smiled.

'You do remember me.'

He didn't. She was as alien to him as the old Will was. Yet something did feel familiar, something he couldn't define. It was as vague a memory as this cave, and maybe not even a memory, just a feeling that stirred inside him.

'Everyone's talking about you in Havensmouth,' she said.

He had the feeling she was waiting for a reply, but he was unsure what to say. She took a step closer, then stopped. He glanced at her hands. One stroked a nearby rock, the other ran its fingers through her hair. He caught another flash of blonde in the gloom.

'They're saying you can't remember anything,' she said. 'But I think there's some things you never forget.'

She took another step closer. He watched the hands, the face, the hands again. They were stretching towards him.

'Will,' she murmured.

He stood there, rigid. The fingers touched his neck, stroked it. He shivered. They stopped moving but stayed on the skin. He made to step back but before he could do so, she took another step forward, locked her hands round his neck and pulled him towards her. He froze. She nestled her head into the crook of his neck, then twisted her mouth up and kissed him on the cheek.

'Will.'

He didn't speak, didn't move.

'It'll come back,' she whispered.

Her mouth touched his. He twisted his face away. She went on holding him.

'Will.'

He took a step back and she let go. Her eyes seemed to darken like the cave. He stared at her, trying to understand.

'I can help you remember,' she said.

He looked down, unable to face her. He yearned to remember. There were so many things trying to come back. He could feel them circling him like ghosts. He looked up at her again. She was watching him as before.

'You liked to be touched before,' she said.

She was right. He knew that. The feeling he could not define was still there, but he was starting to sense what it was.

'Touch me,' she said.

The light caught her hair again. It glowed for a moment, then vanished. She flicked her head back, reached out a hand. He took it. She stroked his fingers, squeezed, coaxed. He stepped closer, breathing hard. She looked up into his eyes, her lips apart. He stared down at them. They were whispering something, something he could not hear.

All he heard was the thunder of surf outside the cave. He felt her hand tighten round his, saw the lips move again, saw the shape of his name upon them. The lips drew closer, carrying his name with them. He let them brush his neck, his cheek, his mouth. He felt her body touch his. He quivered, felt himself freeze again. She moved her head round and murmured into his ear.

'I can help you. I can bring everything back. It'll be just like it was.'

He tensed further. The feel of her had been good but only for a moment. She was too close now.

'Close,' he muttered.

'I know. It's good.'

'No, I . . . '

He pushed her sharply away. She stared back and he saw her eyes darken again.

'I'm sorry,' she said. 'I'm pushing you too fast. Please don't stop trusting me.'

He found he was shaking. She hesitated.

'Do you remember anything about me?'

'Beth,' he said suddenly.

Her face brightened.

'Yes! I'm Beth!'

He stared at her.

'You see?' she said. 'I told you it would come back.'

He shook his head. He had no idea where the name had come from. It had fallen into his mind but nothing else had fallen with it, no memories certainly.

'Black hair, ' he muttered.

'You're talking about Muck.'

He wasn't sure whether this was a question. It didn't sound like one.

'The little boy,' she said. 'I saw you following him along the beach. That's why I crept in here. I thought it meant you'd remembered him, and if you remembered him, then you'd remember me, and this cave.'

She frowned.

'But I was wrong. You don't remember me and you don't remember this cave. And I suppose you don't remember Muck either, do you?' She didn't wait for an answer. 'It doesn't matter. I know it's not your fault. I should be grateful you're still alive. Christ, I must sound so selfish.'

She took a step closer again, saw him flinch and stopped.

'It's OK, Will. I won't touch you again. I can see you're awkward about it.'

He relaxed a little, but still watched her closely, his mind on this new name she had given him. A strange name for a boy.

'Muck,' he said.

'He's not here. He ran in and went straight out again.'

Will glanced round the cave. There was no sign of another exit and no shaft of light to hint where one might be. Yet there must be another way out. The boy hadn't run out the same way he ran in.

The girl called Beth was silent now. So too was the sea outside. Strange that he hadn't noticed the quietness growing. The thunder was gone and in its place was a heavy stillness.

'I've got to go,' he said.

Something felt wrong. He didn't know what. He only knew he wanted to get out of the cave. But it was no good. His body felt fixed and now something was shivering over his feet, up his legs, through his spine. With an effort he moved his eyes to check. Nothing was climbing over him except fear. He gave a low gasp.

'You did that before,' said Beth.

He looked at her.

'You used to shiver and gasp,' she said, 'when you were about to feel stuff.'

He felt his eyes drift from her, round the dark space, up to the roof of the cave, and part of him seemed to drift there too. He heard a moan far away, and listened. It was growing louder, more insistent. The sound of the sea was back, drowning the thoughts that rushed through him, but not the moan, which was now a series of moans, pulsing in his head, around his head, filling the cave with rampant sound.

He fell to the ground.

'Ah!'

He felt Beth's shadow over him, her hand on his shoulder. He felt cold and scared, but the moaning sounds had gone and only the surf was left. Beth's hand was still there. He turned to look up at her. All he saw was her shadow, then gradually it cleared and he saw the shape of her head, and then her face staring down at him.

'Will,' she murmured.

The moaning sounds came back, reaching through the noise of the surf beyond the cave.

'Will.' Again Beth's voice, louder now than all the other sounds. 'I'll be here for you. Like I was before.'

He looked up at her, aching to remember.

'You're still you,' she said. 'Whatever you've forgotten, you're still you.'

She leaned closer.

'Do you trust me now?'

He didn't answer, couldn't answer. She helped him to his feet and put her arms round him. He stood there, his own arms loose.

'Will, please.'

He listened for the moaning sounds, but they were gone. He reached out and pulled Beth closer to him. Her body seemed to soften into his.

'You do trust me,' she said. 'A bit, anyway.'

She drew her head back and looked into his eyes.

'Promise me you always will.'

Still he couldn't answer. She watched him for a moment, then reached out and touched him on the cheek.

'Come on,' she said. 'There's something I want to show you.'

7

He followed her out of the cave. There seemed little point in doing anything else. The boy called Muck was not inside. She stopped on the sand and waited for him, the sun flaming upon her hair. He joined her and glanced up at the headland.

'Breeze Point,' she said. 'Remember it?'

The name meant nothing to him. He stared at the tip. High and sheer, dark rock and white water. It felt as unfamiliar to him as the name. He turned back to Beth and saw her forcing a smile. He tried to smile back but found he could only stare.

'Christ,' she said. 'One thing doesn't change.'

'What do you mean?'

'You're still scary when you stare like that.'

'Like what?'

She studied him in silence for a few moments, then shrugged.

'You used to have a way of staring,' she said, 'like you're peering right through the person you're looking at. You're doing it now. No wonder you freak some people out.'

He blinked and looked away towards the dunes. Figures were moving along the top again, further down this time. Those teenagers: the boy with the bandana and his two companions. He could see them clearly, even from here; and more figures had joined them, also teenagers by the look of them. He counted the group: ten. No shouts or gestures this time but the same sense of hostility from all.

He glanced back at Beth.

'Don't worry about them,' she said. 'They're no big deal.'

The surf crashed upon the beach again. He turned and saw a roller drive in and sweep up the sand towards them. It stopped close to their feet, then drew back into the sea.

'What did you want to show me?' he said.

She walked past him and started to climb, not up the dunes but crosswise towards the rocky shoulder of the headland. He followed, his eyes still on the figures, and then on Beth, and then the path, which he now saw was twisting upwards parallel to the rock, the ground hardening with every step. To his right were the hillocks around the foot of the dunes but the sand was firm here close to the headland, though uneven enough to make him nervous of his footing.

Beth walked ahead, as confident or apparently confident as when he'd first seen her. She seemed unconcerned about the path and not in the least bothered by the figures on top of the dunes, still watching from afar. He followed, wary of them, wary of her.

The path grew steeper and as they climbed higher, he started to feel the force of the wind again. He glanced back at the figures on the dunes, Dad's words running through his mind.

Sometimes you unsettle people. And they go for you.

He saw Beth had stopped and turned. She was watching him closely but it was hard to read her eyes. He caught her up and stopped too, then turned and

57

stared over the sea. A squall darkened the surface as it raced towards the shore.

'Why won't you look at me?' she said.

'I thought you didn't like it.' He went on gazing at the sea. 'You said I freak you out.'

'I said you freak some people out. I didn't say you freak me out.'

He looked back at her and saw her watching him still. The wind caught her hair and flung it over her face. She flicked her head and the hair flowed free. He felt a sudden desire to touch her.

'You can if you want,' she said. 'Touch me, I mean.'

Once again he glanced at the group on the dunes.

'It doesn't matter about them,' she said.

He knew what she wanted. She wanted him to touch her first, make the move; and he sensed she wanted those others to see it. He felt his hands tighten into fists, but they moved no further. She turned and set off towards the top of the headland.

He followed, unsure what to feel. He didn't want to hurt her, but he could see now that for all her confidence, he was causing her pain. Yet again he tried to remember what the old Will knew. All that came back was silence.

And with it a new set of fears. He glanced at the sea again as he tramped after Beth. There was a sluggishness in the surf that didn't feel right, and the moaning sounds were back. Once again he felt the shivering sensation over his feet, legs, and spine. He felt himself shudder but managed to climb on.

Beth didn't look back and seemed unaware of what was happening. He kept on walking, his eyes on her, on the figures on the dunes, but he was moving awkwardly now and he yearned to stop. They reached the top of the headland and Beth continued towards the farther end. He stopped, his body shaking, his mind screaming.

You get these trances.

'Trances,' he murmured.

You lose control.

His body was rigid now. The only movement was in his eyes as they twisted upwards against his will. The sky opened like a red mouth.

'No!' he screamed.

'Will, Will.' It was Beth and she was close again. He felt her hand. It was warm, strong, quite useless. His body was no longer his own, nor was his voice.

'Sickness.' It was muttering now. 'Sickness, it's . . . '

'Will—'

'It's here, it's . . . '

The red mouth widened. He saw shadowfaces swimming inside it. The moaning sounds grew louder and they were coming from the sea.

'Go away,' he pleaded.

The mouth closed, shutting the faces from view. He gave a cry and fell to the ground.

'Ah!'

'It's all right, Will.' She was bending over him again, as she'd done in the cave. 'It's all right. I'll take care of you.'

He stared past her towards the sky. The redness was easing and blue was coming back. He thought of the other girl's eyes—as blue as this, as wide as this. The moaning sounds stopped.

'Black hair, blue eyes,' he whispered.

He saw Beth's face close to his. She was stroking his cheek.

'Thank you,' he said.

'Can you get up?'

'I think so.'

For the second time she helped him to his feet. He stood still for a few moments, breathing hard, unsure what to say or do; then he realized he'd been supporting himself on her shoulder, and let go.

'It's all right,' she said. 'You can hold on to me if you want. You used to.'

'Did I?'

She nodded.

'You used to do it when you had your . . . turns. But sometimes you couldn't stay upright. You kind of blacked out and I had to help you lie down. And you'd keep talking like you did just now. About this . . . sickness.'

He frowned, trying yet again to remember. But as always, nothing came back.

'What else did I say?' he asked.

'Not much. I'm not sure you knew exactly what it was yourself. You just used to say there's this . . . sickness . . . in Havensmouth, and it was like it was driving you crazy not knowing what it was. You kept saying something's really, really wrong here. Most people in town thought you were off your head, and still do. But I reckon . . . '

She stopped suddenly, and looked away.

'What?' he said.

'You'll laugh at me if I tell you.'

'No, I won't.'

She looked back at him.

'I reckon you were close to finding out what it was. This sickness thing. It's just a feeling I had. Something about your manner. You were like a hunting dog on a scent. But then you had your accident.'

He watched her for a moment, then turned and stared about him.

She was right. There was something wrong here. He could feel it like a vapour all around him—on the dunes, in the sea, over the beach, round the headland. He turned and gazed through the gap in the dunes to where the woodland stretched away inland. He could feel it there too, though it was hard to tell how far it reached in that direction.

'Sickness,' he murmured.

The teenagers on the dunes had vanished.

He turned back to Beth and saw to his surprise that she wasn't there. She'd wandered over to the far side of the headland and was standing there with her back to him. He walked over and joined her. Below them was the second beach he'd seen from above the town, with more dunes rolling back from the shore.

And close to the base of the dunes was a tent.

'That's what I was going to show you,' said Beth.

He looked at her.

'There's a strange guy lives in it,' she said.

She paused and he had the feeling she was trying to prompt something from him. A memory probably. He glanced at the tent again. A battered, heavy-duty thing and anything but clean. There was no sign of its owner, or anyone else, but there was a ring of blackened stones outside with the embers of a fire still glowing.

'So you don't remember him?' said Beth. 'This guy?'

'No. Did I know him?'

'You used to, a bit, and his companion. That's another reason why some of the people in Havensmouth weren't too keen on you. You started talking to these two. But that was also when I got the feeling

61

you were starting to work out what's wrong in Havensmouth. What this sickness thing is.'

Will frowned. All these things Beth was telling him—things he'd once known. It seemed impossible that they would ever come back. Yet again he yearned for the old Will to return. If only to tell him what to do.

'What's the guy's name?' he said.

'They call him Crow round here. It's a nickname. Nobody knows his real name.'

'Why Crow?'

'Because he looks a bit like a crow. He's got thick black hair and a thick black beard, and a kind of beaky nose and shifty eyes. And he spends his time scavenging and living off other people's scraps. He's not liked in Havensmouth.'

'And he lives in this tent all the year round?'

'No, no, he's a tramp. He turns up in the spring most years, out of nowhere, and camps on the beach through the summer, then disappears again. No idea where he goes. Spends his time here beachcombing and living off what he can get. Totally weird and he keeps the tourists off this part of the beach, but that's not the reason why the locals don't like him.'

'Why don't they like him?'

'Because he's creepy. And this year people are even more wary of him. He used to come on his own but this time he turned up with a companion. And not just any companion.'

Beth hesitated.

'He turned up with Muck.'

8

A t that moment a form darkened the entrance to the tent. Will stared at it, searching for the boy, but it was a man about Dad's age.

'That's Crow,' said Beth.

Will studied the tramp as he crawled out and stood up. There was indeed something crow-like about him. The thick black hair reached well down over his shoulders, the beard covered most of his face, yet neither obscured the bird-like nose or the restless eyes. He was barefoot and had a torn pair of trousers with braces that stretched up and over an old checked shirt that was unbuttoned almost to the waist.

Then another figure appeared in the entrance to the tent.

'That's Muck,' said Beth.

The boy crawled out and stood in the sand, a scruffy kid of about seven, barefoot like the man, and as roughly dressed: shorts made from cut-off jeans, a tatty shirt and nothing more; and like the man, a shock of black hair.

'He says Muck's his son,' said Beth.

Will watched the pair. Everything about the boy's face and posture betrayed fear. The moment he'd spotted the two figures on the headland he'd snatched the man's arm and pulled himself close. The man reached out with his free hand and pressed the boy's head against his leg.

'Weird, aren't they?' said Beth.

Will looked at her.

'Why don't you like them?'

'I've got nothing against the boy,' she said. 'I feel sorry for him. But I don't like to get too close. He's smelly. He's really disgusting. That's why they call him Muck round here.' She watched them for a moment. 'It's Crow I don't like. He's shifty and stuff goes missing when he's around. I got really uncomfortable when you started talking to him.'

'What did I talk to him about?'

'I don't know. I kept well away. Didn't want to go near him. He gives me the creeps. Can you see why?'

Will didn't answer. He was watching the boy, who was now staring fixedly at him.

'What's Muck's real name?' he said.

'Nobody knows,' said Beth. 'Crow doesn't answer questions very much and the boy never speaks at all. He just hangs around with the tramp. Clings to him. See?'

The boy was indeed clinging to the tramp.

'They're almost always together,' she said. 'Just occasionally you spot Muck on his own, usually on the main beach where you saw him. He runs off quick if he sees someone coming.'

'Into the cave?'

'Usually.'

'And then where? You still haven't told me how he escaped.'

'There's a tiny passage out the other side of the rockface. Too low and narrow for most people but Muck can scramble through it. He ran into the cave when I was in there and crawled straight out the other side.'

'Did he see you?'

'Yes. As he ran past.'

'What did he do?'

'Ran faster. He's scared of everybody.'

'Except Crow.'

'Yes.'

Will went on watching the figures by the tent. Both were now looking up at him. He stared back, trying to gauge their feelings. The boy's were easy to read: he was still scared. The man's face was hard to see with the beard covering so much of it, but his body language, like the boy's, betrayed him.

Contempt, or perhaps more a kind of surliness. Pride certainly. Will narrowed his eyes. There was something else too, something that had just appeared in the tramp's posture: no softening of the stance but something more conciliating. Then suddenly the man turned, Muck's hand in his, and led the boy off down the beach. Muck glanced once over his shoulder, then the pair moved on, picking a path towards the sea.

'They're always beachcombing,' said Beth. 'Crow used to do it on his own but now he's got Muck with him, they both do it.'

Will followed them with his eyes. They were wandering about, peering into rock pools, picking over driftwood, searching the weed. Neither of them kept anything. They just picked things up, looked them over, dropped them and moved on.

'Told you Crow was weird,' said Beth. 'And now he's got Muck living with him, people are getting really suspicious.'

'What do you mean?'

'Well, they think it's dodgy, a creepy guy like that living in a tent with a young boy.'

'But Muck's his son.'

'Nobody knows that for certain. It's just what Crow's said. And if the boy's his son, how come he's suddenly turned up now? Crow used to come here on his own. There's something not right about those two.'

'But the boy's not scared of him.'

'Yeah, but . . . ' Beth leaned closer. 'Who knows what the guy's doing to make him like that?' She frowned. 'You know what people are saying in Havensmouth?'

'What?'

'They're saying it's like what paedos do. Grooming kids and all that. They're saying Crow could be some pervert. Just because the boy's clinging to him doesn't mean everything's all right. It might mean the guy's got him in his power. I'm not saying I believe that. But lots of people think that round here.'

Will stared out over the sea; and the image came back of the angel girl. Her face moved before him like a cloud, then vanished. The water started to darken again. He turned away, anxious not to see it.

'I've got to get back,' he said. 'My parents don't know I'm out.'

'Yes, they do.'

'What?'

She nodded towards the town. He whirled round and saw Mum and Dad hurrying along the top of the dunes towards the headland. They'd seen him and were waving furiously.

'I've got to go,' said Beth.

'But—'

'I'll see you around.'

And before he could speak again, she ran off down the track towards the woodland. A few moments

66

later she disappeared from view among the trees. Mum and Dad reached him, both out of breath.

'Will!' said Mum. Without warning she grabbed him and pulled him close. 'Not already.'

'What do you mean?'

'You're not back five minutes and it's starting all over again.'

'Mum—'

'You can't remember who we are. But you remember how to put us through hell, don't you?'

She pushed him sharply back again and turned away. He stared at Dad.

'We've got feelings too, Will,' he said.

'I know.'

'You've lost your memory but we've lost something as well. You're not the only one suffering here.'

'I know.'

'And we had hoped . . . ' Dad frowned. 'We had hoped you wouldn't be up to this kind of thing quite so soon.'

'What kind of thing?'

'Running off. Going God knows where. And worse still, hanging around with that . . . girl.'

'Beth?'

'Yes,' said Dad.

'What's wrong with her?'

'Did you find her or did she find you?'

'I don't know. We sort of found each other.'

'Do you remember her?'

'No.'

Dad glanced at Mum.

'Maybe that's something,' he said to her.

Will watched them, unsure what to make of all this.

'What's wrong with her?' he said again.

Mum stepped closer and he felt himself draw back. She stopped.

'I'm not going to hit you, Will.'

'I didn't think you were.'

'But you're wary of me.'

'Yes.'

'I'm sorry.' She hesitated. 'I didn't mean to grab you and then push you away. I was just upset. I won't do it again.'

They watched each other for a moment, then Mum stepped forward again. He let her approach and put her arms round him. The wind blew her hair across his eyes but he caught a glimpse of the sea through it. The surface was still darkening.

'Oh, Will,' she said. 'I really hoped this would all be over.'

'What's wrong with Beth?' he said.

'I didn't mean her. I meant all this other stuff. Running off and . . . I suppose you've been seeing things again.'

'You mean having hallucinations.'

'Don't be angry with us, Will. We can't see the things you see. So we don't know what to call them.'

He pushed her hair from his eyes and stared over her shoulder at the sea. It had darkened so much now that the blue had turned to a sickly red. He searched the water for the shadowfaces, sensing they were near; and there they were, floating upon the sea.

'Go away,' he murmured to them.

'Please, Will,' said Mum, 'don't tell me to do that.'

'I'm not talking to you.'

'Don't say that.'

He tried to step back but she was holding him too tightly. He took her hands and gently prised them from him, his eyes still on the water.

'I didn't mean what you thought,' he said.

'Will, look at me.'

He kept his eyes on the sea, unable to take them from it. The shadows were still there: faces staring up at the sky, up at him, and they were spreading, spreading, spreading in size until they seemed to cover the whole surface of the water all the way to the horizon. He felt a shiver run through him. The red was spreading too, seeping out of the water and over the lower stretches of the beach. He watched, trying not to believe in it.

Mum spoke again.

'Will, please look at me.'

The panic in her voice broke his eyes free. He looked at her now, gratefully. She seemed suddenly so fragile. He reached out, then stopped, unsure how to touch her. She took his hand, kissed it, held it, and he looked back at the sea.

It was still dark and so was the beach, but the redness was easing and some of the surf was pushing through. The faces were gone, stretched beyond recognition, and the water was turning grey.

'Will,' said Dad. 'Come back home.'

He didn't move.

'You're pale,' said Dad. 'Come back home. You've seen enough for now, whatever it is.'

Will went on searching the water. The darkness had gone and blue was forcing its way back through the grey, but something of the shadow remained: a heaviness in the air, a heaviness in him. He looked at Dad.

'I'm sorry,' he said. 'I'm really sorry.'

'Come on, Will.' Dad put a hand on his shoulder. 'You need to eat and rest. You've got yourself in a state again.'

Yes, he thought. Again.

'I didn't mean to frighten you both,' he said.

'I know,' said Dad. 'You never do mean to.'

The sea looked almost tranquil now. Beyond the harbour mouth he saw another fishing boat heading towards the point.

'You asked about Beth,' said Mum. 'Well, that's Stu Palmer's boat.'

'Who's he?'

'Beth's father.'

Will watched the boat for a moment, then glanced at Mum.

'Is that why you don't like her? Because she's a fisherman's daughter?'

'I don't care what her father does for a living,' said Mum. 'And I didn't say I don't like her.'

'But you and Dad don't like me seeing her.'

'Maybe, well . . . I don't know . . . ' Mum shrugged. 'We weren't too happy when she took a shine to you. She hangs around with some of the more rowdy teenagers in town. She's a bit like her father—seems to know just about everybody in Havensmouth. She also sees quite a lot of Brad and Micky Wetherby, and I've never been too keen on them. You saw them on the lane. Brad's the boy with the bandana. Micky's his brother. They're both a bit wild. Their parents own The Sea Chest.'

'The what?'

'The pub down by the harbour,' said Dad. 'Come on, let's go home.'

'There's a girl too,' said Will. 'I saw her with them. She's got mousy-grey hair.'

'That's Izzy Wetherby,' said Mum. 'Their sister. And there's a whole tribe of other teenagers they hang around with, including Beth. None of them particularly desirable company. So we weren't too pleased when Beth started spending time with you.'

'Home,' said Dad.

'Hold on.' Will caught them both by the arm as they tried to move off. 'I saw Brad and Micky on the dunes, and that other girl, their sister—'

'Izzy.'

'Yes, and they were really unfriendly—'

'I told you,' said Mum. 'They're not very desirable company.'

'But Beth wasn't like them. That's the point. She even stared them down and made them go away. So why don't you like her?'

Mum and Dad looked at each other.

'Tell me,' said Will.

'She's just a bit full on,' said Dad. 'A bit self-confident. And you're . . . I mean . . . '

'Weird.'

'No, not weird, but you're shy and deep and . . . '

'Different.'

'If you like. You take some understanding.'

'You still haven't told me what's wrong with Beth.'

'Nothing's wrong with her, but . . . ' Dad frowned. 'Let's just say she's a bit too self-confident for my liking. A bit too popular with too many boys, OK? You've got no experience whatever with the opposite sex, and she's got . . . well . . . enough said.'

And Dad set off towards the dunes. Will felt Mum take his arm.

'Come on, Will,' she said. 'Let's get home.'

He looked back over the other beach towards the tent. There was no sign of Crow and the boy called Muck. Probably just as well, he thought. No doubt Mum and Dad would disapprove of them too. The fishing boat drew close to the headland and he read the name on the side.

Spindrift.

Mum squeezed his arm.

'It'll be all right, Will,' she said.

He looked at her and said nothing.

9

The Four Winds and a meal, and then alone at last in his room again, and the long afternoon. It seemed to move as slowly as his thoughts. He sat in the middle of the floor, staring towards the balcony door, and through it to the sky outside. A pale sky, like a face drained of blood.

He looked about him. Piles and piles of paper, and on the walls, the drawings of the girl. He thought of the picture in the sand. There was no question in his mind that it was meant to be her. Someone else knew about this girl, and that person clearly cared enough to want to draw her.

He thought of Muck: the dirty, smelly boy. He'd been on the beach around the time of the drawing, or just after anyway. Perhaps he'd drawn the picture in the sand. Yet why, if the boy was so frightened of leaving Crow, come all this way on his own to draw such a picture? He could just as easily have drawn it on the other beach where it would have felt safer for him.

Unless the picture was meant to be seen by someone in the town. But that seemed a ridiculous thought. It had to be something else. He picked up the nearest pile of papers and took it out onto the balcony. There below him was the spot where the sand-picture had appeared. The tide had covered it now but there was no question that The Four Winds was the best place from which to see it.

But this was crazy. The picture couldn't have been meant for him.

He sat down cross-legged, below the level of the balcony rim, the pile of papers on his lap, and stared at the top sheet. As usual, a sketch of the girl looked up at him. He went through the pages one by one. Again and again it was her. Then he came to a different kind of page.

A page with words, and they were written in a hand he recognized at once from the exercise books and documents Mum and Dad had shown him in hospital.

His own.

> Over my eyes
> Dark water falling.

He pondered them for a moment, then closed his eyes and pictured the girl's. Blue eyes, like the ocean. How deep they were, how wide. Yet the ocean had darkened to black and red; and then the shadowfaces had come. He opened his eyes again and saw the sky stretched over him with the same pale face.

'Dark water falling,' he whispered.

Something dropped into his mind: not an image of dark water but a memory, a clear memory. It had come as effortlessly as Beth's name had fallen into his mouth earlier. There was something gold around the time of the accident. He remembered the tree, the bird, the lane. He remembered the blue and the black and the red. But there was something gold too. He'd clearly seen it. He closed his eyes again.

And the shadowfaces appeared.

He gave a start at the sight of them. They swirled close, as hideous and distorted as before. He tried to will himself to open his eyes again but they seemed to be locked closed. He felt that queasy chill run over his feet, legs, and spine. The faces pressed closer, as though they'd entered through his closed lids and were driving deep inside him.

Something brushed his face. He gave a jerk and his eyes flew open. He was still sitting on the balcony but he had pulled his knees close in to his chest, the pile of papers bundled together in one hand. He looked around him, breathing hard.

No one was on the balcony.

No one but him.

He relaxed the grip on his knees, eased his legs out in front of him, and looked down again at the bundle of pages in his hand.

> Over my eyes
> Dark water falling

On an impulse he crumpled this page up and threw it to the side—then gave another start.

On the page underneath was a picture of the shadowfaces.

He had drawn them. The old Will had drawn them. He stood up, trembling, the papers still in his hand, the picture of the faces still on top. What was happening? This had to be imagination. Maybe Mum and Dad and the experts were right and this was hallucination.

Maybe he was mad.

Something brushed his face again. The wind, a gust of wind, no more. He reached up and felt his cheek. He'd been sure it was something else, but he was so jumpy now it was hard to tell what he was seeing or feeling.

He thought of the old Will again, the Will who unsettled people; and for a brief moment he sensed that the old Will was still there, still inside him, close to the surface. He stared down at the papers in his hand.

The shadowfaces stared back. There was no mistaking what they were. He'd drawn them exactly as they'd appeared to him as he hurtled towards death. He forced himself to study them, as calmly and dispassionately as he could, as though they were just a drawing.

They *are* just a drawing, he told himself. On this page anyway. So study them like a drawing. Be rational. Count them. Start off by counting them. That was a good idea. He hadn't managed to count them before. Whenever they'd appeared, they'd always been moving and he'd been too scared. But here they were, static on the page.

He counted them.

Five.

Already he felt better. He'd felt sure there were more of them before.

'Do it again,' he said aloud. 'Touch them as you count them.'

He went slowly from face to face, touching each one with the tip of his finger as he counted aloud.

'One . . . two . . . three . . . four . . . five.'

Five shadowfaces, long and distorted and painful to look at, but already less scary for being just five, and less scary again for having been touched.

Analyse them, he told himself. Make them even less scary. He ran his eye over them as critically as he could, speaking his thoughts aloud again.

'Badly drawn. I should have done much better than this. The one top right looks shoddy. The lines don't even connect where they're supposed to meet. The one in the middle's out of proportion. The one far left's . . . '

He stopped suddenly. Something was coming from the faces, something he hadn't seen before. It wasn't anything scary—somehow the faces had ceased to be scary now, at least on paper—but it was something else.

He was sure they were speaking to him.

The faces went on staring up at him with silent mouths. He gazed at them, yearning to understand. But it was no good. He could not grasp what they were saying, if anything. He looked up from the drawing and saw a figure moving on the beach.

Crow.

The tramp, the beachcomber, the weirdo, the father of Muck—maybe. And that other word—maybe.

Paedo.

It was a word he hated, a word he wished his memory had not retained. But it was still there. He knew it well enough. He stared at the man as he plodded along the beach just above the level of the surf, heading this way.

'Is that what you are?' he whispered. 'A paedo? Or is that what people want to think?'

He searched for some sign of Muck but he was nowhere to be seen. Perhaps the boy was hiding in his passage in the cave. But figures were now moving again on top of the dunes. Five teenagers, boys, and two were familiar: Brad Wetherby, no bandana this time, and his brother Micky close behind. There was no sign of their sister.

Will watched. As before, Brad was clearly the leader and it was obvious that the others, including Micky, were ready to do whatever he wanted. It was soon apparent what that was.

They'd come to jeer at Crow.

The tramp took no notice of the catcalls and walked doggedly on. The shouts continued, Brad leading the group along the top of the dunes and moving ever closer to The Four Winds. Will stepped up to the rail. The teenagers seemed so far unaware of him, their attention being fixed on the tramp. The man didn't stop and simply pushed on towards the base of the hill.

Suddenly a hail of stones flew down from the top of the dunes. None of them hit the tramp but several thudded into the sand close by him. He walked on, not looking up or increasing his speed. Far away at the end of the beach, something darkened the entrance to the cave.

Will stiffened. It was Muck, definitely. He was hovering in the entrance, half-in, half-out, as though waiting to decide whether to stay or run. A moment later he disappeared inside the cave. Will looked back at Crow. He was now close to the path that led from the beach to the road. The teenagers had drawn back but were watching silently.

Suddenly the tramp stopped and looked up. Will froze. There was no mistaking the direction of the man's gaze. He was looking up at the balcony, his body twisted into the same attitude of surliness it had had on the other beach. Will stared back, wondering what things he had talked about with this man.

Then, to his surprise, a new figure appeared.

A bald man, about thirty, in a loose shirt and jeans. He had clearly come from the direction of the town and was now striding down the path onto the beach. He was carrying a supermarket bag in each hand. Crow continued to stare up at the balcony, then, almost with reluctance, he turned to face the other man.

The two exchanged a few words, then the bald-headed man handed over the supermarket bags, strode back up the track and disappeared from view. Crow put the bags down and poked about inside them. Even from here Will could see that they contained groceries and mineral water.

Brad and the others had disappeared from view.

Crow went on poking through the bags, then suddenly straightened up, holding an apple. He took a bite from it and stared up at the balcony again, then raised his other arm and brandished it. Will watched. It didn't seem like a gesture of hatred. It seemed like . . .

A summons.

But now Crow had turned and without a backward glance was shuffling off towards Breeze Point. Beyond the headland three fishing boats were heading back towards the harbour. Will looked down at the papers in his hand and saw the shadowfaces still watching with their hollow eyes.

'Over my eyes,' he murmured, 'dark water falling.'

As before, he crumpled up the page inside his fist;

and as before he gave a start at what he saw on the next sheet. Words again, but this time not in his own hand, nor in anyone's hand. These were cut from a newspaper and pasted onto the sheet.

YOU ARE EVIL.

YOU aRE DeAd.

10

'Will! Open the door!'
The voices seemed to come from a distant place, a distant time.

'Will!'

'Will!'

He recognized Mum's and Dad's voices, but now there was a third.

'No need to stay inside, Will.'

A man's voice, somehow familiar and unfamiliar at the same time.

'Will, please.' Mum again, pleading. 'Unlock the door. Or at least . . . say something.'

He pulled the bedcovers more tightly over him. Dad's voice came again, more distant than ever.

'Will, we'll have to force the door if you won't open it.'

Will closed his eyes. The shadowfaces appeared at once before his inner gaze.

'Over my eyes, dark water falling,' he whispered.

The faces went on gaping at him as he dug himself further into the cocoon of bedclothes. He screwed his eyes tight, trying to squash the faces into nothing, but they went on swimming before him. He heard a crash as Mum and Dad forced the door, then the sound of heavy steps. A moment later the bedclothes were flung back. He buried his face in the pillow and screamed.

'Will, Will.' It was Mum, soothing. 'It's all right, darling.'

He felt her hand on his shoulder.

'It's all right, Will.'

The hand squeezed, let go, stroked his hair. He felt tears break out and rubbed them off against the pillow. He heard a soft, painful moan. It seemed to come from him.

'Easy, Will.' Dad's voice now. 'It's all right.'

From somewhere far away came the crash of surf. Another distant place, another distant time. He wondered where he was, where he'd been.

'What . . . ' he muttered, his face still pushed into the pillow. 'What . . . time . . . is it?'

'Half past five,' said Mum.

'You mean . . . in the . . . '

'Afternoon. You've been up here for three hours.'

The hand went on stroking his hair.

'We should have checked you earlier,' she said. 'I'm so sorry, Will.'

He rolled over and saw three faces watching him: Mum and Dad, looking frightened, and a man with an expression that was hard to read; a man who looked familiar, a bald-headed man.

The beach. He remembered now. It was the guy who'd handed the groceries to the tramp.

'This is John Shepherd,' said Mum.

'Our vicar,' said Dad. 'You knew him once. But you probably don't remember him now, do you?'

Will shook his head. The man called John Shepherd smiled. Will studied him: strong body, strong face. Same loose clothes he'd been wearing on the beach: shirt unbuttoned at the top, sleeves rolled up, no dog-collar. His skin was brown and weatherbeaten.

'You don't look much like a vicar.'

'So people tell me, Will,' said the man placidly. 'Indeed, you told me so yourself once.'

'John looked in to see how you were,' said Mum. She glanced at the vicar. 'Not too good today, John. As you see.'

John Shepherd said nothing.

'What's going on, Will?' said Dad. 'Why lock the door and hide in bed? And why all this?'

'All what?'

'This!' said Dad, and he gestured round the room.

Will sat up in bed—and gasped. There were new pictures scrawled on the wall, not of the girl but of the shadowfaces; and that was not all. The paper that had littered the room had been moved. The floor was now clear but the balcony was carpeted with white. The sheets had been torn into tiny shreds and now formed a blanket of papery snow. As he watched, the wind caught some of the topmost flakes and whipped them away towards the beach.

He stared. He had no recollection of tearing up the papers, moving them, drawing the new pictures on the walls; no recollection of locking the door and burying himself under the bedclothes. He remembered the death threat, and it must have been that that prompted this—but all that followed was a blank.

'Put some clothes on, Will,' said Mum.

He looked down, still confused. He'd forgotten undressing too. He pulled the bedclothes around him and stared at them.

'You act like you didn't know you were naked,' said John Shepherd.

Will looked at him. He liked this man. He didn't know why. Perhaps the old Will had liked him too.

'Did I use to argue with you?' he said to the vicar.

'All the time, Will. It was rather fun.' John Shepherd paused. 'Are you guessing this or are you remembering? Or did your mum and dad tell you about it?'

'We didn't,' said Mum.

'Maybe you're remembering a bit, Will,' said Dad.

Will kept his eyes on John Shepherd.

'What did we argue about?'

'We didn't argue,' said the vicar.

'You just said we did.'

'I said you argued with me. I didn't say I argued with you.'

'What do you mean?'

'You did all the arguing.'

'What did I argue with you about?'

'All kinds of stuff. But most of all it was the thing you didn't like in my church.'

Mum and Dad stiffened, but John Shepherd went on in the same unruffled voice.

'Can you remember what that was, Will?'

He didn't answer. He could feel that icy movement over his feet, legs, and spine again. With a supreme effort he forced his body to betray nothing. John Shepherd watched him for a moment, then turned to Mum and Dad.

'I think Will needs to put some clothes on. He's shivering.'

'Of course,' said Mum. 'Come on, Will. Get dressed.'

She picked up his clothes from the floor.

'You obviously just dumped these and dived into bed.' She passed him the clothes. 'We'll be downstairs, OK? Come down when you're ready.' She hesitated. 'Will?'

'Yes?'

'You will get dressed and come down, won't you?'

'Yes.' Will thought for a moment. 'And I want to go out.'

'Where?' said Mum.

'To the church.'

'Are you sure?' said Dad. 'I mean, it wasn't exactly . . . your favourite place.'

'What didn't I like about it?'

John Shepherd answered.

'Let's see if you remember when you get there.' He looked at Mum and Dad. 'I'll take Will if you want.'

'You don't have to,' said Dad.

'No, I'd like to. If it's no problem with either of you. Or Will obviously.'

'You OK about that, Will?' said Mum.

'Yeah.'

I suppose, he thought.

'But do you really want to go out?' said Mum. 'You were in such a state just now, I'd have thought—'

'I'm OK,' said Will. 'I really want to go.'

'All right,' said Dad. 'We'll see you downstairs.'

And they left him alone. He climbed out of bed and stood there for a moment. Mum was right, of course. He was still in a state. The death threat had shaken him badly. But he couldn't stay locked in his room. He knew that. He had to find things out about his past.

Or try to.

Downstairs he heard Mum and Dad talking to John Shepherd. He didn't catch the words but the tone was clear: anxiety from Mum and Dad, something hard to define from the vicar. A sort of detachment, not a lack of feeling but a kind of . . . acceptance of things.

The thing you didn't like in my church.

He tried to remember what Mum had said about the incident there.

You got a bit upset and had to be taken away.

He dressed, then walked over to the balcony door and opened it. The wind was still whisking the top layer of paper flakes into the air. Some were swirling away over the edge of the balcony, some back into the room. He stared down. He must have torn the sheets up himself. No one else could have done it. So why couldn't he remember?

He was starting to wonder what memory was. The accident had wiped away his recollection of people and places and events, and yet now, it seemed he'd suffered from memory lapses anyway: moments like this when he came upon things he'd done just an hour or two ago, yet could not recall.

He felt a sudden rush of panic and closed his eyes. Something brushed his face, something warm. He tensed for a moment, then relaxed. He'd felt that before out here on the balcony, when he'd come out to study the pictures. It was just the wind from the sea.

Then he saw her face.

A slow shimmering form, easing from the darkness under his brows, but unmistakably her, even the blue of her eyes now, pricking out from the black. He felt the warmth on his face again.

'Touch me,' he murmured.

But she was gone.

He opened his eyes again. Far down the beach he could see Beth standing by the entrance to the cave. Next to her was Brad. She was retying his bandana. There was nobody else in sight. He heard Dad call from downstairs.

'Will! You all right?'

He stepped back into his room, closed the balcony door behind him, and looked over the walls at the new pictures. The shadowfaces stared back at him.

'Who are you?' he said.

He glanced at one of the pictures of the girl.

'And who are you? An angel or a hallucination?' He reached out and touched the drawing. 'And why did you save my life?'

'Will!' called Mum.

He made his way downstairs.

'We were all getting worried about you again,' she said.

Will looked from face to face. John Shepherd didn't look worried about anything but it seemed pointless to mention that.

'Sorry,' he said.

'Are you still sure you want to see the church?' said Dad.

'Yes.'

'Well, just remember it's . . . you know . . . a sacred place. To be treated with—'

'He'll be fine,' said John. 'And I promise to bring him back.'

'We'll get rid of all that paper from the balcony while you're out,' said Mum. 'I presume you don't want it, seeing as you've torn it to pieces?'

'Thanks,' said Will. He hesitated. 'Sorry about the mess.'

'Be careful while you're out,' she said.

John Shepherd opened the front door.

'We'll see you later,' he said.

11

'So what am I supposed to call you?' said Will as they walked down the hill.

'John seems like a good idea.'

'Not Reverend or Vicar or . . . '

'Your Grace?' A half-smile appeared on John Shepherd's face. 'Your Eminence? Your Holiness?' He chuckled. 'No, I think we'll stick with John.'

They passed the sign pointing to the beach path and headed on towards the town. Below them, just up from the harbour, the church nestled among the houses and shops. Will stared at it, trying to remember what it was he'd once seen there and didn't like.

But it was no good. He simply had no memory of it.

He looked at John. He seemed such an odd sort of vicar. He walked with a brisk, elastic step, more like an athlete than a preacher; he dressed in loose, informal clothes; he insisted on being called John; and he was happy to spend time with a boy who'd argued with him and had a problem with his church.

But maybe there was another motive for this trip.

'I suppose you're going to start talking to me about God and stuff.'

'Did you want me to start talking to you about God and stuff?' said John.

'Not particularly.'

'Then I think we'll pass on that.'

And the vicar walked calmly on. Will looked away, feeling slightly nettled. There was something unnerving about John's self-possession. They passed two men working on a power cable by the side of the road.

'Afternoon, John,' said one.

'All right, John?' said the other.

John nodded to both.

'Fine, thanks.'

Will caught the mixture of messages in the men's eyes: respect for John, something else for him; not exactly hostility but a certain wariness. They passed a woman watering her hanging baskets.

Same again. Respect for John, wariness of him.

And so it went on as they drew closer to the centre of the town. Everyone here seemed to like the vicar. Everyone here seemed to distrust the boy walking with him; and some felt more than distrust.

There was no mistaking the feelings of the two teenage boys riding their bikes up the road. Will stiffened. He remembered seeing them on the lane when Mum and Dad had brought him back from Newton Barnet. They hurtled up the road, then wheelied past, glaring at him. He watched them go, then turned and gazed the other way.

Far over to the right, through a gap between the houses, he could see the headland of Breeze Point. A small black-haired figure was standing at the end, staring out to sea. Further inland, but also on the headland, was Crow, watching. Beth and Brad Wetherby were nowhere to be seen.

Will stopped suddenly, the icy feeling on his limbs again.

'Something's wrong,' he said. 'Something's . . . really wrong. Something in Havensmouth.'

John stopped too and looked at him.

'I know, Will.'

'You do?'

'Yes.'

'Is it me?'

'I don't think so.'

Will stared back at him.

'Then what is it? I can feel something but I don't know what it is.'

'I don't know either.' John thought for a moment. 'Before your accident you used to talk about a sickness in the town.'

'That's what it feels like. I don't know any other way to describe it.' Will frowned. 'Why do they all hate me here?'

'They don't all hate you.'

'Lots do.'

He turned back towards Breeze Point. Crow was now leading the small figure away from the end of the headland. Will glanced at John and saw him watching the figures too.

'I saw you giving that man food today,' he said.

John didn't answer.

'Does he live off your handouts?'

'I don't know,' said John. 'I've never asked him.'

'Some people are saying he's a paedophile.'

'Some people are saying you're mad.'

Will stared at the vicar.

'That's a strange answer,' he said.

'Come and see my church,' said John.

They made their way down the main street of the town, past the bakery, past the souvenir shop, past the garage, and into the little square that housed the church and graveyard. John stopped at the gate and fumbled with the catch.

'Bit stiff, this thing,' he muttered. 'Keep meaning to get it sorted.'

Will gazed up at the bell-tower and then past it into the sky: a familiar, ocean blue. A moment later he heard the groan of the gate as it swung open.

'Come inside,' said John.

He followed John down the path and into the church. There were no other people there. He looked at the vicar, standing just inside the door, as quiet and still as the church itself.

'Is it here?' said John after a while.

A long silence, broken only by the distant crash of surf and the sound of men's voices somewhere down the street. Will said nothing; he was still listening to the sounds and trying to feel whatever he had once felt here. Suddenly, without warning, John closed the door of the church.

Darkness thickened around them.

'Don't be alarmed,' said John.

Another long silence, the surf barely audible now, the men's voices gone. Will went on listening. He could hear John's breathing, slow and deep, and the sound of his own more jerky breaths, though they were slowing down. John spoke again.

'Is it here? The thing you didn't like?'

Will looked round at him. The man's form seemed ghostlike in the dusky space.

'No,' he answered. 'Whatever it was, it's not here.'

Yet something was wrong. He closed his eyes and listened to the silence again. Something had been here, something he hadn't liked, didn't like—and it would come again. The question was: where was it now?

He opened his eyes again.

'I want to go out.'

'Sure,' said John, and he opened the door.

Light came flooding in and the sky seemed bluer than before. Will stepped out of the church and waited by the gate. John closed the door behind him and walked over to join him.

'So you don't remember what it was that you didn't like?'

'No.' Will paused. 'You'll have to tell me.'

'I don't know either.'

'That's helpful. You don't know anything and I don't know anything.'

John smiled.

'I think you know far more than you realize, Will. Even with your memory not working. I can only sense something's not right here. But you see things. And I think, just before your accident, you were close to finding out something really important.'

'Someone else told me that.'

'Really?'

'Yes. She said I was like a hunting dog on a scent.'

'That's a good way of putting it.'

He looked at John.

'What did I do in your church?'

'You stood up suddenly in the middle of my sermon and started freaking everybody out.'

'How?'

'You had a kind of trance, and then started spouting about sickness. That wasn't unusual. You'd done that before, around the town, but it was different this time because you spoke so forcefully and to so many people at once. We had a packed congregation that day.' John took a slow breath. 'But what upset people most was that you appeared to attack the church.'

'What do you mean?'

'You said the sickness was inside the church.'

Will looked back at the ancient building, now bright in the sun.

'That put a lot of people's backs up,' said John. 'We've got a very active congregation here. Your mum and dad are worshippers. You used to come too, sometimes, though I know it was only to please your mum.'

Will shook his head.

'I'm sorry,' he said. 'About the church thing. I didn't mean to upset you.'

'You didn't upset me, Will. Quite the contrary. You interested me. And what fascinated me most was what you said about sickness.'

'Why?'

John leaned closer.

'Because it was as though in that moment in church you'd suddenly understood something, had a gift of clarity, revelation even. You weren't just ranting about sickness in Havensmouth. You'd done that before. This was different. I was sure you'd found something out. And it was something that became clear to you during that service. I felt certain you'd have said more if they hadn't taken you away. And then of course you had that dreadful accident shortly afterwards.'

John reached out suddenly and put a hand on Will's shoulder.

'Take care of yourself, Will. Do you understand what I'm saying?'

'Yes.'

93

'Be a little cautious. No, be very cautious. You've made a few enemies. It's not just the people who were in church that day who know about what happened. Word's gone round the town. And there are some very rough elements in Havensmouth.'

'I know.'

John opened the gate.

'Time to get you home.'

'I'm not going home,' said Will. 'Not yet.'

'But—'

'I've got to . . . I don't know . . . ' Will looked about him. 'I've got to find out what's going on.'

'Will, what did I just tell you about being cautious?'

'I'll be cautious,' said Will. 'I'll be really, really careful. You don't have to follow me about. I can look after myself.'

'You were hiding in bed with the door locked a short while ago.'

'I'm all right now.'

'I promised your parents I'd bring you back.'

'Well, I'm not ready to go back yet.'

'But what did you want to see?'

'I don't know,' said Will. 'Just . . . stuff.'

And he turned down the main street and headed towards the harbour. As he expected, John soon caught him up, moving as before with the same lightness of step. Will threw a glance at him.

'You a sportsman or something?'

'Judo,' said John.

'Judo?'

'Yes. Do you remember what that is?'

'A martial art.'

'Right.' John gave him a quizzical look. 'Strange how your memory works in some places but not others.'

'Yeah,' said Will. 'It works everywhere except the places where I really want it to. You any good?'

'What, at judo?'

'Yeah.'

'Black belt.'

'Now you're showing off.'

John chuckled but said nothing.

'Doesn't it feel a bit odd?' said Will. 'I mean, doing judo and—'

'Working for God?'

Will raised an eyebrow.

'I thought we were going to pass on God today.'

'Sorry,' said John. 'I lapsed. What were you going to say?'

'I was going to say doesn't it feel a bit odd doing judo and living here? I mean, there can't be many people you can practise with in this little place.'

'I drive to Newton Barnet. They've got an active club there.'

They were close to the end of the main street now and the harbour was opening before them. From inside the pub on the corner came the sound of voices. Will glanced up at the sign as they approached.

The Sea Chest.

A moment later the door of the pub burst open and a man of about thirty tottered out. It was clear at once that he was going to miss the step. Will jumped forward but John was quicker and caught the man just before he hit the ground.

'Easy, Davy,' he said.

The man called Davy swung his face round and peered up at the vicar.

'Shepherd,' he mumbled, 'you . . . bloody . . . '

95

Whatever he meant to say was lost as with a violent movement he twisted his head the other way and threw up against the side of the pub. A bearded man came hurrying out, followed at once by a short, capable-looking woman.

'Davy, for God's sake,' she said, then, 'John, get him over to that seat by the harbour wall, can you?' She threw a glance at the bearded man. 'Give John a hand.'

John and the bearded man helped Davy over to the seat where he was promptly sick again. Will made to follow but the woman caught him by the arm.

'Will,' she said, 'it's great to see you back in the land of the living.'

He stared at her, wondering who she was. She smiled.

'I know. I've heard. You can't remember much. Does my face mean anything to you?'

The bearded man gave a laugh and called across.

'It's a few years since your face meant much to anybody.'

'Nobody asked your opinion,' she retorted, and the man laughed again.

'But she can still pull 'em in,' roared Davy, vomit on his chin. 'Can't you? Still pull 'em in, right?'

The woman shook her head.

'Davy, please tell me that's not meant to be a chat-up.'

But Davy was already being sick again. The woman turned back to Will, beckoned him out of earshot of the others, and lowered her voice.

'Don't mind them, Will. Davy abuses everybody when he's drunk but he's quite harmless. And the bearded guy's harmless too. I know that. He's my husband. The point is—how are you?'

'I'm . . . I'm all right . . . '

'Are you sure? After all you've been through?'

'Yeah, I'm . . . '

'Do you remember me at all?'

He stared at her, trying to focus his mind.

'I don't know . . . I . . . '

'Nothing?' she said. 'Nothing at all?'

'I . . . '

'What about my name? Do you remember that?'

If this woman and the bearded man owned the pub, then he could guess the surname from what Mum and Dad had told him. But that would also mean they were the parents of Brad, Micky, and Izzy.

'Do you remember my name?' she said again.

'Wetherby?'

'Good!' she said, smiling. 'Well done! What else?'

He shook his head.

'Nothing?' she said.

He took a slow breath.

'I only guessed your surname because Mum and Dad told me it.'

'How come?'

'I saw your . . . kids . . . on the dunes. Mum and Dad told me their names. Said their parents owned The Sea Chest.'

'Oh.' The woman frowned. 'So it wasn't a memory. It was just a guess.'

'Yes.'

'Oh, Will. I'm so sorry. This must be horrible for you.' She took his arm. 'And my kids . . . please tell me they weren't vile to you. They can be a bit badly behaved sometimes.'

He shrugged, unsure what to say. The woman gave his arm a squeeze.

'It's all right, Will. Say no more. I can guess what they were like. And I apologize profusely. Brad's got a bit of an attitude, Micky does whatever Brad does, and Izzy's gone from goddess to drama queen in a matter of weeks. Don't ask me why. Teenagers are another species as far as I'm concerned.'

The woman gave a sigh.

'Anyway, my name's Sarah, OK? Sarah Wetherby. That bearded lump over there's called Geoff. He was quite good looking when I married him. Hard to believe, I know. And the reason why we know you is because we used to see a lot of you round the harbour. You liked coming here with Beth.'

She glanced towards the others.

'We'd better go and see how Davy's coming along. But don't let him upset you. Remember what I said. He tends to abuse everybody when he's had too many.'

They walked over to the seat by the harbour wall where Davy was now sitting more or less upright. His eyes were blurred but they managed to settle on Will.

'I know you,' he muttered. 'You're the crazy boy who says he sees stuff.'

'That's enough, Davy,' said Sarah.

'So what do you see now? Eh?'

'A drunken jerk,' said Geoff. 'That's what he sees. And so do we.'

'Like I give a toss,' said Davy. 'Eh, Reverend? Like I give a toss.'

'Right, Davy,' said John. 'Come on, Will. Let's go.'

But Will didn't move. He was staring into Davy's eyes, and they were staring back. Another deep blue, almost as deep as the girl's. He peered into them, trying to find a way past the man's anger and into the part of him that was trying to speak. But at that moment there was a shout from the harbour.

'All right! Where is he?'

A broad-shouldered man of about forty was climbing out of a rowing boat onto the quay.

'Now you're for it, Davy,' said Sarah.

Davy simply dropped his head and threw up again. The big man was hurrying towards them. Will felt Sarah take his arm again.

'That's Stu Palmer,' she said quietly. 'He owns *Spindrift*. Davy's one of the crew. When he manages to turn up, that is.'

'Will ought to remember Stu Palmer,' said Geoff. He gave Will a wink. 'Beth's dad. You remember Beth, right?'

Will didn't answer. He was watching Stu Palmer approach. A huge presence, he seemed, even from afar. The man reached them, looked quickly round, then fixed his eye on Davy.

'You waste of space,' he growled. 'Why do I bother?'

To Will's surprise, the man suddenly flashed a glance at him.

'Welcome back, Will. Glad you're still in one piece. Have you seen Beth yet?'

'Stu,' said Sarah. 'Take it slowly. He's still making sense of things.'

'OK, OK.' Stu reached out and gave Will a pat on the arm. 'Give it time, boy. It'll all come back. Come and see us whenever you want. Your mum and dad'll remember where we live even if you can't. I know Beth's itching to see you again.'

'I saw her.'

'Oh, you did? She never said.'

'On the beach.'

'Well, that's good.' Stu smiled at him. 'So come and see us. Come and see us soon.' He looked back at Davy, now bent over his knees. 'I'd better sort out this beer-bucket.'

'Need any help?' said Geoff.

'No, no. I've got plenty of help, thanks. And they're all practised hands at dealing with him, believe me. I just wish they didn't have to be.'

Stu glanced over his shoulder to where three tough-looking men were making their way up the quay. Sarah whispered into Will's ear.

'Robbo, Andy, and Lee. The rest of Stu's crew.'

But Will barely took them in. His mind and his gaze had drifted beyond them to the outer harbour, and from there towards the horizon, where the sky was darkening again.

12

Midnight. Stars pushing through the cloud cover. A vagrant moon. The song of surf, softer now that the sea was calm. The clutch of sand particles between his toes. He stood on the beach and stared out across the velvet waste.

No ship or boat, no sign of life, just the blurred extremities of land on either side: Breeze Point to the right, the harbour to the left. The town itself was a presence he could not see, and did not wish to. The ocean would do. The ocean held all the secrets he wanted right now.

But what were they?

He stared at it, at the darkness on the horizon, still there, still visible, even past the setting of the sun, a darker dark even than this troubled night sky. He sat down on the sand, just above the reach of the surf, pulled his knees into his chest and let his head drop.

'Come to me,' he whispered.

She came, as though on the wind of his thoughts. He felt her first, somewhere close, and looked up and saw her there, standing in the shallow water, facing him, the wash of the sea white around her legs. She was wearing a simple skirt and a kind of smock, and the moon shimmered upon her black hair.

About fifteen, she seemed, yet somehow ageless too, and not really physical at all. Where Beth was beautiful in a tangible way, this girl was not. Her beauty came from something else. She was decidedly not for touching. Yet even so, he yearned to be closer to her.

He stood up. She did not move. She simply watched, her eyes fixed upon him. Even from here he sensed the blue of the ocean in those wide pools. He took a step closer and saw her body fade.

'Wait,' he said, stopping.

She was still there, still visible, still watching him. The water sighed against her, bright and phosphorescent. A gust caught her hair and it streamed out for a moment, then rested on her shoulders again as the breeze died.

'Don't fade,' he murmured.

Her face was half-hidden by the darkness. Only her eyes showed clear in the night. He hesitated, then took another step towards the sea. Again the figure started to fade.

'No.'

He stopped again. Still she was there, still she watched him. He clenched his hands, then relaxed them again. No movement from the figure before him. He took a long, slow breath. It felt rich with the spirit of the sea, and something of the girl came with it.

'Speak to me,' he said.

She did not speak. Yet she understood him. He sensed that clearly; and some part of her seemed to reach out to him through her eyes. He sensed a restlessness in the sea behind her. He took his eyes reluctantly from her and searched the water. No further forms had appeared, just waves moving with the night, yet he sensed the shadowfaces somewhere close. He looked back at the girl, took another slow breath, then eased his foot forward.

One step, no more, his eyes fixed on the girl. She did not move and this time did not fade, though he sensed the fragility of her form. He took another step. Again she did not fade. She was just a short way from him now. Once more he caught the restlessness in the sea behind her. He stared over the water, aware of the shadowfaces close again, though he could not see them.

Another gust sent the girl's hair streaming. A larger wave rolled in, just below shoulder height. He saw it lick past her, race on towards the beach and crash onto the shore, its wreckage bubbling up the sand to die at his feet. He looked back at the girl. She was still there, glistening with the remnants of the wave. He stared past her again, searching for the shadowfaces. They were even closer now. He knew it, though they were still hidden.

Then he heard a voice behind him.

'What are you seeing?'

He whirled round and saw Crow watching him from further up the beach. He was carrying some driftwood in his arms.

'Eh?' said the tramp.

Will looked back at the sea. The figure of the girl was gone, as he'd somehow known it would be. The waves washed over the space where she had been, bearing the thought of her but nothing more. The shadowfaces too had somehow withdrawn.

Yet darkness remained on the horizon.

He turned and faced the man. The tramp hadn't moved but his scratchy eyes were only partly watching. Even as they kept a check on Will, they were darting about the beach. Will caught a movement close to the headland.

'He's over there,' he called to the tramp. 'By the entrance to the cave.'

Crow turned his gaze in that direction. Muck had clearly been watching but he froze at once on seeing them both stare at him. The tramp gave him a wave, but the boy still seemed frightened and a moment later disappeared inside the cave. Crow looked back at Will.

'What are you seeing?' he said again.

'A girl. In the water. A beautiful girl, like an angel.'

'Where is she now?'

'She's gone.'

Will started to walk up the beach. Crow watched him suspiciously but did not move. Will stopped a short distance away, picked up a stick of timber from the sand, and walked with it towards the tramp. The man took a step back.

Will shook his head.

'It's for your collection, not your face.'

Crow stopped moving but still looked wary.

'I'm a friend of John Shepherd's,' said Will. 'He gives you food, right?'

'He's a good man. One of the few.'

'Well, I'm a friend of his. So I'm not going to hurt you. Or little Muck.'

The tramp seemed to relax a little. Will held out the stick.

'Here,' he said. 'For the fire. Or whatever you want it for.'

Crow took the stick.

'This girl you just saw . . . '

'What about her?'

'Is she dead?'

Will looked down at the sand.

'Angels don't die,' he said.

He felt a heaviness inside him and with it a savage pain. He gazed out again towards the horizon. Something hard touched his arm and he looked round. Crow had reached out with the stick and prodded him with the tip.

'You were meant to come back. You weren't meant to die in that accident.' The man paused. 'Maybe you're an angel too.'

'I don't think so,' said Will. 'You're called Crow, aren't you?'

'It's one of the names people give me round here. I've got others. Paedo's quite popular.'

'Did I know you before my accident?'

'We were starting to talk.'

'Then why were you wary of me just now?'

'I'm wary of everybody,' said the tramp. 'I've learned to be.'

'What did we talk about?'

'Muck.'

Will glanced towards the cave again but there was no sign of the boy.

'He won't come out till you've gone,' said the tramp. 'He's got a little hiding place in there where no one can get him.'

'The passage that leads out to the other beach. Beth Palmer told me about it.'

'Well, it's his little place. He crawls under there and no one can reach him. But he won't be there right now.'

'Where's he right now?' said Will.

'Just inside the entrance to the cave. He'll be watching us to see what's going on. He'll only crawl into his hole if he thinks he's in danger.'

'Which he does most of the time.'

'Ah, you remember that, do you?' said the tramp. 'Or maybe you don't. Maybe you've just seen it.'

'I don't know what I remember any more. But I know what I see.'

'And what do you see?' Crow leaned closer and peered into his face. 'With those scary eyes of yours?'

'I see this girl, this . . . beautiful girl. She keeps appearing. I saw her when I was lying by the side of the lane after the accident. She brought me back. I know it. I'd have died without her. And I see these . . . other faces. Like shadows. They've got these horrible gaping mouths, like they're trying to swallow me, drink me up.'

He felt the heaviness inside him grow.

'And then it's like . . . there's this darkness, this . . . sickness hanging over the town. I don't know where it's coming from. I just know it's there.' He looked at the tramp. 'But you see stuff too. I know it.'

'Maybe.'

'What do you see?'

'I see a barefoot boy on a beach in the middle of the night. He's standing right in front of me. He probably doesn't even remember sneaking out of the house. He certainly won't have told his mum and dad about going out. That's because he can't risk being stopped. He's got to come out. He's just got to. Because he sees things and he knows something's wrong. And he knows the answer's somewhere out here.'

'You do see things,' said Will.

'Not like you,' said Crow, 'and that's why you got to be careful, my young friend. But you know that already. Like I do, and Muck does. Because we got enemies of our own.'

'Maybe they're the same enemies as mine.'

'Maybe they are.' The man gave a wheezy cough. 'Want some of John's soup?'

'Why not?'

'Come on, then.'

Crow turned and set off in the direction of the headland. Will stared once again at the entrance to the cave but there was still no sign of the boy.

'You won't see him,' said Crow, watching him. 'He'll have spotted us heading his way and be burrowing down into his hole.'

They walked on over the sand, the sea now sparkling to their left. Will searched the horizon again. Something was wrong out there too. Whatever this sickness was, it wasn't just in the town. Crow headed towards the foot of the dunes, well away from the cave.

'We've got to climb over the headland,' he muttered. 'Can't wriggle underneath the rock like little Muck.'

He led Will up a track that ran to the top of the headland. They stopped there for a few moments to catch their breath and Will looked back over the town. A few lights were on here and there but otherwise all was dark and still. No sign of life or movement at The Four Winds, and no figures to be seen on the beach or dunes.

'Come on,' said Crow.

They crossed the headland, made their way down to the other beach and headed for the tent. A fire was already burning outside. Crow threw down his bundle of sticks.

'We'll let those dry for another day.' He glanced at Will. 'You can take a walk while I heat up the soup.'

Will wandered down to the water's edge and stood there, thinking. The surf was gentle and the sea even calmer than when he'd seen the girl. There was no sign of her now. He stared at the horizon again, wondering about the darkness he'd felt there, then he heard another wheezy cough behind him. He turned and saw Crow approaching with a small saucepan in his hand.

'We'll have to share this,' said the tramp. 'I don't have any mugs or bowls.'

They stood there in silence for a while, taking turns to sip from the pan. Will glanced towards the headland.

'Where does Muck's passageway come out?'

Crow pointed.

'Close to that rock. He's probably watching us from just inside. I could maybe see him if my eyes were better.'

Will couldn't see him either but he said nothing.

'I found him on the shore a few months ago,' said Crow. 'Same day I got here myself. Hadn't even had time to pitch my tent.'

'He's not your son, then?'

'Course he's not my son.' Crow gave a snort. 'I just tell people that to try and get them off our backs. Some believe me, some don't. Most people think I'm doing stuff to the kid. Like I would.'

He turned away from the headland and pointed again.

'I found him down there at the other end of this beach. You can't see the spot from here because of the curve of the shore. But if you walk down that way for about a mile, you'll come to an old stone slipway. No one uses it and there's a deserted track running off it through the woodland behind the dunes. He was sitting there, where the slipway meets the track. Shivering and crying. All on his own.'

'Any idea how he got there?'

'None at all. Anyway, he just clung to me. I took him down the beach and put up my tent, and gave him some food, and waited for someone to come and claim him. No one did. So I thought I'd better take him to the police. I don't like them much and they don't like me, but I didn't know what else to do.'

Crow turned and spat on the beach.

'I didn't need to go looking for the police. They came looking for me, like they always do when I turn up somewhere. To check me out and all, make sure I know I've got to be a good boy. It's called community policing. I don't mind that, even when they're rude. Only you should have seen Muck. Moment he saw them coming, he was screaming and grabbing hold of me. He was that scared of them.'

'What did you do?'

'Told the police he's my son. Since me and Muck look a bit alike. Well, the hair anyway.'

'Did they believe you?'

Crow shrugged.

'Don't know. Don't really care. But I'll tell you one thing. Muck freaked them out, and it must have helped my story, him being terrified of them but OK with me. I told them his mum and me split up years ago. Said she's a drug addict who's always looked after him, but she's gone off the rails now with heroin and stuff, so I'm looking after him.'

'And they left you alone?'

'After a fashion. The police are never far away. Same as the locals. I kept the story going with them too, once I saw how scared the boy is of everybody. I've never seen terror like it. I'm the only person he seems to trust. How's that for crazy? No one in the world trusts me except a boy who doesn't trust anybody else. He's even scared of John Shepherd.'

'Does he ever speak?'

'I've never heard him. But his face speaks. I'm telling you. And I'll tell you something else—when you moved to Havensmouth a couple of weeks after I found him, something changed in him. And I knew you and Muck had a connection.' The tramp paused. 'Don't remember, do you?'

'No.'

'You got here and you started spouting all that stuff about sickness. Something being wrong in Havensmouth. Moment you got here, you were doing it. Boy, do you know how to make enemies. You're worse than me. But it all got me thinking. I'm thinking here's Muck, a little kid of seven or however old he is, and he's scared out of his wits, and he's taken to me. Don't ask me why. I don't even like kids. I just want to be left alone. But he's taken to me.'

Crow took another sip of soup.

'And suddenly there's all these other people interested in him as well.'

'What other people?'

'I'm not sure. I never see them clearly. But I catch sight of them on the dunes sometimes, watching him.'

110

'They might be watching you.'

'No, it's Muck they're interested in. I get lots of attention—I'm used to that—but it's a different kind of thing when it's directed at me. Round here it's mostly kids throwing stones. These other people are different. They always seem to show up when Muck and me are apart a little bit. Doesn't happen very often. He sticks with me pretty close. But sometimes he runs to the other beach or down the end of Breeze Point. And when I go looking for him, I see those figures on the dunes. Or just the glint of their binoculars.'

Crow held out the saucepan. Will shook his head and the tramp went on.

'Luckily, the boy's natural instinct is to run and hide. But I worry about him. And I've been even more worried about him since you started cranking up the community. Because I'll tell you something, my scary friend. Everything you've been saying is right. There is bad stuff in Havensmouth. There's real evil here. And it's something to do with Muck. You know how I know?'

The man's eyes narrowed.

'Because of the way he looks at you. He watches you like he watches nobody else. And he's speaking to you. I can see it in his face. He might be scared of you—no, he is scared of you—but he's trying to tell you something. And you might just be the only person in the world who'll understand him. I certainly don't.'

Will said nothing. He was sure he'd heard a sound somewhere close by. He thought of Muck but quickly dismissed the idea. It hadn't been the sound of a small boy but someone or something larger. He listened again but all was quiet now. Crow leaned closer and lowered his voice.

'I'll tell you something else. We've got to watch out. You, me, and Muck. Because this is a dangerous place for all three of us.'

In the silence that followed, Will caught the sound again; and this time he saw a movement along the top of the dunes.

13

Figures, several, crowded together. They were close to the headland, blocking any escape that way. The tramp had spotted them too.

'Keep still, boy,' he murmured. 'I don't think they've seen us yet.'

Will counted them: five figures. For a moment they made him think of the shadowfaces. But these were solid people and he didn't like what he saw.

'Do you know them?' he said.

'No.'

'They could be teenagers or adults.'

Crow grunted.

'What difference does it make how old they are? They're all looking for trouble.'

Will strained his eyes to see more clearly but the figures were still hard to make out in the darkness. Size seemed to be distorted by the night. Then he saw something.

'They're wearing balaclavas.'

'I've noticed,' said Crow.

No wonder they were so difficult to make out—and there was no mistaking their intent now. Crow suddenly turned to him.

'You got to get away. You can't stay here. They'll see you the moment they hit the beach.'

'They might not come down.'

'They will. They're looking for trouble. So get going. Not home. Not yet. You won't get past the headland. Run along the beach. Go as far as the slipway I told you about. The one where I found Muck. You should be all right there. But go now. They won't see you if you keep close to the water's edge.'

'But what about you?' said Will. 'What about Muck?'

'They won't find Muck. He'll stay put.'

'You, then?'

'I'm too wheezy to run.'

'Too proud, you mean.'

'Call it what you like but get going.' Crow glanced back at the figures, now descending towards the beach. 'I'm more used to this kind of trouble than you are.'

'But—'

'Just go, for Christ's sake.' Crow glared at him. 'You'll only make things worse by staying. But listen—' The tramp grabbed him by the arm. 'If anything happens to me, promise you'll take care of Muck. Promise me you'll do what you can for him.'

'But I can't just—'

'Promise me, you mad, scary kid!' The tramp shook him hard. 'Do it!'

'I promise.'

'Now get going. And don't make a sound. You're no use to Muck if you're dead.'

And without another word, Crow pushed him away, tipped the rest of the soup onto the sand, and set off towards the tent. Will started to run down the beach, keeping close to the water. Over to the right, he could see the fire still burning outside the tent and far above it, the dusky group of figures still descending.

He stopped, in spite of Crow's warning. Running suddenly seemed a bad idea. If he could see the figures from here, they could surely see him. He was less likely to draw their attention if he moved slowly. He carried on, walking now, his eyes still fixed on the group.

Everything about these five people spelled danger. Again he felt a powerful urge to stay. For all his fear of them, it seemed wrong to leave Crow alone with them. Yet the tramp was walking confidently towards the tent as though he had no anxiety at all. The figures were closer to it now, still keeping tightly together. There was no sound of voices, just the crackle of burning wood and the ever-present heave of the sea.

Will stopped again. It was no good. He couldn't just run away. Muck was there too. He might be hidden and Crow had insisted the boy was OK, but that didn't mean it was right to leave these two. The figures had now reached the bottom of the dunes and were spreading out around the tent. Crow was already there, poking at the fire.

Will clenched his fists. He had to go back. He had to do something.

But now there was a new development.

One of the figures broke clear and started to run down the beach towards Muck's hiding place. On an impulse, Will made to hurry back, but then to his horror he saw two more figures break from the group.

And these were heading straight for him.

He turned and fled down the beach, the way the tramp had told him to go. His mind chafed with guilt and fear, but fear was stronger and Crow's words were coming back.

You're no use to Muck if you're dead.

He checked over his shoulder. The two figures were still racing after him but they were some distance behind and it was hard to tell whether they were gaining or not. A wave broke on the shore close by. He moved right to avoid it and checked over his shoulder again.

The figures were closer.

He drove himself on as hard as he could, running, running, running. The shore was curving to the right, as Crow had said it would, and it was growing stonier too. His bare feet smarted as they pounded over it. He ran on for another couple of minutes, then checked over his shoulder again.

No sign of the figures yet. The curve of the beach had blocked them from view. But suddenly they appeared again, and they were closer still. He ran on, panting now, his feet throbbing with pain. Another wave crashed on the shore.

He forced himself on. The beach had straightened again and he scanned the stretch ahead. A short way down the surf broke upon what looked like a spit of land. He stared at it as he ran. Crow had talked of a stone slipway that led to a track through the woodland. If he could just make it there, he might be able to lose his pursuers in the trees.

He checked over his shoulder again. The figures were still close but no closer than they had been a moment ago. He put on speed, determined to reach the track in enough time to disappear into the trees without them seeing which way he went. Another check over his shoulder and at last he saw he was starting to edge away. Not much but it might be enough.

Here was the slipway before him. It was the thing he'd thought was a spit. He could see now that it ran between the dunes all the way down to the water and some way out into the sea. But there was no time to think of that now. He cut right, heading for the point where the slipway met the track, the point where Crow had found little Muck.

There it was, just a short distance away. He jumped onto the slipway and tore up it onto the track, softer underfoot and welcome to his aching feet, but slower too with its mud and grass. The dunes rose on either side but they were soon past and here was woodland opening before him, cleft by the track.

He ran on for a few metres, then glanced back again. No sign of his pursuers yet but they would be here any second. He blundered off the track, cut into the trees to his right and headed for a small copse. Another check behind—still no sign of pursuit—and he crouched behind a clutch of small trees.

And waited, panting.

The track was visible through gaps in the foliage. He watched, his heart pounding inside his chest. His breath was still coming in thick, heavy gasps and he was trembling feverishly. He tried to calm down. If they came along the track now, he felt certain they'd hear him or detect him in some way.

A figure appeared on the track, alone. Will stiffened, watched, holding his breath now. The second figure appeared a short way behind. Both were still wearing balaclavas. He held himself rigid as he peered between the leaves.

There were still no clues as to who these people were. They could be some of the teenagers he'd seen. They could be adults. Whoever they were, they were big enough to be dangerous.

The slitted eyes turned his way.

He froze. The leaves round his face moved as a gust caught them; the wind died and they fell still again. The figures walked on down the track and a moment later disappeared from view.

He slumped to the ground, his back against one of the trees. He couldn't stay here, that was for certain. He had to get home, had to wake Mum and Dad—if they weren't already awake and worrying about him—and get them to call the police. And somehow he had to avoid not just these two pursuers but the others who'd gathered by the headland.

He tried to think. One part of him knew that he ought to sneak after the figures, keeping just out of sight, and watch to see if they took off their balaclavas. He might be able to use that knowledge. But another part of him knew he couldn't do it. He was just too frightened—and here they were coming back.

He heard them before he saw them. No voices, just the soft tread on the track. He twisted slowly round and peered between the leaves again. The same two figures, still wearing the balaclavas. They didn't stop this time and continued past the copse. A few moments later they disappeared again, heading towards the beach.

He waited several minutes, watching the empty track in case it was a trick, but they appeared to have gone. He climbed to his feet, checked the track again, and tried to work out which way to go. The simplest way back would be to follow the line of the dunes while keeping in the trees.

If that was possible. He didn't remember this place at all and had no idea if there was a path. An alternative might be to head down the track, not back to the beach but the way his pursuers had first gone, and see where it ended up. Crow had said it was deserted so he was unlikely to meet anyone and there must at some point be a road or lane that linked up with it and led back to the town.

But even a deserted track felt too exposed right now.

The trees, then, and hope for a path to follow.

He set off, scrambling over roots, ducking under branches, trying to keep the dunes in view over to the right. Most of the time they were easy to see, usually with the moon sailing over them, but after a while he lost them. He'd strayed too far inland and the trees were now denser than the ones by the track and different in species. These were mostly conifers and he appeared to be on the fringes of some form of plantation.

He walked on, weary and disorientated and growing more frightened again. A patch of gorse opened up, then he was through that and facing orderly ranks of spruce and pine. A path ran through them and he hurried down it, unsure where it led but anxious to reach somewhere, anywhere—and then it came.

A memory.

A clear memory.

Something before the accident. He'd been here. He knew this place, or something about this place. He tried to grasp what it was but no picture would come. He walked on, shivering slightly, and then suddenly the trees fell away and he saw a clearing in front of him with a lane leading off to the right.

In the centre of the clearing was a house.

14

A light was on in an upstairs window, the only one visible in that dark shell. He stared up at it and edged forward. He could feel grass under him now, soft and damp after the harder ground of the woods. His trouser legs felt damp too, and in some places caked with mud. He stopped at the house, just below the lighted window.

Again he felt it.

The memory. He knew this place, and more than this place, he knew who lived here. He called out.

'Beth!'

From inside the room came a sound of footsteps. A shadow appeared at the window and a moment later the curtains were flung back. He saw Beth's face peering down. She gave a start and opened the window.

'Will!' She leaned out, her nightdress loose about her. 'What's happened?'

She didn't wait for an answer.

'Stay there!' she called and disappeared.

He waited, breathing hard. His mind and emotions were in a whirl, not just with what had happened, his fears for Crow and the boy, but with the stress of his pursuit and now this strange, unexpected memory. He saw lights flashing on inside the house and a few seconds later the front door opened and three figures burst out.

He felt a moment of panic and stepped back.

'It's OK, Will,' called Beth. 'I'm here too.'

He stopped, still breathing hard. Yes, there she was, and the other figures were clear now: the big man he remembered from the harbour, her father, yes, Stu Palmer, that was his name; and the woman must be her mother. All three were in dressing gowns.

'Easy, Will,' said the man. 'Easy, boy. Everything's all right.'

The three figures stopped on the other side of the pond just up from the front door. He faced them across it, aware suddenly that the fountain in the middle had been trickling all this time. He hadn't heard it before.

'It's all right, Will,' said the woman. 'All friends here. Nothing to be frightened of.'

He heard a voice. It didn't sound like his own. But he knew it was.

'They're going to kill him. Are you listening?'

They stared back in silence. The water went on tinkling from the fountain. He heard his voice continue.

'I should have stayed. I should have stayed and helped him.'

'Who?' said Beth.

'Crow.'

Will felt his eyes start to move. He didn't want them to. He wanted them to stay fixed on the three figures. But they were moving, round and round the circular pond, up and over the little stone figure in the middle—an urchin boy, his face and eyes lifted to the sky, his arms outstretched, two streams trickling from the palms of his hands.

But they were red.

He stared. It wasn't right, it wasn't real, and yet

121

suddenly everything was red: the water, the hands of the statue, even the statue itself.

'They're looking for him,' he said.

'Looking for who?' said Beth. 'The tramp?'

'The boy.'

'Who?'

'Muck. They want to kill him.'

The palms of the statue were growing redder. He could see it clearly in spite of the darkness. He pointed to it.

'It won't stop unless we stop it.'

'Will—'

'It's not just his blood. Don't you see? It's all the others' too. It's their blood too.'

'Will—'

'Can't you see it?' He nodded towards the hands, now streaming red. 'Can't you see it?'

'All I can see,' said Stu, 'is that we've forgotten to turn off the fountain again.'

Will looked from face to face; and the faces looked questioningly back. Then Stu smiled and stepped round the pond.

'Come inside, Will. We'll make you something to drink and ring your mum and dad.'

'But we've got to do something!' Will stared at him. 'There's been some trouble down on the beach. People in balaclavas and Crow and—'

'Then we'll call the police as well,' said Stu. 'But we'll do that inside, OK? Come on.'

Will turned to the fountain again. The red was gone and all he saw was clear water falling. Beth and the woman walked slowly round to join them.

'I'm Beth's mum,' said the woman. She put an arm round him. 'You probably don't remember me, but we were good friends before your accident. You used to come round here to see Beth. And you and I used to talk in the kitchen while I made tea. And you used to eat all my biscuits. If I let you. Do you remember my name?'

'Rose.'

'Well done. Did Beth tell you that? Or is it a memory?'

He didn't know and he couldn't think of that now. All he could think of was the pictures flooding his mind: the boy, the tramp, the red mouth opening.

'Rose,' said Stu. 'We need to get him inside.'

'I know,' she said. 'Come on, Will.'

She guided him into the house, down the hall, into the kitchen. He liked the feel of her arm but wished it was Beth's. They stopped in the middle of the kitchen, Rose's arm still round his shoulder.

'You never answered my question, Will,' she said. 'Was it a memory getting my name right or did Beth tell you?'

'Mum,' said Beth. 'Don't hassle him. He's in a state.'

'Of course,' said Rose. 'Sorry, Will.'

She smiled and gave him a hug. He tensed suddenly.

'What is it, Will?' said Beth.

He didn't know but he could feel an icy tremor rising up his body. He sensed Beth draw near, felt her hand on his shoulder. Rose was still holding him.

'Let go of him, Mum,' said Beth. 'He wants me to hold him.'

He felt Rose's hands leave him and Beth's pull him close. He dug his chin into her shoulder. She moved her head, rubbed it against his, her blonde hair falling over his eyes. Through it he saw Rose and Stu watching him, the glow of the kitchen light on their faces, on the gleaming cutlery laid out for breakfast, the shiny saucepans on top of the cooker.

The ice ran up and down his body. He closed his eyes. The red mouth opened before his inner gaze. He searched for the shadowfaces. There they were, drenched in red like the statue. He looked for the girl. She too was there. She too was drenched in red. He thought of Muck and trembled.

'It's all right, Will.' It was Beth's voice, soothing. She pulled him closer. 'It's all right, it's all right.'

'I'll ring his mum and dad,' said Stu. 'Make a hot drink, love.'

'OK,' said Rose.

The sound of footsteps hurrying away, a kettle being filled, a voice on the telephone down the hall: 'Mrs Bly . . . Stu Palmer . . . yes, he's here . . . '

All was red now. It swallowed everything: Stu's voice, the bubbling kettle, the warmth of Beth's body. His mind, heart, being were red. Crow's words floated before him. They too were red.

Promise you'll take care of Muck.

'I promise!' he screamed.

The sound of his own voice broke him free. The red mouth closed. The faces vanished. His eyes pricked open and he saw other faces through the mist of Beth's hair: Rose watching him, kettle in hand, Stu by the door, and next to him a boy about seventeen in a dressing gown.

'It's me, Will,' said the boy.

Will stared at the strange new figure. Beth relaxed her hug a little and whispered into his ear.

'It's only Jack. My brother.'

Will frowned. He didn't remember this boy at all.

'What's going on?' said Jack.

'You didn't wake up,' said Beth. 'That's what's going on.'

Jack edged past his father and walked over. Will watched the boy's face loom closer and stop. A large, open face. It studied him for a moment, then turned to Stu.

'What's happened, Dad?'

'Will's had an unpleasant experience,' said Stu. 'But he managed to find his way here.'

'While you were sleeping,' said Beth.

'Yeah, yeah.' Jack yawned. 'You still haven't told me what's happened.'

Stu came forward from the doorway.

'Will, let's sit down and have some tea, and wait for your mum and dad. They're on their way. And if you can, tell us what happened. I need to know if I've got to ring the police.'

'Yes!' Will pulled back from Beth. 'You've got to call them right now!'

'Sit down first, Will, OK?' said Stu. 'Just . . . you know . . . ' He hesitated. 'What I'm saying is . . . you've said some strange things in the past and . . . before I call the police out at two in the morning, we just need to hear what you remember.'

Rose put a mug of tea in Will's hand and sat him down with her at the table.

'Will,' she said, 'I know this is horrible but let's find out what happened. First question—how did you end up on the beach by yourself at midnight, or whatever time it was?'

He stared at her.

'I don't know. I just did.'

'Don't you remember going out of the house?'

'No. I must have sneaked out.'

Rose looked up at her husband.

'Did Mrs Bly say anything about Will going out?'

'No,' said Stu. 'They saw him go to his bedroom around ten and they thought he'd turned in, but then they looked in a while later just to check he was all right and found him gone.'

'Have they called the police?'

'They were about to when I rang. They've been out looking for him in the town. Thing is, they didn't ring the police straightaway because it's . . . you know . . . '

'Happened before,' said Will.

'Yes,' said Stu.

'Lots of times.' Will looked away. 'You probably all think I'm mad.'

'We don't, Will,' said Stu.

'Maybe I am mad. Maybe I'm a basketcase.'

'You're not,' said Beth.

'Tell us what happened on the beach,' said Rose.

'I saw her.' He looked round at them. 'The girl. She's beautiful. She's an angel. She's got long black hair and these . . . kind of . . . deep blue eyes. Like an ocean. I don't know how I got to the beach. I must have just . . . slipped out or something. I felt pulled to the sea. There's something out there, offshore. I don't know what it is. But it's something to do with this . . . ' He swallowed hard. 'Sickness.'

He felt Jack shift on his feet close by.

'You definitely think I'm mad,' he said to the boy.

'I didn't say that,' said Jack.

'But you're thinking it.'

'Well, you have hallucinated before,' said Jack. 'That's what people are saying round here.'

'Shut up, Jack,' said Stu.

'I'm only reporting what people say.'

'I saw her,' said Will. 'She appeared in the sea. And then Crow came and talked to me, and we went away and had some soup.'

'And what about the angel?' said Jack. 'Did she have some soup too?'

Beth cuffed her brother round the top of his head.

'Ow!' he said.

'Don't be horrible.'

'I'm not. It's just that . . . you know . . . it's a bit far-fetched, all this.'

'I'm not lying,' said Will.

No one spoke.

'I'm not,' he said. 'I saw the girl in the water, and then Crow came and we went to the tent, and he made some soup and we talked, and then these people in balaclavas turned up, and closed round Crow, and one of them broke off to look for Muck in his hiding place, and another two came running after me. But I escaped and came here.'

There was a long silence.

'You don't believe me,' he said. 'None of you do.'

'Will,' said Rose. 'It's not that we don't believe you. It's just that—'

'You don't believe me.' He turned away and stared at the far wall. 'Nobody ever believes me.'

He heard the sound of a car approaching.

'That'll be your mum and dad,' said Rose.

'You must call the police,' he said. 'Crow's in danger. Muck's in danger.'

'We'll call the police.'

He looked at her.

'No, you won't.'

He heard the car stop outside the house, heard two doors open and close, then footsteps on the gravel. He looked down at his untouched mug of tea. For a moment it seemed to turn red before him. The door-bell rang. Stu touched him on the shoulder.

'It'll be all right now, Will. Here's your mum and dad to take you home.'

'They haven't come to take me home.'

'What do you mean?'

Will looked up at him.

'They've come to take me away.'

15

The late-afternoon sun. The long garden of Acacia Court, high above the town. Gulls wheeling over the harbour, house-martins over the roofs. The conversational murmur of other patients sitting in chairs about the garden. His own chair facing the sea.

And all its secrets.

But he barely had the clarity of mind to think of that now. Since the drugs he'd felt more muddled than ever, though not so muddled that he hadn't taken in his surroundings. It was a pleasant enough place: friendly nurses, good facilities, comfortable rooms, a beautiful garden.

He just wished he wasn't here.

'But, Will,' said Dad, 'I keep telling you. Crow's gone and so has the little boy. They just went, OK? No one saw them but that's not unusual. It's what tramps do. It's certainly what Crow's always done. Everyone says so. He comes and he goes.'

'You never believe me,' said Will. 'Nobody ever believes me.'

'Will,' said Mum, 'we're not saying you didn't see anything.'

'Just another hallucination.'

'Don't be like that,' said Dad. 'As we've explained to you before, we can't see the things you see, so we don't know what they are. We can only try our best to understand.'

Will said nothing.

'And this tramp,' Dad went on, 'OK, you had some soup with him. Maybe that really happened—'

'It did.'

'And maybe—'

'You keep saying maybe. You see? You just don't believe me.'

'OK,' said Dad. 'You did those things. You had soup with him. Then you say some people from the town turned up looking for trouble and two of them chased you off.'

'They did. I'm not lying.'

'Dad's not saying you are, Will,' said Mum. She pulled her chair closer to his. 'What he's saying— what we're both saying—is that you don't know what happened next on the beach because you weren't there. You said that yourself. You ran off down the beach and ended up at Mr and Mrs Palmer's house.'

Will looked away.

'Didn't you?' said Mum.

'Yes.'

'So you don't know for certain that something terrible happened to Crow and the little boy.'

'Why've they gone, then?' said Will. 'Why've they disappeared?'

'They just have,' said Dad. 'Look, we rang the police. They already knew because Stu Palmer had rung them as well to report a possible incident.'

'Possible. See?' Will glowered at him. 'Stu Palmer's as bad as you with your maybes.'

'But what else could we all do?' said Dad. 'We've reported the incident and the police have been down to the beach to investigate. And they've told us there's no sign of the tramp or the boy.'

'So doesn't that look suspicious?'

'Not necessarily,' said Dad. 'Like I said, tramps like Crow come and go. I don't suppose it was particularly comfortable living in that tent and if some of the louts from town did come along and make trouble, he probably thought enough's enough and let's move on. And the little boy would have gone with him, seeing as the man's the only person he seems to trust. For some strange reason.'

Will closed his eyes. Darkness fell upon him, a darkness which so often contained the things he feared most. But for now there were no shadows watching him. He looked for the girl, but she was not there either. All he saw was a deep, dark space.

He heard Mum's voice.

'You've got a visitor.'

'John Shepherd,' he said.

'How did you know that, Will? You've got your eyes closed. And we weren't expecting him.'

'I don't know.'

He opened his eyes and saw the vicar standing behind Mum's chair. He was wearing the same open-neck shirt and loose trousers but now his bald head was protected by a floppy white beach hat.

'Hello, Will.'

'You still don't look much like a vicar.'

'So you keep reminding me.'

'Have you come to save my soul?'

'Does it need saving?'

'You tell me.'

John considered for a moment.

'I think your soul's in pretty good shape.'

'Just the rest of me that's screwed up, yeah?'

'Is that what you think?'

'Who cares what I think?' said Will. 'It's what everybody else thinks that seems to matter round here.'

John pulled up a spare chair and sat down on it.

'And what do they think?'

'They think I'm a head case.'

'Will!' said Dad.

'That's not true,' said Mum. 'We don't think that.'

'They think I'm hallucinating,' said Will. 'They've always thought that. Everybody's always thought that.'

'I don't think that,' said John.

'What about my trance in your church?'

'What about it?'

'Wasn't that a hallucination?'

'I don't know what it was. I didn't experience it. You did.'

'So I'm the only person who can decide what I experience. Is that it?'

The vicar didn't answer. Will looked away over the sea. Far away on the horizon the darkness was growing again, and it had that uncomfortable reddish tinge. He tensed suddenly.

She was standing at the end of the garden, her back to the sea, and she was gazing towards him, her hair streaming to the side as the gusts caught it, just as it had done last night when he'd seen her standing in the shallows. She was wearing the same simple skirt and smock, and her face seemed more grave than it had ever been.

He stood up, staring.

'Will?' said Dad.

He didn't answer.

'What are you seeing, Will?' said John.

'My angel. Over there.'

Nobody answered but he felt them all stand up. He kept his eyes fixed on the girl. She was walking closer, closer, just a few steps away now. Then she stopped.

'Who are you?' he said.

'Will?' said Mum. 'Who are you talking to?'

He said nothing. He was watching the girl, waiting to see if she would speak. But she remained silent.

'It's all right,' he said to her. 'You don't have to talk.'

Something in her face reassured him that she understood.

'Will,' said Dad, 'we can't see whatever you're seeing.'

'She's right here in front of you,' he said, his eyes never leaving the girl. 'You must be able to see her.'

No one answered. She turned suddenly and started to walk back the way she had come. He saw the breeze catch her hair again as she neared the end of the garden where the ground fell away to the town below. It caught her skirt too, and her smock, both moving with the gusts. She stopped at the end of the garden and turned to look back at him.

'She's trying to show me something,' said Will. 'I've got to follow her.'

'Will, don't,' said Mum. She caught his arm. 'Please don't do something wild again.'

'I've got to follow her.'

He shrugged his arm free and started towards the figure at the end of the garden. She turned again and set off towards the steps that led from the gardens down to the town. He hurried after her but it was no good. The drugs were still working and his feet were sluggish. Someone caught him by the shoulder.

'Get off!' he shouted. 'Don't try and stop me!'

'Will, it's all right.'

He turned and saw one of the nurses holding him.

'It's all right,' she said.

He tried to break free but she moved her arm round his shoulder and held him more firmly.

'Easy now, Will,' she said. 'We don't want you heading down the steps into town. It's not quite the time for that. Let's stay safe in the garden, shall we?'

'Let me go!' he bellowed.

He threw a glance towards the end of the garden. The girl was now moving down the steps, but she was looking back at him.

'I've got to follow!' he shouted. 'She wants me to go with her!'

Again he struggled to break free but now more hands were clasping him and he was surrounded by figures in white. He saw Mum and Dad watching anxiously, John standing back. A man he didn't recognize had also appeared.

'Easy, lad,' he said.

'The girl!' Will screamed. 'I've got to follow the girl!'

'There is no girl,' said the man.

'But—'

'She's not there, Will,' said Mum. 'She never was there.'

He turned towards the steps and saw that she was gone. He felt a wave of despair.

'Come back!'

He thrashed his arms about in an effort to escape

but there were too many hands upon him now; and suddenly he was sitting again, on the edge of the chair he'd just left. The end of the garden seemed a blank, pointless space. He gazed at it, his mind numb with pain and a growing confusion.

'It's the drugs, Will,' said Dad. 'They're probably having a funny effect on you.'

'I thought it was the drugs that are supposed to stop me seeing things,' he heard himself say. 'Not the other way round.'

One of the nurses spoke.

'The drugs are designed to calm you, Will. And help you sleep. They're not hallucinogenic. They won't have caused whatever it is you think you just saw.'

He went on staring towards the end of the garden.

'She was there,' he said. 'And I've seen her before.'

He looked round at them all. They seemed less of a blur now that he was sitting down again and there weren't quite as many people as he'd thought there were when he was struggling to break free. Just three nurses, the unknown man, Mum, Dad, John, and an old biddy who seemed to have joined them by mistake. A young woman was already guiding her away.

'Nothing for you here, Gran,' she was saying. She glanced round at them as she led the old woman away and mouthed, 'Sorry.'

Will stared at the faces watching him. Kind faces, all of them. He just wished they'd all go away. He looked at the vicar.

'You're the only one who believes me.'

'Tell us what your angel looks like,' said John.

'You'll laugh at me. Well, you won't but they will.'

'They won't,' said John. 'What does she look like?'

'She's about fifteen. She's got long black hair down over her shoulders. Eyes so blue it's like looking into an ocean.'

'Where did you first see her?'

'I must have seen her before my accident because I've drawn pictures of her. But I don't remember any of that. The first time I remember seeing her was when I was lying by the roadside. I saw her face as I was about to die. She saved my life.'

He looked quickly round at the other faces.

'You all think I'm lying.'

'Nobody thinks you're lying, Will,' said Dad.

'Hallucinating, then. Or whatever word you want.'

'Will—'

'They're not hallucinations!' He stood up again and roared. 'They're not hallucinations!'

'Easy, Will.' One of the nurses took him by the arm. 'No one's making judgements about you. Come on now. Sit down again.'

He glared about him, aware for the first time that the garden had cleared. Only two people were left, and they were being helped back towards the house.

'It's all right, Will,' said Dad. 'All friends here.'

He glanced round at them again: all friends. Yeah, right. He looked at the unknown man. About John's age, good looking in a smooth kind of way, clever, a little cool.

'Do I know you?' he said.

'You have met me before,' said the man, 'but you won't remember. My name's Peter Blanch. I'm the senior consultant here.'

'So you think I'm deluded.'

'Is that a question?'

'No, it's what you think.'

The man shrugged.

'No one's saying you're not seeing something, Will. And it's obviously something that's extremely upsetting for you.'

'But?'

Peter Blanch frowned.

'The problem is—what's causing all this? You don't know and we don't know. You see this stuff—this angel or whatever—and you tell us about it. But we can't see it. So how do we know if you're delusional? How does anyone?'

'Great,' said Will. 'So much for science.'

Peter leaned forward.

'Do you know what scientists are saying about the brain right now? They're saying it's more complex than we ever dreamed it might be. It's like a computer with programmes so sophisticated we're barely scratching the surface in terms of understanding it. They're saying the wiring is so intricate it's easy for us to be tricked or misled into thinking we're perceiving something mystical or psychic when it's simply a disturbance of brain function.'

'So?'

'So we need at least to consider the possibility that the things you're experiencing could be—I repeat could be—caused not by some mystical intervention but by some trickery of the brain. Do you understand what I'm saying?'

Will said nothing. Peter leaned back, still watching him.

'I'm not attacking you, Will. Just asking questions, OK?'

'Peter,' said one of the nurses. 'This maybe isn't the time.'

Peter looked at her, then back at Will.

'Is it the time, Will?'

Will looked back over the sea. The redness was starting to seep over the surface again and as before, it was at the horizon where the greatest darkness lay. He heard Peter's voice again.

'It probably isn't the time to be talking about these things.'

'But you're going to anyway,' said Will, still watching the horizon.

'All I'm saying,' said Peter, 'is that our brains are complex and they're subject to different impulses. These impulses affect us in different ways. You look at Havensmouth and you see a place full of some terrible sickness. I look at it and I see a pretty seaside town with two nice beaches, great surfing, sand dunes, woodland, a harbour with lots of fishing boats, a nice pub down by the quayside, lots of great people, a quaint little church with an active congregation, and a slightly eccentric vicar who likes martial arts.'

As if from a great distance, Will heard a ripple of laughter. The shadow went on spreading across the sea.

'John sees it,' he murmured. 'John sees the sickness.'

He went on staring over the sea. John spoke.

'I don't see it like you do, Will.'

'But you know it's there.'

'I sense something's not right in the town. But I don't see things the way you do. Not clearly anyway.'

'You need to get Peter to re-programme your brain.'

Another ripple of distant laughter—a strained, reluctant sound.

'He's in danger,' said Will.

'Who?' said Dad.

'Muck. He's in terrible danger.'

'We can't do anything more about it, Will. We've reported everything to the police and it's over to them now.'

'They won't be able to stop what's happening. Not on their own.'

He looked sharply round at them. Their faces seemed like masks now, fixed and unchanging. They were all frightened of him, he thought. Even John. Why couldn't they see that he was the one who was most frightened here?

'When can I go home?' he said.

'Tomorrow morning,' said Dad. 'Right, Peter?'

'I think that's best,' said Peter. 'Will, we want to keep you here tonight under close observation. Just to make sure you're OK.'

'Why can't I go home now?' said Will. 'I won't be any better for staying here.'

'Tomorrow,' said Dad. 'Peter thinks it's best. And so do we.'

Will looked out to sea again. It was now a deep red all the way to the shore.

'What are you seeing now, Will?' said John.

'Nothing,' he answered.

16

So much for close observation, Will thought. Sneaking out of Acacia Court couldn't have been easier. Act dozy all evening—not too difficult since he was already worn out with the drugs—then around ten at night feign sleep. Piece of cake after that.

A few checks from the nurses, and after eleven practically nothing, certainly nothing to stop him creeping out, collecting his clothes and dressing, and slipping unseen out of the library window. Not a movement or a murmur from the duty staff.

He pressed himself against the wall and tried to decide which way to go. All his instincts told him it had to be the steps at the bottom of the garden. That was the way the girl had gone. He didn't suppose he'd see her there again tonight, though there was always a hope, but either way it seemed the right way to go.

She'd been trying to show him something, take him somewhere, and that was the way she'd gone. Even if he didn't see her, there might be a clue by going that way. If he left by the main entrance and took the road down into the town, he might miss something.

The only problem was that the garden steps meant stealing past the windows of the big sitting room and it was just possible one of the staff might be in there looking out. But he knew he had to take the risk. He checked around him, then, keeping close to the wall, crept down to where the sitting room windows started.

Below him the garden stretched away towards the steps at the bottom. Below that, even from here, he could see the roofs of the town, the spire of the church, and the sea beyond the harbour, glistening under the moon. He edged as far as the first window and peeped round.

Nobody inside the sitting room. The big standard lamp in the corner was on but nobody was in the chair beside it and nobody anywhere else. He stared at the door of the room. It was open and the light from the hall was pushing through. As he watched, a shadow moved across it.

Peter Blanch.

There was no mistaking the consultant. But the man didn't stop and walked straight past the opening in the direction of the wards on the other side of the building. Will waited a moment longer, his eye fixed on the opening, but nobody else appeared.

Now was the time.

He ran across the lawn towards the steps. Nobody called after him and he soon reached the bottom of the garden. He stopped for a moment and looked back. No sign of anybody watching from the windows, no lights going suddenly on. He hurried down the steps, and immediately hit the first problem.

The gate just below the level of the rise. He hadn't seen it from his chair in the garden but it had presumably been open then for the use of residents as he'd seen several of the patients come and go that way with their carers.

But now it was locked.

He ran his eye over it. Too high for a comfortable climb over the top but with a bit of care, he should be able to clamber round it and onto the steps on the other side. There was certainly no point in going back to the main building and taking the road into town.

He checked the firmness of the gate and the fence. Solid iron, bedded into the rock. He eased himself up, hand by hand, and made his way slowly round the side of the gate, his feet on top of the safety rail that ran along the outer edge of the steps.

Below him was an almost sheer drop to the roofs below.

He clung on and, to his relief, was soon round the gate. He jumped back onto the path and continued down the steps, his heart pounding, not just at the return to security with the hill on his right and the safety rail on his left, but at the thought of the girl coming this way earlier.

He'd been looking for her from the moment he left the garden, even while clambering round the gate, and in spite of his earlier thoughts that he wouldn't see her here again, he was starting to change his mind. He wasn't sure why. There was no visible indication that she was close.

But he could sense her again.

He thought of the super-cool Peter Blanch. No doubt the man would say this feeling of the girl's closeness was just the brain playing tricks; but he didn't much care what the consultant thought right now. He had clues to follow and whether they were real or illusory didn't seem to matter: they were worth following either way.

'Where are you?' he whispered to the girl.

He hurried on down the steps, still talking to her.

'Show me what you wanted me to see this afternoon.'

He looked over the town below. There were still plenty of lights on, even though it was so late. He stopped for a moment to check his surroundings. Far over to the right was the hill with The Four Winds on top. No lights on there that he could see. He hoped Mum and Dad were sleeping. He didn't suppose they slept much these days with all the worry he caused them.

He pushed the guilt from his mind and let his eye move from The Four Winds to the beach and dunes, and the dark shoulder of Breeze Point. No lights there at all. He thought of the cave at the base of the headland, and Muck's refuge underneath. If the angel girl had been trying to lead him somewhere, it could well have been there.

Yet for some reason he found his gaze moving left, back along the white line of surf, past the houses on the beach side of the town, and then inwards, passing roofs and narrow streets, to the centre of the town. From this high point he could see the intricacy of the roads and alleyways, the main street twisting past the church towards The Sea Chest and the harbour beyond.

He could see figures too. A surprising number of people were moving about the town, mostly up and down the main street. He thought of the figures with balaclavas and wondered where they were right now. And the girl. Where was she? He couldn't sense her presence anywhere near the beach or dunes or Breeze Point. If she was anywhere close, it was down there in the town itself. But there was no sign of her in the streets and alleyways.

'Show me where you are,' he whispered.

He stared further out towards the harbour. The water inside it glowed round the moored fishing boats.

'Show me,' he whispered.

There was something about the harbour. He found his eye didn't want to leave it.

'Are you there?' he murmured.

It was hard to see anybody clearly from this far away, even with the height to help him, yet two figures appeared to be moving along the quayside. He stared at them, trying to make out what kind of people they were. A man and a woman, as far as he could tell, certainly not a young girl.

Then he stiffened.

There was another figure. He was sure of it—someone right out at the end of the harbour wall: a figure sitting, or so it appeared. He strained his eyes to see more clearly.

'Is it you?' he whispered.

The figure seemed to lengthen. He watched through narrowed eyes. Whoever it was had stood up, and he was certain . . .

He peered through the darkness.

He was certain it was someone with long hair. But he could well be wrong. The glow of The water in the harbour and the lighting from The Sea Chest further up the quay seemed to distort rather than help things.

'Turn round,' he muttered. 'Turn round so I can see you.'

The figure did not turn.

'Then I'll come and find you.'

He hurried on down the steps. He had no idea whether the figure was the girl but even if it wasn't, he was certain she was either near the harbour or calling him there for some reason. There was something about the place that felt significant right now. He drew close to the bottom of the steps and slowed down again.

Now he had to be careful. There were plenty of people about who would recognize him, and if the staff at Acacia Court had found out he was missing, they'd be looking too. He stopped at the gate that opened onto the road round the base of the hill. Like the gate at the top of the steps, it was locked.

He climbed up and dropped over onto the other side.

The sound of a car reached him from the direction of the town centre. He moved to the side of the pavement and turned his head away. The beam of head-lamps fell over him and quickly passed. He saw a car disappearing round the bend on its way out of Havensmouth.

He hurried on towards the centre of town.

He'd already decided from the high vantage point of the steps how he was going to get to the harbour. He'd take the little lane that ran parallel to the main street and then cut back at the last minute to the harbour. It looked a straightforward route and since most of the people who were out were hanging around the main street, it should be easier to avoid being seen.

But the lane proved anything but easy to follow.

It had looked so simple from above but now that he was down here—especially with his memory not working—it seemed utterly confusing. The road twisted and turned far more than he'd thought it did from up on the steps and the poor street lighting only made things worse.

But at least it was free of people and for the moment that was the vital thing. He hurried on, aware of the harbour somewhere over to the right. He couldn't see it yet from here with the houses blocking the view, but he sensed it—and he sensed something else.

'Is it you?' he said to the girl.

He'd been hoping it would be her, this thing that was drawing him, but he was starting to wonder. Something was calling him from the harbour, but what it was he couldn't tell. He walked on, even so, his eyes searching the alleys and lanes that ran off this one. Now and then, through some of the gaps, he caught glimpses of the main street and people in it: young men and women mostly, but some older folk, and at least two small groups of teenagers, none of whom he recognized.

He walked on, checking for dangers around him. Nothing appeared in the dark spaces, nothing to fear so far. But now the lane was twisting to the right. There was the end of the main street. There was The Sea Chest, the harbour, the seat where John Shepherd had helped Geoff and Sarah Wetherby prop up the drunken guy from Stu Palmer's fishing boat. He tried to remember the man's name.

Davy, that was it.

And here he was again.

Will stopped. The man was slumped against the wall that ran round the top of the harbour. No one was with him. From inside The Sea Chest came the sound of men slurring out a song.

'Ten green bottles, hanging on the wall . . . '

Then Sarah Wetherby's voice, friendly but firm.

'Thank you very much, boys. All done for tonight.'

The singing broke off. A short distance away, Davy stirred. Will moved into the shadow of the wall, unwilling to be seen or stopped now that he was so close to the harbour. Davy's chin was resting on his chest but his eyes were half-open and he might just make a nuisance of himself.

At that moment the doorway of the pub filled with people. Will ran his eye over them: five men and two women, one of the men still murmuring the remnants of the song.

'And if one green bottle should accidentally fall . . . '

'Yeah, yeah,' said one of the women.

And the group drifted off down the main street.

He glanced back at Davy. The man's eyes were closed now and it was probably safe to slip past him. But before he could move, more figures appeared in the doorway of the pub, and these he recognized: Geoff Wetherby and the three members of Stu Palmer's crew.

Robbo, Andy, and Lee.

He was sure those were the names Sarah had whispered in his ear. Hard-looking men, whatever they were called. Late thirties, early forties, tough as teak. They didn't appear to have noticed him, but they spotted Davy right away.

'Bloody hell,' said one.

'Better get him home,' said another.

And they set off towards Davy, leaving Geoff Wetherby behind in the doorway of the pub. Sarah Wetherby joined her husband and the two watched as the men hauled Davy to his feet and helped him off down the main street. Will waited till Geoff and Sarah had disappeared inside the pub, then hurried forward.

Now was his chance to check out the harbour. He could still feel that pull, that sense of something or someone calling him, and it was close, really close. But he had to move quickly before someone else appeared. He reached the main street and checked down it. The men carrying Davy were pushing ahead and not looking back.

He glanced at the pub. No one in the doorway but the lights were on downstairs and he knew someone could come out again at any moment. There were lights on upstairs too, and to his surprise he saw a face looking down at him from one of the windows.

A girl.

He gave a start. But it was not the girl he was looking for, nor was it Beth. It was the girl with mousy-grey hair he'd seen following Brad and Micky Wetherby: Sarah and Geoff's daughter.

Izzy.

A sour-faced character, he decided, now that he could see her more clearly. He thought of what Sarah Wetherby had said about the girl: goddess to drama queen in a matter of weeks. Izzy saw him looking up, lit a cigarette and drew the curtains across. He turned quickly back to the harbour.

Still the sense of being called, but still no clue as to what it was. It was nothing to do with Izzy or Davy or Sarah or Geoff, or those men from Stu's boat. That much he knew. He stared round. There were no figures on this part of the quay and none that he could see on any of the boats, nor on either of the walls that formed the outer limbs of the harbour. Yet the wall to his right . . .

It was at the farthest end of this wall that he had seen the figure from up on the path. There was no such figure there now. Yet still he could feel that pull, and it was growing stronger. He was certain now that it wasn't the girl. It was something else. Something important.

He walked down onto the quayside, turned right and started to make his way along the wall. Below him, in the harbour, the water glowed around the fishing boats, pleasure craft, and dinghies. He glanced the other way and saw waves rolling in from the sea. The wall stretched out in front of him, curving like a claw.

He reached the end and stopped at the place where the figure had been. A short distance away he could see the tip of the opposite wall, and below him, between the two points, the water moving duskily through the harbour mouth. He followed it with his eyes, out into the sea.

And there, floating past the gap, was a dark form.

He knew at once what it was.

A body.

17

It was Crow.

His head was down, his hair streaming, his arms
thrown out on either side. His shirt and trousers
billowed out, the braces trailing loose. His body was
half-floating, half-sinking, as though water and air
were fighting for possession of it. He appeared to have
drifted from the direction of the beach and was
already moving past the harbour mouth towards the
coastline beyond.

'No!' Will shouted.

He pounded his fists against his sides. He should
have stayed with the man. He should have done something. This was all his fault. He tried to think. The body
had to be recovered before it drifted any further. He
had to get help. He had to call the police. He whirled
round and saw five figures standing before him.

Wearing balaclavas.

'How you doing, mad boy?' said the nearest.

A male voice, not adult but older than him. Will
forced himself to speak.

'There's a body in the sea. We've got to help. It's
Crow.'

'Yeah, kooky,' came the answer. 'And I've got
horns in my head.'

The figures crowded round. He felt a hand seize him
by the hair, jerk his head back. He saw eyes leering

at him through the slits in the balaclavas. The same figure spoke.

'Or maybe you're the one with horns in his head. Maybe you're the Evil One.'

A fist thundered into the side of his face.

'Ah!' He staggered back, lost his footing and slipped towards the side of the wall. Below him he saw the moon-glow on the water and even from here the shadow of Crow's body as it drifted away. A hand caught him before he rolled over the edge, and here was the voice again.

'Not yet, crazy kid.'

He felt himself yanked to his feet and thrown against the wooden boarding that housed the lifebuoy. Somehow he stayed upright but his head was spinning now and he was losing balance. The balaclavas loomed over him again.

'Crow,' he murmured. 'We've . . . we've got to do something.'

'Yeah?' said the voice. 'Do what?'

Before he could answer, the fist smashed into his face again. He clutched the boarding and somehow stopped himself from falling. The fist squeezed itself under his chin and levered him back until he was pressed against the lifebuoy.

'Tell me, crazy boy,' said the voice, 'can you feel the sickness now?'

'Sickness,' muttered Will.

'That's right, kooky. We know all about that, don't we?' The fist worked its way into his throat. 'Cos you told the whole town, didn't you? Prophet of doom, ain't you? See stuff, yeah?'

He was gasping for air now, desperate to breathe, escape, think. The fist pushed hard against his windpipe.

151

'Thing is,' said the voice, 'we don't like people like you round here. Weird people, crazy people, people who tell us we're sick when they're the ones who are sick. They're the ones who bring all the bad stuff. We don't like people like that. And we don't like people like that wacky paedo either. So if something's happened to him, how much do you think we care?'

Will tried to speak but all he could do was gasp.

'This much?' said the voice, and the fist pushed harder into his throat.

Will gave another gasp but the fist kept pushing.

'This much?' said the voice.

The fist moved away, only to drive straight back into Will's stomach.

'Ah!' He doubled up and felt blackness engulf him. Somehow he stayed conscious but before he could gulp in air, he felt himself yanked upright again, and here was the balaclava back in his face.

'Or this much?'

And he was picked up by all five.

'No!' he shouted.

But they were already bundling him towards the end of the harbour wall.

'No!' he screamed, his eyes on the water beyond. Even now some part of him was searching for Crow's body, but all he saw was black water rushing close.

Then suddenly a light fell upon the sea.

In that instant everything changed. He fell, not into the water but onto the hard stone floor of the harbour wall. From behind him came the sound of running feet. He dragged himself back from the edge and twisted round to look.

The figures were tearing off down the quay. They cut behind the sheds and sail lofts to the left of The

152

Sea Chest and a moment later disappeared from view. Outside the pub was a police car, the beam from the headlamps thrown over the harbour.

He struggled to his feet but his head was swimming. He clung to a bollard for support and stared at the police officers. He had to call them, had to attract their attention somehow, but he was finding it hard to breathe, and even harder to stand.

'Come on,' he muttered. 'You've got to catch them before they drive off.'

Shouting wouldn't work. He didn't have the breath. He'd have to make himself walk. He let go of the bollard, took a step and fell. Darkness swirled about him. He hit the stone floor with a thud, rolled to the side and struck his head on a metal ring.

'Ah!'

His eyes blurred with tears and as they did so, he saw the beam of the headlamps change direction as the police car turned in the road.

'No,' he moaned, 'don't drive off, please . . . '

But it was no good. With a roar of the engine the car disappeared.

He lay back on the hard stone, tears running down his cheeks. He was shivering now and his body ached. The moon stared indifferently down. He thought of Crow's body floating under it. Then a new figure appeared over him.

He stared up. It was hard to see the face clearly through the tears but it was a male build and similar to one of the balaclava figures. He braced himself for another blow. But it never came. Instead, the figure turned and whistled back down the quay.

There was a sound of steps approaching. Will lay there, unable to move. Another face and this time he recognized it: the girl he'd seen at the upstairs window of The Sea Chest.

'Izzy!' called another voice. 'Who is it?'

She didn't answer but her companion did.

'Come and see!'

A third face appeared. Will's eyes found their focus at last, and the three figures became clear: Brad, Micky, and Izzy Wetherby. Brad knelt down and Will braced himself again. But the boy simply spoke.

'What happened to you?'

It wasn't a friendly voice. Not even an interested one. But it was better than another fist. He tried to answer.

'The tramp . . . drifting . . . '

'Eh?'

'Crow . . . he's . . . floating in the sea . . . he's . . . dead . . . '

He heard more footsteps approaching, then another voice.

'Will!'

He felt a wave of relief. It was Sarah Wetherby. She knelt down next to Brad.

'Will! You poor boy! What's happened?' She took him by the hand. 'It's all right, don't answer.'

She turned quickly to Brad.

'Got your mobile?'

'Yeah.'

'Ring the police and give me your phone the moment they put you through. Izzy, run back to the pub and get Daddy. Micky, check round the wall and see if Will's dropped any of his things.'

Will lay there as the others busied about. Brad soon had the police on the line.

'Give me your mobile,' said Sarah.

154

He handed her the phone.

'Hello?' she said. 'It's Sarah Wetherby from The Sea Chest in Havensmouth. I've got a boy injured on the harbour wall. His name's Will Bly and he's from The Four Winds. He's been beaten up and we'll need medical assistance as well.'

'Body,' murmured Will. He squeezed her hand as tightly as he could. 'There's . . . '

'What's that, sweetheart?'

'Crow . . . the tramp . . . he's . . . he's . . . dead . . . '

Somehow he blundered through what he'd seen while Sarah repeated it into the phone. Geoff Wetherby appeared with Izzy a few steps behind.

'Bloody hell,' he said.

'Quiet!' said Sarah. 'I'm on the phone.'

Will could feel his breathing starting to calm down but he was still shivering badly.

'Here,' said Geoff.

The man took off his coat and laid it over him. Sarah rang off and turned back to Will but before anyone could speak again, the police car had reappeared at the top of the harbour. Two policemen hurried across the quay.

'Will,' said Sarah, 'I'm going to ring your mum and dad. Can you tell me the number?'

'Done it,' said Geoff.

She looked round at her husband.

'You what?'

'I rang them from the pub before I came out.'

Will gave a sigh. Somehow, even now, all he wanted was to be left alone. He heard another car pull up at the top of the harbour. Again the sound of car doors opening and closing, then another engine, and suddenly it seemed as though everyone was around him: Mum, Dad, the police, the medics, Peter and a nurse from Acacia Court, the Wetherbys. A small group of onlookers had also gathered outside the pub.

Will closed his eyes and let the medics fuss around him.

'Please tell me someone's looking for Crow's body,' he said.

'Yes, we're looking,' came an answer.

One of the policemen, by the sound of it. Will didn't open his eyes. He knew the man was lying. Any other witness and they'd have organized a search. But not the boy who saw things that weren't there.

'You must believe me,' he said.

'We do believe you, darling.'

Mum's voice, also lying.

He stared into the darkness of his mind and saw a picture of the tramp floating through a murky sea; and floating with him were the shadowfaces, strangely sad, not frightening at all now; and then the girl. So beautiful, so strong. She too had ceased to be scary.

He heard another voice.

'Will!'

A familiar voice, a female voice. He opened his eyes and saw Beth pushing through from the back of the group. Jack was standing just apart, his arm round another girl's waist. Beth knelt down beside the medics.

'Will, what's happened to you?'

'Got beaten up.'

'Oh, Will!'

'And I saw . . . I saw . . . '

'Easy, Will . . . '

156

'Crow . . . floating in the sea . . . only . . . nobody believes me . . . '

A murmur of protest ran round the group.

'You don't!' Will shouted at them. 'None of you do. I'm just that weird boy, that crazy kid.'

Several people started speaking at once. The police wanted to question him about the balaclava figures, the ambulance men wanted to take him to hospital, Peter wanted to take him back to Acacia Court.

'No!' shouted Dad.

The voices ceased. Dad glared round at them all.

'Will's coming home with us. The police can question him when he's had a rest. And he doesn't need any more medical care right now. We're really, really grateful to all of you for your help. But he needs to be home now.'

Will reached out and touched Dad on the arm.

'It's not your fault, Dad.'

'It is our fault.' Dad glanced at Mum, who nodded. 'It bloody is our fault,' he went on. 'We shouldn't have been so quick to hand you over to other people.'

'Not that we're not really grateful,' Mum added, looking quickly round. 'But it's time we got Will back where he belongs.'

Sarah Wetherby put a hand on Mum's shoulder.

'We'll leave you to it, Julie,' she said. 'But don't forget where we are if you need anything. Will, drop by when you're feeling better, OK?'

'Thanks for your help,' said Dad.

'No problem.'

And the Wetherbys set off back to The Sea Chest. Will watched them go, then turned and looked into Beth's face. She leaned forward, kissed him softly on the mouth, then straightened up.

157

'I believe you,' she said quietly. 'And if there's anything I can do, just say.'

'There is something,' he said.

He felt Mum and Dad stiffen close by. Beth's expression didn't change. She simply looked back and waited for him to speak.

'I want to go out in your father's boat,' he said.

'What for?' said one of the policemen. 'To look for the tramp's body?'

Will turned his head away and stared towards the horizon.

'No,' he answered.

18

'Cast off!' shouted Stu.

Robbo cast off and *Spindrift* started to chug out of the harbour, the morning sun already bright upon her. Will stood next to Stu at the wheel with Beth to his left, and Mum, Dad, and Jack just behind. Stu nodded towards the harbour entrance.

'And that's where you saw Crow's body, you said?'

'Yes,' said Will.

'Has anybody reported seeing it?' said Dad.

'Not that I've heard,' said Stu.

'I saw it,' said Will. 'I did see it.'

'Nobody's doubting you there, boy,' said Stu.

Yes, they are, Will thought. But he said nothing.

They steered out of the harbour, then Stu eased off the engine until the boat was barely moving.

'OK, Will,' he said. 'Over to you.'

Will frowned. It was hard to know how to go about this.

'I'm not quite sure what I'm looking for,' he said eventually.

'Well, that makes two of us,' said Stu.

'I'll try not to waste your time.'

'Don't worry about that, Will. I'm glad to help if I can.'

'This is so good of you,' put in Dad. 'We do appreciate how busy you must be.'

159

'Not a problem,' said Stu.

Will felt the attention of all of them upon him. He wished he could be left alone for a while. A few minutes by himself and he felt sure he'd know what to do. He particularly disliked having Beth's brother there with all his cynical looks and comments. But Jack had wanted to come for the ride and there was nothing he could do about it.

Beth spoke suddenly.

'Will needs to be quiet for a minute. He can't think with us hassling him.'

'We're not hassling him,' said Jack.

'He needs to be left alone for a bit,' she said.

Will looked at her gratefully.

'Beth's absolutely right,' said Dad.

He put an arm round Will's shoulder and guided him to the rail outside the door of the wheelhouse.

'Will, no pressure, OK? Just take your time. But obviously . . . ' He lowered his voice. 'At some point we'll need to give Stu an idea of where . . . '

'I know, I know.'

Will looked round at the others. Everyone seemed to be watching him: Stu, Mum, Jack, and Beth in the wheelhouse; Dad standing here; Robbo, Andy, and Lee down in the waist of the boat. He turned and stared towards the horizon.

The redness had come from out there, but where the exact source was he couldn't tell. Perhaps he wouldn't find the spot. He clenched his jaw. He had to try, especially now that Stu Palmer had offered to help. He might not get another chance. He pointed straight ahead.

'Can we go that way?'

'Dead ahead?' called Stu.

'Yes. Right out to the horizon. I'll tell you when to stop.'

'OK.'

The engine roared into life and *Spindrift* headed towards the open sea. Dad rejoined the others in the wheelhouse but Will stayed at the rail, gazing towards the horizon. There had to be a clue out there as to what was wrong in Havensmouth. Again he thought of Crow's body and wondered where it was—and where little Muck was too.

He leaned on the rail, thinking hard and glad that the others had left him alone. But now Andy, Robbo, and Lee were wandering towards him. He tried to remember which one was which. Beth had introduced them when he came aboard but he'd been so jittery about setting out that he hadn't paid much attention. He'd also been slightly nervous of them. They were even more rough-looking up close. But at least the tallest of the three had a smile for him.

'Forgotten, ain't you?' said the man. 'Our names, like.'

'You're Robbo.'

'Well done. What about the other two?'

'Andy and Lee but I can't remember which one's which.'

'No big deal,' said Robbo. 'But it's easy to remember.' He glanced at the man to his right. 'Andy looks handy, right?'

It was true. Will couldn't imagine anyone wanting to pick a fight with Andy.

'So the other guy's got to be Lee.'

Lee looked every bit as handy as Andy but Will made no comment. He thought of the other crew member, the one who wasn't here.

'What happened to Davy?' he said.

All three laughed at this. Andy started to roll a cigarette.

'He'll be sleeping off whatever he had last night. And we won't miss him. He ain't pulled his weight for a long time. Skip won't be using him no more.'

'So if you know anyone who's looking for a job,' said Lee, 'and is mad enough to want to go fishing . . . '

The three laughed again, then Robbo leaned forward.

'So what's this trip about? Skip didn't tell us much. Just said we ain't fishing and come along for the ride if we had nothing else to do.'

Will frowned.

'I'm hoping to do some fishing of my own,' he said.

He felt a hand on his shoulder and saw Beth standing next to him, her hair streaming in the breeze. He felt the men glance her way.

'All right, guys?' she said.

'We are now,' said Lee.

Robbo clipped him round the head.

'Behave.'

Andy lit his cigarette and laughed.

'Do you want some beer?' said Beth. 'Dad's brought some.'

'Why not?' said Robbo.

And the men lumbered below to the cabin. Will watched them go, feeling slightly uncomfortable. He wasn't sure whether it was the sight of them flirting with Beth that unsettled him or something else. Beth gave him a smile.

'Nice guys,' she said.

He looked down.

'Will?'

He looked up again.

'You all right?' she said.

'Yeah.'

'Does that mean no?'

He shrugged.

'Do you want to be left alone?' she said. 'So you can think?'

'I'm all right.'

But he wasn't. He could feel that eerie coldness inching up his feet, legs, and spine. The breeze was still warm but it made little difference. He twisted round to face the other way. Astern he could see the town fading in the distance, though some of its features were still visible: the harbour, The Sea Chest, the spire of the church; the rocky coastline to the right; Breeze Point and the beaches and dunes to the left.

Again he thought of the tramp—and the little boy.

'Muck,' he murmured to himself.

'Nobody's seen him,' said Beth.

He looked at her with a start. He hadn't intended her to hear.

'Nobody's seen him,' she said. 'So Dad says, and he'd get to hear. He knows everybody.'

Will shivered again. The coldness was still running over his skin. He turned back to face the bows. Somewhere ahead there had to be a clue as to what was wrong. *Spindrift* ran on, away from the shore. Lee, Robbo, and Andy reappeared with beer cans and wandered forward to lean over the bows. He watched them absently, his mind on the chill that was growing around him, and the fear that was growing with it. Beth hooked an arm in his.

'You're cold,' she said.

'I'm fine.'

'You're really, really cold. Are you having one of your—'

'I'm fine, OK? I'm really fine.'

He looked away.

'Will?'

'I'm all right.'

'You're avoiding my eyes.'

'I'm all right.'

He needed to be by himself suddenly. He needed to feel what was happening. There was something drawing close that he didn't like and he needed to place it. He felt his breathing speed up. He tried to calm it down, but without success. Beth still had her arm linked with his.

'Will, are you sure you—'

'I'm OK, really.' He looked hard at her. 'Please, just—'

'OK, I won't fuss.' She leaned closer. 'I know you feel stuff nobody else does. I know you're different.' She drew back. 'I'll give you a bit of space. Shout if you need me.'

And without another word, she let go of his arm, climbed down to the waist of the boat and wandered over to the bows to join Robbo, Andy, and Lee. They made a space for her between them and then all four leaned forward together, gazing ahead. Will watched, feeling another twinge as they joked with her. But the awkwardness didn't last. The other feeling— whatever it was—was starting to overwhelm it. It was starting to overwhelm everything.

Spindrift forged on. He stared ahead, beyond the bows, and there at last was the darkening of the sea he'd expected: that deep, reddish blot that seemed even now to be spreading towards them. No one else seemed to have noticed it. The faces in the wheel-house had not changed. Robbo and Lee were laughing up in the bows. Andy was pointing out a floating crate to Beth.

Will turned and looked astern again. The land had slipped away faster than he'd expected it to and was now far distant. Mum and Dad joined him at the rail.

'All right, Will?' said Mum.

'Thought you'd be looking forward, not back,' said Dad. 'Isn't it out there the thing you're looking for? I mean . . . whatever it is . . . '

Will went on staring at the shore.

'It's back there too,' he murmured. 'It started here but it's there too.'

'But what, Will?' said Mum. 'What started here?'

He turned back towards the bows and gazed over the sea. The red blot was deepening in colour and widening. He felt the chill over his skin grow stronger. He saw Beth wandering back, followed by Robbo and Lee. Only Andy remained in the bows. The other three climbed up and joined him at the rail with Mum and Dad.

'Any sign of the thing you're looking for?' said Robbo.

Will pointed to the red shadow.

'Can you see it?'

They all stared over the rail.

'I can see water,' said Robbo. 'Plenty of water.'

'It's called the sea,' said Lee.

'Very funny,' said Robbo. 'The sort of rubbish my son comes out with.'

'Can't you see anything else?' said Will.

Robbo shook his head. Will looked round at the others.

'Can't anyone see anything else?'

They were entering the shadow now and the sea was turning to a bloody pool. Even the bow wave was tinged with red.

'Just water,' said Mum. 'Nothing strange.'

Will looked at Dad.

'Sorry, Will.'

'Beth?'

She too shook her head. Suddenly Andy gave a shout from the bows.

'Look! Over there!'

He was pointing into the very heart of the shadow where the red was most intense. Will stared at it and as he did so, he felt the coldness grow worse. Where before it had run over his skin, now it was seeping inwards and closing round his lungs.

'Another crate!' called Andy. 'See it? I bet that came from the same boat that dumped the last one.'

Will felt the coldness inside him tighten, not just round his lungs but his heart as well. He started to struggle for breath. Robbo called out to Andy.

'See anything else?'

'Like what?' came the answer.

'I don't know. Like . . . something funny.'

'Bit of seaweed that looks like your face. That's pretty funny.'

Will started to gasp.

'Will?' said Dad. 'Are you all right?'

Will clutched at the air.

'Get me away from here,' he spluttered.

From inside the wheelhouse came the sound of a mobile ringing.

'Dad.' Will gripped his father's shirt. He could feel himself losing consciousness. Dad's arms locked round him and held him steady. 'Dad . . . '

The mobile went on ringing.

'Dad . . . get Stu to turn back.'

The mobile fell silent.

'Stu!' bellowed Dad.

Stu didn't appear but Jack did.

'What's up?' he said.

'Get your father to turn back!' roared Dad. 'Do it now!'

Jack disappeared inside the wheelhouse again.

Will felt himself eased to the deck, still held in Dad's arms. He saw faces above him: Mum's, Dad's, Beth's, Robbo's, Lee's—and then other faces, not unexpected. Somehow it made sense that they should come to him out here.

The shadowfaces, and the girl, mingling with the others.

'Who are you?' he said to them all.

'It's us, Will,' said Mum. 'Just us.'

He stared at the ghostly forms. How strange that he had once found them frightening. They were not frightening at all. They were just sad.

'It's us, Will,' said Mum again.

From the wheelhouse came a shout. He only dimly heard it. Something from Stu about heading back to the shore and then a question: did Dad want him to call the air ambulance?

'Yes,' said Dad.

'No,' said Will.

He didn't need the air ambulance. He knew that. They were leaving the red shadow now. He could tell without looking. He could feel his breath returning.

'Just give me a moment,' he muttered. 'Till we've left that place behind.'

No one spoke for several minutes and gradually the coldness released its grip on his heart and lungs. The shadowfaces and the girl started to fade. Beth took his hand.

'Are you all right now, Will?'

He looked up at her, unsure what to say. Stu's face appeared.

'Christ, Will,' he said. 'You know how to scare us.'

'I'm sorry.'

'No need for apologies.' Stu glanced at Robbo. 'Take the wheel, can you? I've left it with Jack but you know what he's like.'

Robbo disappeared inside the wheelhouse and Stu turned back.

'Will, I don't know if you're ready to hear this, but . . . ' He frowned. 'I've just had a call on the mobile from Geoff Wetherby. The police have found Crow's body washed up further down the coast. The hunt's now on for the little boy.'

19

The cave was just as he remembered it from last time: musty and dim. Mum, Dad, Beth, and Stu stood close by. In the far corner DI Cutler and DC Drake were bent over the ground with their torches.

'It's further to the right,' said Beth.

Both policemen looked round at her.

'Can you show us the exact spot?' said DI Cutler.

She walked over to the officers and pointed.

'There. To the right, see? You've got to climb over those small rocks and then you'll see it underneath the overhang.'

DC Drake shone his torch in that direction and the two men peered along the beam. Will watched too. Even from here he could see that the stony wall barely rose above the ground before jutting straight out into the cave. The men stared at it with obvious distaste.

'You'd have to be pretty tiny to get under that,' said DI Cutler eventually.

He clambered over the small rocks until he reached the overhang, then bent down and stared into the space beyond.

'Christ,' he said. 'It gets even lower further along.'

'Can you see the passage?' said DC Drake.

'Part of it. But not much. It's too narrow to see clearly.'

DI Cutler straightened up again and looked round.

169

'And this passage comes out the other side of the headland?'

'Yes,' said Beth. 'On the other beach.'

'And it's as narrow as this all the way through?'

'I don't know,' she said. 'I've never been in there. Don't know anyone who has, apart from Muck. He seems to be able to crawl through anything. But the other side's as narrow as this where it comes out so I suppose it's probably as narrow all the way through.'

The officers studied the opening for a few more minutes, then turned and clambered back to join the others.

'And you think it's possible,' said DI Cutler, 'that the boy might still be in there?'

'He could be,' said Stu. 'If he's somewhere in the middle, out of sight of both ends. But I don't know how we check.'

Mum shuddered.

'I hate to think of that child stuck down there. Maybe too frightened to come out.'

'Or dead,' said Stu. 'Not a nice thought but . . . you know . . . we've got to face the possibility.'

'Could you send a dog down?' said Dad to the officers.

'That would terrify the boy,' said Mum.

'I mean a friendly one. I'm sure the police must have special dogs for things like this.'

The two officers exchanged glances.

'We'll sort something out,' said DI Cutler after a moment.

Will looked away. It made no difference what the police said. He could tell the real level of their interest from their faces. They'd check out the passage, no doubt, though he sensed Muck wasn't there. They'd look for the boy along the coast and make enquiries in Havensmouth and Newton Barnet, and other places. They'd make enquiries into Crow's death.

But they weren't really interested. He didn't suppose most of the locals were either. Who cared about the death of a man no one liked and the smelly little boy who hung around with him? Crow's body had shown no signs of violence, the police had said. It was death from drowning. Maybe it was murder but there was no proof. He could have just fallen into the sea and got washed down the coast. And the kid ran off.

Two misfits gone. Good riddance.

As for the balaclava gang, who said they even existed? Only one person claimed to have seen them: the mad boy, the loony with the big mouth, the boy who makes stuff up, causes trouble. So someone knocked him about a bit on the harbour wall. Well, he had it coming. He's upset so many people. Who says it was a balaclava gang? No one else has mentioned a balaclava gang.

Just the boy who sees things that aren't there.

And now he's seen a red blur in the sea.

So what?

He looked round at the faces watching him. Polite faces, showing all the things they meant to show and most of the things they didn't. He turned to the officers.

'You've got to keep looking for Muck.'

'We will,' said DI Cutler. 'And hopefully we'll find him somewhere safe. There's no reason at this stage to suppose foul play.'

DC Drake nodded.

'It's highly unlikely he'll stay unnoticed for long,

unless he's had an accident in some remote place. More likely someone'll take him in and let us know.'

'But he's an edgy kid,' said Stu. 'He might not be willing to let anyone help him. Crow was the only person he trusted. I'm not quite sure why. I mean, I know the guy claimed Muck was his son, but no one really believed that round here.'

'Muck wasn't his son,' said Will. 'Crow told me. It was just a story he put round to get people to leave them alone.'

DI Cutler shrugged.

'Well, we can only hope the lad turns up.'

He shone his torch over the passageway again.

'I don't suppose he's in there,' he muttered to DC Drake, 'but we'll get DC Griffiths to check it out. It's more her province. Can you speak to her?'

'Leave it with me,' said DC Drake.

DI Cutler turned back to Will and frowned.

'What?' said Will.

'Your face is an open book, young man.'

'So's yours.'

'You think we don't believe you.'

'I know you don't believe me.' Will scowled at him. 'Only what about these bruises on my face? I suppose I did that to myself, did I? Or maybe I walked into a wall.'

'Nope,' said the policeman. 'Somebody whopped you, no question.'

Will said nothing.

'I'll be honest with you,' said the officer. 'I don't quite know what to make of you. You come out with claims no one can verify—'

'That doesn't mean I'm lying.'

'I'm not accusing you of lying.' DI Cutler's eyes

narrowed for a moment. 'I'm just saying it's hard to know what to make of you. We get lots of people claiming this, that, and the other. Nutters, drunks, druggies, weirdoes, religious fanatics. You name it, we get it.' He paused. 'But you're different.'

Will felt Mum and Dad tense, as though they were about to leap to his defence. He looked at them and shook his head. Neither spoke; but neither relaxed. The officer glanced at them, then back at Will.

'You say there's a sickness in this community.'

'Yes.'

'But you don't give any specifics.'

'It's deep and it's bad.'

'But you don't say what it is.'

'I don't know what it is. I just know it's there.'

'You just know it's there.' DI Cutler paused again. 'You've got nothing to back up what you say. You just know it's there.'

'That doesn't mean I'm lying.'

'You keep saying that,' said the officer. 'And I'll repeat what I said a moment ago: I'm not accusing you of lying.'

Outside a wave crashed on the shore.

'Normally,' DI Cutler went on, 'I'd be reluctant to push this too hard without any firm evidence. As I just mentioned, we get lots of people claiming weird things. But like I say, you're different. Don't ask me why. And now a body's turned up and a boy's gone missing. And an ally's come forward to defend you.'

'Who?'

'John Shepherd.'

'Good man,' said Stu. 'Best vicar we've had for years. Everybody says so.'

'Yes,' said DI Cutler, 'but maybe a little out of his

depth on this one. Though I've no doubt he means well.'

Another wave crashed on the shore outside.

'What's John done?' said Will.

'Spoken up for you,' said the officer. 'Seems a little strange to me. I'm surprised he wants anything to do with you after you upset his congregation.'

'There's no need for that kind of talk,' said Mum.

DI Cutler glanced at her.

'I'm not passing judgement on Will.'

'Yes, you are,' she said.

'I'm just stating it the way it is.'

'The way you see it, you mean.'

The officer shrugged and looked back at Will.

'John Shepherd's been to see us anyway, and although, like you, he hasn't got anything concrete in the way of evidence—nothing more than a feeling, as he puts it, that something's wrong in Havensmouth— he's been urging us to take you seriously. He's even asked us to give you something.'

'What's that?' said Dad.

'Police protection.'

'Blimey,' said Stu.

'Which of course we can't offer.' DI Cutler looked at Will. 'I'm sure you'll appreciate that's just not possible. We don't have the resources for something like that and anyway, there's no justification for such a thing.'

'But Will's got enemies,' said Dad. 'You can't deny he's got enemies.'

'Of his own making, some might say.'

'There you go again,' said Mum. 'Making judgements.'

'I'm just putting it the way many might see it,' said

the officer. 'I'm not saying we won't do our best to keep an eye on Will, but we can't give him special protection, whatever John Shepherd might think.'

'Then we'll give him special protection,' said Dad.

'So will we,' said Beth. She looked quickly at her father.

'Definitely,' added Stu. 'We'll help.'

The two police officers looked at each other.

'Well, that's all to the good,' said DI Cutler eventually. 'But it would surely be best if you took Will away.'

'No!' said Will firmly.

He saw all eyes fix upon him.

'No!' he said again. 'I'm not being taken away!'

'For your own safety,' said DC Drake. 'There's clearly bad feeling towards you in Havensmouth. We think the vicar's overreacting but he's probably right about being cautious. It might be in everyone's interests if you—'

'No!' said Will. He glared at DC Drake, then round at the others. 'I'm not doing it!'

'Easy, Will,' said Stu. 'This gentleman's only trying—'

'I won't go. I can't.' Will looked down. 'I can't . . . leave them.'

'Leave who?' said Mum.

Will shook his head.

'I don't know. I . . . '

He pictured the shadowfaces, the girl, the little boy, all somehow linked; and for a moment the sandy floor of the cave seemed to take on the form of their faces. He stared at it until the images left.

'I don't know who they are,' he muttered. 'I only know I can't leave them.'

Silence, broken only by the surf—then DI Cutler's voice again.

'Well, we might as well go outside. There's nothing more to discover in here.'

Will followed the others out. To his surprise, the beach and dunes were now crowded with figures: walkers, sunbathers, surfers, swimmers, others just standing around. Police officers too were dotted about, even on the harbour wall.

Watching.

He looked round at the others. The officers were already striding off towards the town, DC Drake talking into his radio. Mum, Dad, Stu, and Beth were standing together, waiting for him.

'Will?' said Mum. 'Are you coming home now?'

He turned and stared towards the horizon, where the red darkness still lingered.

'Will?' said Mum.

He looked at her.

'Don't take me away,' he said. 'Please.'

He walked slowly up to her.

'It might be safer, Will,' she said.

'Your mum's right,' said Stu. 'It might not have to be for long. Just until things settle down.'

'They won't settle down, not if I go. It's gone too deep now, this thing.'

He saw Beth crying, close by.

'You know, don't you?' he said to her. 'You know something's wrong.'

She wiped her eyes and nodded.

'But I don't know what it is either,' she said. 'I just know . . . this isn't a happy place any more.'

Mum reached out and put an arm round Beth's shoulder.

'But, Will,' said Dad, 'what can you possibly do by staying?'

Will turned back to the sea.

'I can try to put things right,' he said.

20

Muck stood before him. Will stared up from the bed and saw the boy framed against the door to the balcony, the night sky behind him bright with stars. Red streams poured from the child's eyes, nose, mouth, and ears and flowed down his chest and arms. His hands were held out like those of the statue in Stu Palmer's fountain. They too oozed red, which fell in splashes onto the floor. Will sat up and screamed.

Dad's voice called out from the next bedroom.

'Will? Are you all right?'

He didn't answer. He was staring at Muck's face. So much red now covered it that it was hard to see the eyes clearly. Yet somehow they spoke to him; and somehow he understood.

'Not mine,' the eyes said.

'I'll help you,' said Will. 'I promise I'll help you.'

He heard a knock at the door, then Dad's voice again.

'Will?'

The door swung open and he saw his father standing there, followed a second later by Mum.

'What's happened, Will?' she said. 'You screamed.'

He turned back to face the balcony door, but there was no boy. All he saw was the stars beyond, and the shadowy headland of Breeze Point at the far end of

178

the beach. He stared over the carpet. It had no traces of red. But he'd expected none.

'Not mine,' he murmured.

'What did you say?' said Dad.

'Nothing.'

Mum came forward and sat down on the bed.

'Will,' she murmured.

'I didn't mean to frighten you both,' he said.

'I know you didn't. What did you see?'

'Do you really want to hear? I thought you didn't like my hallucinations.'

She gave a sigh.

'We've never said they were hallucinations. You know that. It's just one of the theories some people have suggested.'

He looked down.

'I saw the little boy,' he said after a moment. 'He had . . . '

He pictured the figure, swimming in red.

'Not mine,' he murmured again.

'I don't understand,' said Mum.

'Neither do I.' He looked back at her. 'I saw the boy anyway.'

'I wish we could see him too,' she said.

'You wouldn't want to. Not the way I just saw him.'

Mum watched him for a moment, frowning.

'Well, maybe you're right,' she said. 'Even so, I can't help wondering where he is, poor thing.'

'I'll tell you where he isn't,' said Dad. 'He's not in the passage under Breeze Point.'

Mum looked round at him.

'How do you know?'

'Stu Palmer rang and told me.'

'Did he? When?'

'Earlier this evening, when you were out in the garden. I forgot to tell you. The police did a search but Muck wasn't there. Stu heard it from one of the officers.'

'Good of him to let us know.' Mum hesitated. 'I was wrong about Beth, Will. I'm really sorry. She's been great. And so has her father.'

'I agree,' said Dad. 'Though I have to say I still don't care for Jack very much.'

Will said nothing. He was still worrying about Muck. He'd never expected the police to find the boy in the passage. He lay back in bed again, thinking. Muck felt strangely close, and not just as a hallucination, or whatever he'd been a moment ago. The solid, physical boy felt close too.

And that was not all. Something else felt close, something equally solid and physical, but it was hard to work out what it was. He only knew it was something that was out of place. He glanced round the room as secretly as he could, anxious not to worry Mum and Dad any further. But they were watching him too closely to miss what he was doing.

'What are you looking for, Will?' said Dad.

'Nothing.'

'Have you seen something else?'

'No, just . . . looking round.'

They went on watching him.

'Honestly,' he said. 'It's nothing. I'm probably just being a bit jumpy. I'll be all right now. Thanks for coming in.'

'Call us again if you need us,' said Dad. 'If you're frightened or anything.'

'OK.'

Mum leaned down.

'We do believe you, you know. These things you see. We do believe you.'

'I told you before, Mum,' he said. 'You're a terrible liar. But I love you for trying.'

She smiled at him.

'That's the first time you've told me you love me. Since the accident, I mean.'

'Did I tell you before?'

She bit her lip.

'All the time,' she said quietly.

She leaned down and kissed him.

'Goodnight, darling.'

'Goodnight.'

'Sleep well,' said Dad.

'Yeah, right.'

And they all managed a laugh.

He waited till the door had closed, then sat up in bed again. It was still there, this other thing. It wasn't the boy. He was clear about that. It was something else. It didn't feel like the girl or the shadowfaces. It felt like something physical. But perhaps he was wrong. Perhaps he was just being jumpy, as he'd said.

He looked about him, searching the room. He wasn't even sure it was something in here. He took a long, deep breath, trying to calm himself, trying to make sense of this new feeling of danger. Yes, he decided— it was a feeling of danger. And there it was again, that hint of solid presence.

He stood up, switched the light on and dressed, apart from his shoes; then, after a moment's thought, he put his trainers on too. Somehow he felt safer with his clothes on. He looked about him again. No sign of anything dangerous in the room but he didn't feel reassured. He walked towards the balcony. The door was closed but he could see clearly through the glass, though the right and left corners closest to the wall of the house were hidden from view from inside the room.

He stopped at the point where Muck's form had appeared. Beyond the door the stars were still bright in the sky and the moon had now emerged to throw down a ghostly light. He pushed open the door and stepped out. The sound of the surf seemed strangely distant. He remembered the hidden corners of the balcony and quickly checked.

But no one was there. He stepped back into his room, walked through it and out onto the landing. From inside Mum and Dad's room came the sound of snoring, but then, to his surprise, the door suddenly opened and he saw Dad standing there in his pyjamas.

'Will,' he said quietly, 'I heard you moving about. What are you dressed for?'

'I thought . . . ' Will hesitated. 'I thought . . . '

'Have you seen something again?'

'No.'

'Heard something?'

'No.'

The sound of snoring stopped, then Mum called out.

'Chris?'

'It's nothing,' said Dad. 'Go back to sleep.'

He closed the door behind him and joined Will on the landing.

'What's up, Will?' he whispered.

Will looked at his father's face. Even with the landing light off he could see Dad's desperate attempts to hide his frustration.

'Nothing, Dad. Honestly. Can't sleep, that's all.'

'It's not that. It's something else.' Dad switched on the landing light. 'What is it? Tell me.'

'Can we search the house?'

'You think someone's broken in?'

Again he saw Dad struggle to conceal his frustration.

'Dad, listen, we don't have to.'

'No, let's do it.'

'But—'

'It's OK, Will. Let's make sure.'

They went through the rooms, one by one, upstairs first, switching lights on, checking the obvious places of concealment, then downstairs.

'Kitchen first?' said Dad.

'OK,' said Will.

But his heart was sinking. Everything felt wrong. He was starting to doubt himself again. There was clearly no one here and Dad's growing impatience— much as he tried to hide it—only made things worse. As expected, there was no one in the kitchen.

'Sorry, Dad. Let's go back to bed.'

'No, we'll check everything.'

'We don't have to.'

'No, no. Let's do it.'

Nothing in the lounge, nothing in the study, but the window to the garden was slightly open.

'That's my fault,' said Dad, closing it. 'I meant to shut it when I came upstairs and forgot. Do you want to check the garden?'

'No, it's all right. I'm really sorry, Dad. I know you're fed up with me.'

'I'm not fed up with you at all,' said Dad. 'But I am tired, Will. Really, really tired.'

183

'I know.'

'And it's the wee small hours, you know?'

They made their way upstairs again and stopped outside Will's room. Dad switched off the landing light.

'Give me a hug, Will,' he said.

They held each other for a while, then drew back.

'Thanks, Dad,' said Will.

They smiled at each other. From inside Mum and Dad's room came the sound of snoring again.

'She's knackered too,' said Dad.

'Did she always snore?'

Dad gave him a quizzical look.

'I can't remember,' said Will. 'Remember?'

Dad shook his head.

'You seem so like you always were I sometimes forget you can't remember things. She's always snored a bit. When she sleeps on her back. I have to coax her to roll over onto her side and then she's all right.'

'You'd better get in and do that, then.'

'OK. Night, Will.'

'Night.'

And Dad disappeared. Will waited for the door to close behind him, then turned towards his own room—and there was that feeling again. A solid presence, no ghost or vision or hallucination. Maybe not in his room, but somewhere close to it, or close to the house, or in sight of it.

He stood on the landing, unwilling to enter the bedroom and glad of the soft darkness around him. From inside Mum and Dad's room the snoring continued and soon it was joined by the sound of slow breathing from Dad, clearly audible in spite of the closed door.

The door to his own room was ajar. He pushed it fully open, watching from the threshold. Everything appeared to be just as he'd left it. The door bounced off the rubber stop on the floor and started to swing back towards him. He put out a hand to hold it still and went on peering into the room. All was clear with the light on.

There was nobody in the room, and even from here he could see there was no one under the bed. Whatever he had felt was not here. He walked slowly in and stopped in the centre of the room. Still nothing dangerous to be seen, and yet that sense of something close. He walked towards the balcony and stopped again on the spot where Muck's form had stood.

Then he saw it through the balcony door.

The tiny figure of Muck racing across the beach, his black hair brightened by the moon. But he was not heading for the cave. He was running in the direction of The Four Winds. In another moment he would be hidden from view by the rim of the balcony rail. And there was something else.

Behind the boy were more markings in the sand, not a drawing this time but letters: large, untidy letters scrawled above the tide-line. It was impossible to read what they said from here. Will hurried out onto the balcony and craned over the edge. Muck was now tearing along the beach path and round the base of the hill.

But he looked up and their eyes met—once—before he disappeared from view behind the curve of the hill. Will turned back to face the beach and stared at the letters in the sand. Only one word was written there. He read it aloud.

'Dream.'

Then he heard a sound behind him.

He whirled round and saw a figure crouching in the corner of the balcony. The face was hidden by a balaclava. He opened his mouth to call to Mum and Dad but before he could do so, the figure sprang forward, clapped a hand over his lips and forced him back against the rail.

He struggled to break free but the grip was too strong. An arm locked under his legs and lifted him towards the edge. Far below him the beach swam like mist. He saw the eyes in the slits draw closer. He recognized them at once from the harbour wall—and the voice that growled in his ear.

'You are evil. You are dead.'

21

Will clutched at the arm under his legs, wriggling as he did so in an effort to break free. From under the balaclava came the sound of hard, heavy breaths. Somehow he checked the movement and kept his feet on the balcony. But the pressure continued. He reached up and plucked at the hand over his mouth. If he could just manage a scream, Dad might hear and come running.

But the fingers only dug deeper into his cheeks, squeezing the sound away. Then the hand pushed harder, easing his head back. He felt his body follow, helped by the arm under his legs. Wriggling again, he kicked one of the legs free and dug the foot into a crack in the balcony floor.

Then he grasped the rail with both hands and clung on. But still he was being edged back, the hand clamped over his face. He twisted his head from side to side and somehow opened his mouth just wide enough to feel one of his attacker's fingers slip in.

He bit hard.

From the figure came a stifled yelp, but not enough to wake Dad, and here was the pressure again, forcing his face back. He bit again, harder. Another yelp, stifled as before, but this time there was a momentary pause in the pressure on his face. He opened his mouth wider to scream but before he could do so, the hand came down again.

No fingers to bite now. The grip over his mouth was firmer, more careful. Whatever pain he'd caused, it was not enough, and he sensed a greater determination now in his attacker. He could feel his foot slipping from the crack in the floor and though he still had his hands round the balcony rail, his grip was loosening as the strain grew.

On an impulse, he released one of his hands and fumbled over his attacker's body. The pressure doubled on the hand still holding on but his other hand found the groin, clutched, and squeezed. A groan from the figure, stifled as before, and still the pressure continued round his mouth. But the hand that had been holding his legs let go and tried to prise his fingers from the groin. He squeezed again, felt the figure recoil, and struggled back onto the balcony.

The attacker lunged at him again. He felt his hand knocked away from the groin, then they fell to the floor, the figure on top of him. The hand that had never left his mouth was still there and now the other was feeling round his throat. He kicked out, desperate to free himself or make some noise, but the eerie silence continued, broken only by their hoarse breaths. He fumbled again for the groin but now he was losing strength.

He clutched at the balaclava, trying to pull it loose. The figure reared up, slapped him in the face, then knocked his hand free, and now the vice was round his throat, both hands, squeezing, destroying. He felt consciousness start to fade and he knew he couldn't stop it. His attacker leaned close and whispered in his ear.

'This is the end, mad boy.'

Will looked up into the eyes within the slits. The voice whispered again.

'I hope you can fly.'

And suddenly he was being lifted again, and the edge of the balcony rail was rushing close, and there was the beach below, and the word in the sand.

'Dream,' he heard himself say.

And then realizing that the hand was no longer clasped over his face, he opened his mouth and screamed.

'Help!'

It was more of a croak than a scream but it had an instant effect. The figure dropped him to the floor of the balcony and vanished into the bedroom. Will struggled to his feet and stumbled after him. There was no sign of his attacker, nor any sound of footsteps, but Dad was calling from the room next door.

'Will!'

Will hurried through to the landing. No sign of the figure here either but a trickle of moonlight was cutting through the hall below. He limped downstairs and saw the front door open.

'Will!' called Dad.

But Will was already halfway down the path. He stopped at the front gate and stared down the hill. Far down the road the figure was running into town, the balaclava still on. A moment later he disappeared from view round the bend in the road. Mum and Dad burst out of the house in their night clothes.

'What's happened?' said Mum.

Will stared at them, his mind still in turmoil.

'You called out,' said Dad.

'I called for help,' he muttered.

'I didn't hear that,' said Dad. 'Just a muffled noise.'

'It was me.' Will dropped to his knees, fighting tears. 'I was attacked.'

'What!' Dad knelt down beside him. 'Who? When?'

'I don't know.' Will looked at him. 'A figure in a balaclava. He must have got into the house and slipped upstairs while we were searching the downstairs rooms. He was on the balcony. He tried to throw me over the rail.'

'My God!' said Mum.

'He let go of me when I called out. I just saw him running down the hill into town.'

Dad clenched his fists, stared down the road. Then he looked back.

'I'm going after him.'

'Chris, no,' said Mum.

'Don't try and stop me,' he said, and ran past her into the house.

Mum threw her arms round Will.

'Come inside the house,' she said.

He didn't move.

'Come on,' said Mum. 'It's two in the morning. Better inside than outside.'

She made to stand up but he clung to her.

'All right, darling,' she said. 'No problem. We'll stay here for a moment. We'll go in when you're ready.'

She pulled him closer and they stayed there by the gate, neither speaking. Dad reappeared, fully dressed. Mum looked up at him.

'You're not going anywhere,' she said.

'I am.'

She let go of Will and stood up.

'Chris—'

'I'm going out, OK?'

Mum and Dad glowered at each other. Will stared at them, an uneasy understanding starting to grow inside him. He stood up.

'You don't believe me,' he said slowly. 'I can tell. You're pretending you do but you don't. You think it's another hallucination.'

'We don't think that,' said Dad. 'And I'm going to check this guy out.'

And before anyone could speak, he ran off down the hill.

'Chris!' called Mum. 'Come back!'

But Dad simply ran on. Will turned quickly to Mum.

'I'm not making this up,' he said. 'It's really true. I nearly got killed just now.'

'We're not doubting you, Will.'

'Don't lie to me. I know when you're lying to me.'

He glanced down the hill at Dad's disappearing form.

'Phone the police, Mum,' he said. 'I'm going after Dad.'

'No!'

She grabbed him by the arm but he shook himself free.

'I've got to,' he said. 'He doesn't realize it's dangerous. He thinks I'm imagining it.'

'Then why's he gone looking?' She caught him by the arm again. 'Tell me that.'

'Because he's acting!' Will scowled at her. 'Because I've driven him mental tonight and he can't take any more. So he's run off. But he hasn't gone to look for this guy. He's gone off to clear his head.'

'That's not true.'

'It is true. He's pretending. You're both pretending. I know it's because you love me. But you've got to believe me. There's people out there. It's me they want but if Dad gets involved, they'll kill him too. Phone the police, Mum. Tell them what's happened.'

And before she could answer, he shook himself free again and raced after Dad.

'Come back!' she shouted.

He ignored her and tore down the street. Only at the bend did he look back. She was still standing by the gate, staring in horror. She shouted again.

'Come back!'

He ran on, trying to block her from his mind so that he could focus on finding Dad. Dad was all that mattered. There was no sign of him ahead, no sign of anyone, even where the road flattened out and continued into town. He stopped, breathing hard. He still had tears in his eyes, and he was shaking. He had to control himself or he'd be useless if anything happened.

He looked about him. Several roads led off this one but there seemed no point in doing anything other than head straight into town. But he'd try to glance down the other roads as he passed them in case he caught a glimpse of Dad in one of them.

At least the moon brightened things. There were fewer places in which to hide, though there were long moon-shadows in which a person could lurk unseen. He listened. Nothing to hear save the music of the sea. He walked on, his eyes searching.

'Dad,' he muttered, 'where are you?'

And where, he wondered, were his enemies?

He reached the main street and started down it, running his eye over the houses and shops. Over to the right he could see the water sparkling beyond the alleyways that ran down from the main street. The church tower loomed above the buildings, dark and proud.

A figure appeared further down.

He moved into a shop doorway and watched. Whoever it was appeared not to have noticed him and was bent over, lighting a cigarette. A second figure appeared from a side road and joined the first, and this time he recognized them: the two teenage boys he'd seen on bikes around Havensmouth. About his age and every bit as unfriendly as Brad and Micky Wetherby.

He studied them. Both had powerful builds and either could have been his attacker on the balcony. The first handed the cigarette to his friend, who used the tip to light one of his own, then they sloped down the main street towards him. He moved further back in the doorway, keeping as low as he could.

Neither glanced his way as they passed.

He waited until they had gone, then slipped out again. Still no sign of Dad. He had no wish to go near the harbour, not after his last experience there, but he knew he had to check it out. He started to walk down towards it. He could see it clearly at the far end of the street. The lights in the buildings were mostly off, though one or two still glowed in the night.

He reached The Sea Chest and stopped. The pub was dark and quiet. He looked up at the window where he'd seen Izzy Wetherby looking down at him. It was closed and the curtains were drawn across. On the ground directly beneath it was a mess of cigarette ends. Down in the harbour the water was still, though the sea beyond the mouth moved gently in the night. *Spindrift* rocked for a moment as a ripple passed under her.

No sign of Dad at all.

But he could hear footsteps somewhere near. He turned around. There was no one in the street, no one he could see anyway. He hurried round past the pub and cut down towards the sail lofts on the beach side of the town. The sound of footsteps ceased. He stopped and listened. The sound started again, somewhere to the right.

He glanced down the first of the alleyways that ran in that direction. It was too narrow and dark to see clearly, especially with the clutter of boxes, bins, and crates that filled it, but he was fairly sure no one was hiding in there. He walked on, aware of the footsteps continuing to the right.

Another alleyway. He stopped at the entrance and peered down it. More boxes, bins, and crates; a tangle of ropes halfway down; at the end, a rocking horse on its side. Still the footsteps. He stared at the far entrance to the alleyway. There was no sign of anyone approaching from the road on the other side.

Yet he should try to find out who it was.

It might be an enemy, but it could be Dad.

He ran his eye over the alleyway again. It was so cluttered there had to be a better one to use to cut through to the road. He walked on to the next alleyway and stopped. As he did so, the sound of footsteps ceased again. He held his breath and listened. There were no sounds at all now over to the right. But then . . .

A low murmur, barely audible. He went on listening. Silence again. He waited a moment longer, then peeped round the corner of the wall into the alleyway.

Up at the far end were two people, but they didn't look at him. They were intent only on each other.

Very intent.

And now he recognized them: Peter Blanch from Acacia Court with one of the nurses. Neither seemed aware of him. He watched for a moment, unsure what to think, then slipped away down the road. He had to get on, had to find Dad. He ran to the next alleyway and looked down it. To his surprise, it was completely empty. He hurried through to the end and stopped, listening hard.

Footsteps again.

He could feel panic starting. He looked up and down the road and saw another alleyway leading in the direction of the church. He could run down that way and with any luck it should connect with the main street. He listened again. The footsteps sounded closer and he was convinced now that they were coming down this road.

It could be Dad.

Yet it didn't sound like him. He was sure he remembered Dad setting off in trainers—much softer shoes than the ones he was hearing. He made up his mind, crossed the road to the other alleyway, and slipped down it in the direction of the church. A few minutes later he was outside the low wall that bordered the graveyard.

He stopped and looked about him. All seemed safe for the moment, but there was still no sign of Dad. Then he heard the footsteps again—and they were close. He looked frantically about him. Somebody was coming along the alleyway he had just used himself, and he was certain now that it wasn't Dad. He clambered over the wall into the graveyard, crouched behind the largest gravestone he could find and peered round the side.

A figure appeared and stopped.

Will stared. A man certainly, but the end of the alleyway was deep in moon-shadow and it was hard to tell more. The figure turned to the side and a moment later there was a trickling sound. Will didn't need to look to know what that was. Then the trickling sound stopped and the figure emerged from the shadow.

It was Davy.

22

Will went on looking. He was fairly sure Davy hadn't seen him behind the gravestone and if he was drunk, there was almost certainly no danger from him. But Davy did not look drunk at all. He was standing erect, an old bag slung over his shoulder, and seemed fully alert. A shaft of moonlight fell upon him.

No, Will decided: definitely not drunk with eyes that bright; and then he noticed something else. He hadn't seen it before when Davy was the worse for wear, but now, with the moonlight full upon him, it was clear just how physically strong the man was.

Will frowned.

Davy had seemed such a pathetic creature, and perhaps he was, but he was obviously in good physical shape, though he appeared to be doing all he could to change that as rapidly as possible. As if to echo this, the man reached into his bag, pulled out a small bottle, and took a couple of long swigs.

Then, to Will's alarm, he climbed over the low wall into the graveyard.

Will ducked out of sight and waited, holding his breath. From the other side of the big gravestone came the sound of feet tramping over the grass. He crouched as low as he could, hoping that if Davy sloped past, he wouldn't look this way. But Davy had no intention of moving very far. With a heavy sigh, he flopped to the ground on the other side of the gravestone.

Will listened, still keeping out of sight. The sounds of slurping made it easy to picture what Davy was doing. He'd almost certainly slumped against the other side of the gravestone, his feet stretched out in front of him, and was now drinking himself into another stupor, or starting to. Then suddenly the man spoke.

'So what brings you out on a night like this?'

Will tensed.

'Eh?' said Davy on the other side of the gravestone.

Will was just trying to decide what to say when an altogether different voice answered the question.

'Can't sleep.'

He stiffened. It was John Shepherd. He couldn't see the vicar but there was no mistaking the voice. He must have come along the same alleyway and be standing where Davy had just stood to urinate. Davy gave a snort.

'So you haven't come out to convert me, Rev?'

'At this time of night? I'd rather have a few hours' sleep.'

'I thought God never slept.'

'God probably doesn't. But I do. When I can.'

There was a silence. Will stayed low, keeping behind the gravestone. There seemed no reason to remain hidden now that John Shepherd had turned up. Neither of these men were surely dangerous. Yet he said nothing. He wasn't sure why. Davy took a noisy swig and smacked his lips.

'Don't mind me using your graveyard, then, Rev?'

Will heard the taunt in the man's voice; and John's even reply.

'It's your graveyard too, Davy.'

Another silence, a heavier one this time, as though Davy felt the need to digest this last remark. Then John spoke again.

'I'll see you around, Davy.'

'Not if I see you first, Rev.'

And there was a sound of footsteps receding down the alleyway. Will looked about him. Davy appeared to be still slumped against the other side of the gravestone, and he was taking swig after swig. This was surely the time to slip away. If he crept across the grass to the back of the church and then stole round the side of the building, he'd probably escape without Davy ever knowing he'd been there.

Then Davy spoke again.

'You still there?'

He froze. Davy couldn't be speaking to him. It had to be someone else. Maybe John Shepherd had come back. Another swig from the other side of the gravestone, another smack of the lips.

'I said . . . are you still there, mad boy?'

Will crept back a few feet from the gravestone. On the other side, still hidden from view, Davy gave a cough. Then his face appeared at the edge of the gravestone, peering round. His eyes met Will's with a satisfied sneer.

'You are still there,' he said.

And the face disappeared again.

Will stood up and stepped round the gravestone, keeping well clear. As expected, Davy's legs were stretched out over the grass, his body half-slumped against the stone. The bag was on his lap and he was in the process of putting an empty bottle into it and taking a new one out. He turned a baleful eye up at Will.

'You know who's buried here, mad boy?'

'No.'

'James John Erasmus Henry Parker Bell,' he said, not looking at the stone. 'Must have had the parents from hell to dump a name like that on him. Know who he was?'

Davy didn't wait for an answer.

'Rector of this parish, that's who he was.' Davy's eyes remained fixed on Will's face. 'Born 1837, died 1868. How old does that make him?'

Again he didn't wait for an answer.

'Thirty-one. That's how old it makes him. Guess how old I am.'

'Thirty-one?'

'Clever boy. Read how he died.'

Will didn't move.

'Go on,' said Davy. 'Read how he died.'

Will stayed where he was, just out of reach, but craned his head forward a little and tried to read the words on the gravestone. They were too faded to see clearly, even with the moonlight upon them, but fortunately once again Davy didn't wait for him to speak.

'Victim of his own zeal,' he said. 'See that? It says, "Victim of his own zeal." What a tosser! The guy worked himself to death. Still, I don't suppose I'm going to outlast him, and I ain't even got a job now Palmer's shoved me.'

And he took a long swig from the new bottle.

Will straightened up, his mind on Dad, and on getting away. There was nothing to be gained by staying here. But then suddenly Davy reached out and clutched him by the arm.

'They're all tossers, mad boy,' he spluttered. 'Palmer, Shepherd, the whole lot of 'em. And you. You're all tossers.'

'Why's the word "Dream" been written in the sand?' said Will.

He didn't know why he was asking. There seemed no point. Davy was growing angry and he might even turn violent. Yet the word in the sand had fallen into his mind.

'Dream?' muttered Davy. His eyes were glazing now but he managed to focus them on Will. 'Yeah, wouldn't you like to know.'

'Why's it there?'

'I'll tell you why, mad boy. It's cos that's all you got left. An effing dream.' Davy's eyes were clouding further, but he muttered a few more words. 'You're going to hell, mad boy. Maybe you're there already. Yeah, you know what? I think you are.'

He let go of Will's arm and started to cry, moaning as he did so. From the other side of the church came the beam of a torch, then a shout.

'Will?'

It was a policewoman he didn't recognize.

'Will?' she called. 'Is that you?'

'Here,' he answered.

She looked quickly over her shoulder.

'I've found him!'

More figures appeared: three policemen, then Mum and Dad. They hurried over and crowded round. Davy remained sprawled on the ground, staring ahead.

'Will,' said the policewoman, 'I'm DC Griffiths. Are you all right?'

But Will was looking at Dad.

'Are you OK?'

Dad glowered at him.

'You shouldn't have run out after me.'

'But are you OK?'

'Yes.' Dad took a slow breath. 'I'm OK.'

'Did you see anybody?'

'No.'

Dad turned away, still glowering. Will watched him for a moment, then looked at Mum. She too had turned away. He glanced at Davy. The man had stopped crying now and was cradling the bottle to his chest.

'Come on, Will,' said DC Griffiths. 'We'll drive you and your parents home. And we might as well drop Davy off as well.'

'I can make my own way,' Davy slurred.

'I don't think so,' she said.

Mum took Will by the arm and steered him away from the gravestone. Dad walked alongside, his mouth tight. Behind them the police officers were helping Davy to his feet.

'The police car's in the main street,' said Mum.

He looked at her.

'I'm sorry.'

She didn't answer.

'I'm really sorry,' he said. 'I've put you both through it again. But you didn't believe me about the guy on the balcony. And I was telling the truth. I really am in danger.'

'You certainly will be if you run out of the house in the middle of the night,' muttered Dad.

'You ran out first,' said Will. 'And you shouldn't have done. I only ran out because I was worried about you getting caught by the same people.'

'That's ridiculous,' said Dad.

Will bit his lip and said no more. They reached the main street where he saw two police cars parked a short way down. At the end of the road a figure was turning off down a side street. It looked like Peter Blanch. There was no sign of the nurse. Will looked at Mum and Dad again but both seemed to be avoiding his eyes.

They reached the first of the police cars.

'We'll wait here for DC Griffiths,' said Dad.

'I had to run out, Dad,' said Will.

'We'll talk later.'

'You might have been in danger too.'

'I said we'll talk later.'

'Even more danger,' said Will, 'because you weren't looking for trouble.' He shook his head. 'You weren't taking me seriously.'

Dad spun round.

'You want to talk now?' he snapped. 'OK, we'll talk now. We're leaving tomorrow. Got that? We're leaving Havensmouth. Whatever's going on here, or not going on, we're taking you out of it.'

Will stared at him. Yet somehow, even now, all he could see was the boy standing in his room, streaming red.

'We can't go, Dad.'

'We can and we will.'

The police officers appeared in the main street, two of the men propping Davy up. DC Griffiths and the fourth officer hurried ahead.

'Sorry to keep you waiting.' DC Griffiths unlocked the car. 'Jump in the back.'

They all climbed in. Through the windscreen Will saw the two men helping Davy into the other car. DC Griffiths chuckled from the front seat.

'We'll give the other boys the pleasure of Davy's company.' She looked round at Will. 'OK, let's get you home.'

The cars set off in convoy. Will sat in the middle of the back seat, wedged between Mum and Dad. He could feel the anger still burning inside his father. Mum too looked tense and withdrawn. He was glad neither of the officers bothered with small talk.

The other police car was just ahead and appeared to be heading the same way as they were, but then suddenly it pulled over to the side of the road. DC Griffiths glanced at her colleague.

'Stop a moment, Charlie, can you? Just to make sure they're all right.'

The officer drew up behind the other car.

'They should be OK,' he said quietly. 'Davy looks pretty far gone.'

And so it seemed, as the other two officers bundled Davy out of the car, through a front garden and across a vegetable patch to a cottage just back from the roadside. He was hardly able to stand now.

'Is he dangerous?' said Will.

'Not when he's like this,' said DC Griffiths. 'And he's usually all right when he's sober. But he has black moods and you're best keeping away from him.'

'I reckon he's getting worse,' said the other officer, watching the trio struggle to the front door. 'More argumentative.'

'Maybe,' said DC Griffiths. 'Ah, she's been waiting.'

An elderly woman had opened the door before the officers had had time to reach the bell.

'Is that his mum?' said Will.

'No, that's Mrs Weller. His auntie. He's lived with her since he was a boy. No one knows what happened to his parents. But they're not around anyway. So he lives with Mrs Weller. Just the two of them.'

'She's a good sort,' said the driver. 'Goes to church and all that. Don't know how she puts up with him.'

Dad shifted on the back seat.

'Can we get Will home, please?'

DC Griffiths looked round at him.

'Of course, sir.'

They set off again, without the other police car. Will turned and stared back at the cottage. The front door was closed but lights were going on downstairs. He twisted back in the seat and saw the hill to The Four Winds just ahead. Five minutes later they were parked outside the house.

DC Griffiths looked round again from the front seat.

'Now, Will, we'll need to take another statement from you. Your mum's explained some of what's happened but we'll obviously need to get all the details from you. We can do that now or let you get some rest and do it in the morning, whatever you prefer.'

Will shrugged.

'There's no point taking a statement. Nobody's going to believe me. Nobody ever does.'

'Don't be rude, Will,' said Dad.

Will glared at him and said nothing.

'We still need a statement, Will,' said DC Griffiths. 'Even if you don't think it's important. But I'm sure you're very tired right now, and a bit upset, so what I suggest is you get a bit of rest and we come back in the morning and—'

'No.' Will looked at her. 'We'll do it now. In the house. There's no point you coming back in the morning. We might just as well get it out of the way. I'll give you my fabrication of events—'

'Will!' said Dad. 'These officers have just brought you home. Don't be so offensive.'

'It's all right, Mr Bly,' said DC Griffiths. 'We're not offended. And Will's got every right to feel uptight. You all have, to be honest.'

'Will,' said Mum quietly.

He looked at her.

'Please,' she whispered.

He took a slow breath, then turned back to DC Griffiths.

'I'll do the statement inside. Now, if it's OK. And you can decide for yourself if it's . . . worth anything.' He looked down. 'I'm sorry I was rude.'

They climbed out of the car and made their way into the house.

He told the story as best he could, leaving nothing out; and after the police had gone, and Mum and Dad had turned in, he wandered out onto the balcony again, and stared over the sand. The tide had risen now and washed away all traces of the word that had been there.

'Dream, mad boy,' he murmured to himself. 'That's all you've got left.'

The sound of the words faded in the night. Below him the surf drove upon the beach. Restless now, it seemed, where before it had been calm. He let his eye wander along the shore, then over to the headland, dark and strong against the skyline, then out again beyond the shore and away towards the horizon.

And there his attention stayed.

23

It was still there at dawn. The red shadow was growing with the light, deepening with every minute,
always in the same place, far out to sea. He stood
there, his hands clasped round the balcony rail, and
went on watching. But he was weary now and he
yearned for sleep.

He didn't suppose there was much chance of that,
even if he went to bed. He slumped down on the floor,
his back against the side of the balcony, and closed his
eyes, hoping for a miracle. But it was no good. He
remained sleepy but awake. He hated this unbroken
consciousness. He kept his eyes closed for a while
longer, then gave up and opened them again.

Above him the roof of the house sloped away in a
smooth line towards the sky. He felt a breath of wind
from the sea and breathed in a deep draught of air. His
body still ached from the struggle last night. He
thought of the balaclava thrust against his face, the
eyes inside the slits, the voice mocking him, just as it
had done on the harbour wall.

He thought of the fall to the beach below.

And for a moment he wondered what the locals
would have felt about his death if his attacker had
succeeded. Not much, probably. No grief certainly,
perhaps even the opposite: a collective sigh of relief. If
he'd died, it would have been two unwanted characters

out of the way: the tramp and the mad boy; and no evidence of foul play. No marks of violence on Crow's body and none would have been found on his own if the guy had managed to throw him straight over the balcony.

It would have been two tragic accidents, and in the case of the mad boy, a probable suicide. Certainly nothing suspicious. Firstly the kid was already unstable, and secondly the boy's father had gone round the house with him beforehand checking all the rooms; and there was nobody there.

Will remembered the hands round his neck and shuddered. He had no doubt that those same hands had locked round Crow's neck as they forced the tramp's head under the water and drowned him.

He took another deep draught of air. At least the dawn was reviving some part of him. He listened for a moment to the sound of the surf down on the beach. It was heavier than it had been yesterday, much heavier, and he could hear gulls mewing over Breeze Point.

He could feel Muck, too, somewhere close.

'Where are you?' he whispered. 'Show me, little friend.'

The child was near. He knew it. Physically near. Not in the house, not close to the house, but somewhere in the town or around the town. There was something about the boy that he could feel, some deep pain beyond that of loneliness. He was part of the shadow that hung over Havensmouth.

Will frowned. He couldn't leave this place, however risky it was to stay. Muck was in as much danger as he was, probably more. He had to find the child before others did. He let his head rest against the side

of the balcony, and against all expectation fell asleep.
When he woke, he found Dad standing over him.

'Are you all right, Will?'

He wiped his eyes and stared up.

'I'm OK,' he muttered. 'I think I just slept a bit.'

'You're still in your clothes. Haven't you been to
bed?'

'No.'

He waited for the reproach but Dad simply knelt
down and put a hand on his shoulder.

'I'm sorry I was snappy last night. I didn't mean to
be.'

'I don't blame you.'

'I shouldn't have been like that. But I was worried. Well, frightened really.'

'It's OK,' said Will. 'I'm being a pain. I know I am.'

Dad gave a wry smile.

'You are being a pain and you're scaring us witless,
but I still shouldn't have been snappy with you. So
I'm sorry. Again.'

'I'm sorry too.'

Will gazed up at the sky. It was a deep blue now
and almost cloudless.

'What time is it?' he said.

'Half past eight. Mum's downstairs making some
breakfast, but I've left a cup of tea and a couple of
croissants by your bed in case you can't wait. Have a
shower and a clean up, and then come down when
you're ready. We need to . . . you know . . . '

'Talk.'

'Yep.'

And Dad left him.

Will yawned and stretched. A talk, yes. He'd
expected a talk, and he knew what they were going

209

to say. He hauled himself to his feet and leaned on the balcony rail again. The sun was now bright upon the sea and the surf was white and strong. He could see several figures wandering over the beach, some alone, some with dogs, some in pairs or small groups. Others were strolling along the top of the dunes.

Havensmouth had woken up while he'd been sleeping.

He saw Beth far down the beach. She was walking in the direction of the town with Brad and Micky Wetherby, both boys breaking off every now and then to skim stones. There was no sign of Izzy. He saw two more figures below, much closer to The Four Winds.

The two teenage boys with bikes, the ones he'd seen last night wandering down the main street as he crouched in the doorway. They'd ridden down to where the beach path merged with the sand and were lounging in the saddles, staring at Beth and the Wetherby boys. He looked them over: a rough-looking pair. They turned suddenly and started to ride back up the beach path towards the road. As they did so, they glanced up at the balcony.

And one gave him the finger.

Will turned back into his room. Downstairs he could hear Mum and Dad bustling about. It didn't sound much like breakfast being prepared. He drank the tea and ate the croissants, then undressed, had a quick shower, and put on some fresh clothes. The bustling sounds continued below. He took a deep breath and made his way downstairs. It was as he'd suspected.

They were packing.

'I'm not going,' he said, staring at the boxes, bags, and suitcases.

'You are, Will,' said Mum. 'It's not up for debate.'

'But—'

'Whatever's been happening,' said Dad, 'you can't stay in Havensmouth any longer. So neither can we. If what you say is true and you've been attacked—'

'See?' said Will. 'You said "if". You never did believe me.'

'If what you say is true,' Dad went on, 'then you're in danger and we should take you away. And if it's not true, well . . . you're still seeing things and saying things and—'

'Causing trouble.'

'Call it what you like,' said Dad.

'Will,' said Mum. 'It's the old story. But you don't remember, do you?' She shook her head. 'It's not your fault. We know that. But you've forgotten.'

'Forgotten what?'

She moved closer to him.

'Will, have you any idea how many times we've had to do this?'

'Do what?'

'Move house.'

He looked down.

'I'm sorry.'

'Will, look at me.'

He looked up at her.

'I'm not saying you mean to cause trouble,' she said, 'but it just seems to happen wherever you go. It follows you about. And this time it's the worst. In the past it was . . . well . . . not so serious.'

'What do you mean?'

211

'You'd upset people. You'd see things and say things and people wouldn't like it, and they'd round on you, and it was horrible, for you and for us. But it was never so bad that we thought your life was in danger. We'd move on and hope things would be better, but after a while, it would all start again.'

She looked at Dad.

'She's right, Will,' he said. 'This time it's different. A man's died. A little boy's gone missing. There's some really bad feeling in the town. And now you say someone's tried to kill you.'

'They have. I wasn't lying.'

'So we're taking you away. We'll find somewhere to rent temporarily—'

'A good way away,' said Mum, 'where no one can find you. And then we'll put the house on the market. We'll start again, like we've always done.'

The doorbell rang.

'We've made up our minds,' said Mum.

'I'll get the door,' said Dad, and he left the room.

Will sat down at the table, unsure what to say or do. From the hall came the sound of voices, then footsteps, and a moment later Dad returned with John Shepherd. The vicar looked slowly round the room.

'Are you leaving?' he said.

'Yes,' said Mum.

'I see.' John paused. 'When?'

'As soon as we've packed,' said Dad. 'Today definitely. We're not having Will stay another night here.'

'Have you got somewhere to go?'

'Not yet,' said Dad, 'but I'm sure we'll find a cheap guesthouse or something. We'll take enough stuff to last us a few days while we decide on a more permanent place to go. Then Julie and I'll come back and fetch the rest of our stuff, and put The Four Winds on the market. But Will won't be coming back.'

'Ever,' said Mum.

'I see,' said John again. He looked round the room again, then turned to Will. 'So this is it, Will. This is goodbye.'

'This is goodbye,' said Dad.

Will stood up and wandered over to the window. Through it he could see Geoff and Sarah Wetherby walking a dog along the beach, just above the line of the surf. There was no sign of Beth, Brad, or Micky. The sea was now a deep blue like the sky but the red stain still glowed out on the horizon.

He turned back to John Shepherd.

'What are you here for?' he said.

'To ask if you wanted to come to church this morning. For Sunday Service.'

'We just told you, John,' said Dad. 'We're leaving today.'

'Yes, of course.' John's eyes stayed on Will. 'You're leaving today.'

'No, we're not,' said Will.

There was an uneasy silence. John looked at Dad.

'I can understand you wanting to get Will away. I hear he bumped into Davy last night.'

'How do you know?' said Mum.

'I just met Mrs Weller. His auntie, as you probably know. She told me about it, what she got from the police anyway. I'm not sure how much Davy's told her. I expect he was a bit drunk and abusive. I saw him myself in the graveyard. He wasn't too bad when I met him but he swigs the stuff down so quickly it never takes him long to become surly.'

'Davy was the least of Will's problems last night,' said Dad. 'Someone broke into the house before that and tried to kill him.'

'My God!' said John. 'I had no idea.'

'Only no one believes me as usual,' said Will. 'They think it's just a story I made up.'

'Will,' said Mum, 'don't start again.'

'No one believes me. No one ever believes me.'

'I believe you,' said John.

'Thanks.'

'That's why I've been urging the police to give you protection.'

'They're never going to do that.'

'Exactly,' said Mum. 'Which is why we're taking Will away.'

'I understand,' John said to her. 'And I won't try to dissuade you. I suppose I just . . . selfishly . . . '

'What?'

'Wanted to see if Will still found my church a sick and evil place.'

'I didn't last time,' said Will.

'It was empty last time.'

'Apart from you and me.'

'Yes.' John frowned. 'But the time you had your trance and freaked everybody out, it was full, as I told you before. And it'll be full again this morning, assuming the usual people turn up. And I wouldn't be surprised if we have even more. There's a lot of fear in Havensmouth right now and people tend to head for church when they're frightened.'

Will turned to Mum and Dad.

'I want to go.'

'But why?' said Dad.

'I don't know. I just feel I must.'

Dad shook his head.

'I don't like it. You're so unpopular now and another confrontation with John's parishioners is only going to make things worse.'

'There might not be a confrontation,' said John.

'But there might be.' Dad scowled at him. 'That's the point, John. And what's the purpose of this experiment anyway?'

'Dad?' said Will.

'What?'

'It's not an experiment.'

There was another long silence, broken only by the familiar crash of surf. Will thought of Muck, and the angel girl, and the shadowfaces; and Muck again.

'It's not an experiment,' he said. 'It's something else, something . . . really important.'

'Look,' said John, 'this is obviously something you need to discuss without me here. I hope I haven't caused a family dispute.'

'You haven't,' said Will.

Dad grunted.

'Well, I'm sorry if I have,' said John. 'It wasn't my intention to cause trouble.' He gave a quick smile. 'I'll be on my way, OK? May or may not see you. But Will, if you do come—'

'He won't,' said Dad.

'But if I do?' said Will.

John hesitated.

'If you do, then don't come by yourself. Keep someone with you at all times. Just to be on the safe side. I'll see myself out.'

And without waiting for an answer, John hurried from the room. A moment later the front door clicked and he was gone. Will looked back at Mum and Dad.

'I've got to do this,' he said.

They didn't speak, but he knew they were pleading. Yet somewhere close he could feel Muck pleading too. The doorbell rang again.

Dad left the room and returned with Beth.

'I came to see if Will's all right,' she said. 'Dad just called me on my mobile and told me about the business with Davy in the graveyard. He heard it from Mrs Weller.'

'I'm fine,' said Will.

He saw Beth's eyes taking in the bags and suitcases. Mum and Dad remained silent.

'Beth,' he said quietly, 'I was attacked last night.'

'What!' She stared at him. 'By Davy?'

'No.' He told her about the figure on the balcony, aware of Mum and Dad stiffly listening. 'That's why we're a bit . . . tense this morning.'

'Oh, Will.' She reached out and took his hand. 'Are you sure you're OK?'

'I'm fine, only . . . Beth?'

'Yes?'

'Will you come to church with me this morning?'

She looked hard at him.

'Are you sure?'

'Yes. I want to go to Sunday Service. Will you come with me?'

'OK.'

He hesitated, then turned to Mum and Dad.

'And will you come too?'

They looked at him, still silent, then both nodded together.

24

But the walk to the church turned out to be anything but straightforward. There was an uneasy atmosphere in the town and he felt open hostility from many of the passers-by; and there was another thing.

'I've arranged to meet some people,' said Beth.

'What people?' he said.

'Jack and his girlfriend. And Mum and Dad. And some of the Wetherbys maybe. I forgot to tell you. I said I'd see them in the Harbour Café. If it's a problem, I can ring Dad and tell him I'm not coming.'

She looked round at him suddenly.

'Though actually, if you don't mind, I did promise Jack I'd come. He's got this new girlfriend—as of yesterday—and he wants me to meet her. Sisterly approval and all that.'

'But you're younger than he is.'

'I know, but he still wants sisterly approval. Sad, isn't it? But we've got time. If we make for the Harbour Café first, I could quickly see Jack and his girlfriend, and then we could go on with Mum and Dad and the Wetherbys to church afterwards.'

'Your family go to church? And the Wetherbys?'

'Mum and Dad do,' said Beth, 'and Sarah Wetherby does. Geoff Wetherby goes sometimes. Brad, Micky, and Izzy don't go. Jack doesn't. And I don't.'

'But you're going this morning.'

'For you,' she said simply.

'Thanks.' He shrugged. 'I'm not really a church person either. I'm only doing this because . . . I don't know . . . '

'You don't need to explain,' she said.

And he saw from her face that he didn't. He glanced over his shoulder at Mum and Dad, walking about thirty metres behind but watching closely. Mum caught his eye and forced a smile. He called back to them.

'We're going to the Harbour Café first. Beth's meeting her family there. Stu and Rose might be coming with us. And maybe Sarah Wetherby. We can go to the church from there. Are you OK with that?'

'We're fine,' called Dad.

They didn't look fine, Will thought, turning back to Beth, but he said nothing. He was glad Mum and Dad were there, just as he was glad Beth was there. Havensmouth felt a scary place right now. Beth hooked her hand inside his arm.

'If your memory was working,' she said, 'you'd remember about my parents going to church.'

'Are they really into it?'

'Mum's the religious one. Dad's more sort of dutiful. But he likes John Shepherd. Everybody does round here. Dad says the numbers in church have been growing steadily since John became vicar. All kinds of people go. You remember Robbo from Dad's boat? The big guy?'

'Yeah.'

'He goes to church quite often with his wife and kids. Don't think Andy or Lee ever go. But Davy turned up once.'

'Davy?'

'Yeah. Only he was drunk and his auntie had to take him out.'

'How did John react to that?'

'Wasn't fazed at all, Mum said. He's not bothered who turns up or what they believe. He's kind of accepting.'

'He's a funny sort of vicar.'

'He's a good sort of vicar. Dad reckons people trust him because he doesn't bash them over the head with his beliefs. He's not fussed if people don't agree with him. You know Peter Blanch? The senior consultant at Acacia Court? You must have seen him.'

Will thought of the alleyway last night. The two figures, unaware of him.

'I've seen him,' he said quietly.

'He thinks religion's a load of rubbish. But he's a really good mate of John's. You often see them in the Harbour Café arguing over a cup of coffee about science and Darwin and the Bible and all that. Peter even goes to church sometimes.'

'You're joking.'

'No, I'm not. His wife's religious, like Mum is, and Peter goes with her. He doesn't agree with the service but he thinks John's doing a lot of good in the community and he wants to support it. Because this is one mixed-up place. But you know that already. Oh, no, there's Buzz Murley.'

She was staring straight ahead. Will followed her gaze and saw one of the two teenage boys he'd spotted on the beach earlier. He was just emerging from a side road on his bike. He shot round into the main street, rode up towards them and then skidded his bike to a halt a short way down.

There was no sign of his friend. Beth walked confidently on and Will made himself do the same. The boy watched them morosely as they approached. Will leaned closer to Beth.

'What did you say that boy's name is?'

'Buzz Murley.'

'I saw him from my balcony this morning. He stuck a finger up at me.'

'I'm not surprised. He's trouble.'

'I've always seen him with another boy.'

'Del Kenyon,' she said. 'He's trouble too. Not surprising with a father like Fraser. I'd keep away from Del and Buzz if I were you. Especially Buzz.'

'He doesn't look very bright.'

'He's not but Del is, and Buzz worships him. He'll do anything Del says. And Del's got a nasty streak.'

They walked on down the road, both watching Buzz. He studied them for a few more moments with the same sullen expression, then whisked his bike round and pedalled off down another side street. Will glanced over his shoulder again and saw Mum and Dad still following at the same discreet distance. Beth squeezed his arm and he looked back at her.

'Are you nervous?' she said. 'About going into the church?'

'Petrified.'

'I thought you were.' She pulled him closer as they walked. 'I'll be with you, OK? And your mum and dad'll be there. And my mum and dad. And John Shepherd. You won't be alone.'

'I know but . . . I still feel alone.'

He felt her hand tighten round his arm.

'I won't let you feel alone,' she said.

They walked in silence for a few minutes, the street growing busier as they neared the centre of town. He glanced over his shoulder again and saw that Mum and Dad had let them get a little further ahead, though they were still in view of each other. The church was just a short way down now and several people had already gathered outside the gate.

Some of them had spotted him and others were turning to look. He stared at the faces. None of them were familiar, yet all seemed to know him. He supposed they must all have been there on the day he'd had his trance and upset the congregation. All seemed wary of him.

'Walk on,' said Beth. 'There's no point winding them up before the service starts. And we've got plenty of time to get to the Harbour Café and back.'

It was then that he heard the voice.

'Get off!'

He felt a shiver run through him and stopped.

'Get off!' said the voice again.

It hadn't come from the direction of the church but from the other side of the road. He turned and saw a narrow lane running off at an angle to the main street. High stone walls rose on either side of it and there was a large wooden gate just a few metres down. From somewhere behind it the voice came again.

'Leave me alone!'

He shivered again. He knew that voice. It was the voice of the girl who'd used his mobile, the girl who'd phoned the ambulance. But he couldn't see her. He still didn't know who it was. He turned to Beth but she was already hurrying across the road.

'That's Izzy's voice,' she said. 'Something's wrong.'

Beth ran on towards the lane. But as she neared the entrance, the gate in the wall opened and a boy stepped out. Will recognized him at once. It was Buzz Murley's friend.

Del Kenyon.

The boy caught sight of Beth and stopped. Beth did the same and the two eyed one another for a few moments with obvious dislike. Will started forward but a hand caught him by the shoulder. He looked round and saw Mum and Dad standing there.

'Let go, Dad,' he said.

'Don't get involved, Will. It's nothing to do with you.'

'Yes, it is.'

'Will.' Mum hurriedly moved across to block his way. 'Don't, please.' She glanced over her shoulder. 'See? Nothing's happened. No need to get involved.'

Will stared past her and saw Del slinking away down the street and Beth disappearing inside the gate.

'Stay here,' he said.

'Will—'

'Please.' He looked at them both. 'Just . . . stay here. I'll be all right. You said yourself nothing's happened. I just need to check Beth's OK.'

He saw them both frowning.

'It's a friend of hers who's upset,' he said. 'Nothing more than that. Stay here.'

And he ran over to the lane. To his relief, they didn't follow but stayed where they were, watching. He stopped at the gate and looked through. It opened onto a path that led round the back of the shops on this side of the main street. There was little in it apart from dustbins and boxes.

And two figures a short way down.

One was Beth, kneeling, her hands reaching down over Izzy's shoulders. Izzy was sitting on the ground facing away from him, her legs out in front of her on the stony ground, the gold of her T-shirt strangely at variance with her mousy-grey hair. It was clear even from here that a struggle was going on with Beth trying to wrench something from Izzy's grasp.

'Let go, Izzy,' she was saying. 'Come on, give it to me.'

He crept nearer and stopped just behind the two girls. As he did so, Beth prised what she wanted from Izzy's hand. Izzy gave a moan and let her body slump forward, her face turned away from them. Beth sensed his presence at her shoulder.

'Take this,' she said.

She held something out to him. He stared. It was a small, open penknife, dark along the blade. He took it from her.

'Close it and put it out of sight,' she said, and turned her attention back to Izzy.

He looked at the penknife: a tiny, cheap thing but there was no doubting what had caused the discolouration along the blade. The blood was still moist.

'Close it and put it away,' said Beth.

She wasn't looking at him. She was cradling Izzy, and now murmuring into her ear.

'He's not worth that, Izzy, OK? You know it and I know it. And he knows it. He's not worth that. Come on. Let's clean up your wrist.'

'No!' Izzy stirred at last. 'I'll . . . I'll . . . '

She twisted round and seemed to notice Will for the first time. For a moment she stared at him, then she dug her chin into Beth's neck, her eyes cloudy with pain, her arms hanging loose. He saw the marks of the blade on her wrist. She hadn't cut deep, but she hadn't had much time. He shuddered at the thought of what even this tiny blade might have done if they hadn't arrived when they did.

He closed the penknife and slipped it into his trouser pocket.

'Izzy,' he said. 'Listen . . . '

She turned her head away and he knew she didn't want to speak to him. Yet he had so much he wanted to ask her. He thought of the tree, the lane, and that strangely musical voice. Today was the first time he'd heard Izzy speak since he'd come back to Havensmouth. Yet this was the girl who had phoned for help—and then disappeared.

'Izzy,' he said, 'please—'

'Not now, Will,' said Beth. 'This isn't the time.'

She was still cradling Izzy but the girl was fighting her now, pushing her away.

'No!'

'Izzy, it's all right.'

'No!'

Beth took her hands away and the two girls stared at each other, Izzy's eyes wide open and streaming tears. They rolled down her cheeks and neck and started to soak her T-shirt. Will stared at them and felt another memory slip into his mind.

Gold.

There'd been a sense of gold that day, as he was lying at the base of the tree, gold emerging from grey. He'd remembered it briefly that time on the balcony and now he remembered it again. It was probably Izzy's T-shirt he'd seen, this T-shirt, and now that gold was wet with tears. She wiped at them with her hand, leaving a streak of blood behind.

Then she stood up.

'Izzy,' said Beth, 'I'm going to phone your mum and dad.'

'No!' Izzy shook her head. 'Don't you dare!' She stared at Will for a moment, her face gaunt, then turned quickly to Beth. 'Just . . . just . . . leave me alone!'

And without looking back, she raced down the path and disappeared down one of the alleyways to the right. Beth pulled out her mobile and punched in a number.

'Beth,' said Will. 'She said she didn't want—'

'I don't care. She's just tried to cut her wrist, for God's sake. I've got to tell Sarah Wetherby.' Beth waited for a moment, listening. 'No answer. She's probably at the Harbour Café or on her way to church. I'll catch her there.'

'What about Brad and Micky? They must have mobiles.'

Beth shook her head.

'I'm not telling them. They'll overreact and go for Del. They hate him.'

'They hate me too,' he said. 'Come to think of it, so does Del. So does Buzz.'

Beth put her mobile away and looked at him.

'Is that an issue for you?'

'Well, I—'

'Del hates you because he doesn't understand you.' She thought for a moment. 'Actually, that's most people's problem with you. They just don't get you. It's certainly Del's problem. Buzz hates you because he does whatever Del does. Micky hates you because Brad does. And Brad hates you because he knows I like you. I mean, in a way I'm never going to like him. OK?'

'OK.' Will hesitated. 'What about your brother?'

'Jack? What about him?'

'Why does he hate me?'

'Because he's a jerk.' Beth looked at him impatiently. 'Any more questions?'

'Tell me about Izzy,' he said. 'Quickly, before Mum and Dad come and get us.'

Beth frowned.

'Izzy's OK but she's strange. Kind of moody and really, really clingy with her mum. Brad and Micky treat her like she's a fragile doll. They're ultra-protective. But she's gone a bit weird lately. She never used to be stroppy but she's started having tantrums at home.'

'But why the slit wrist?'

'It's got to be something to do with Del Kenyon. He's been after her for ages. He tried it on with me but I told him where to get off. So he's been going after Izzy. Only she's not confident, you know? Not good at telling people like Del to get lost.'

Will heard the sound of footsteps approaching the gate.

'That'll be Mum and Dad,' he said. 'I can't believe they've left us alone this long.'

'Maybe they thought we were having a little moment.'

He saw a half-smile on Beth's face.

'Maybe they did,' he said, with a half-smile of his own.

Mum and Dad appeared at the gate.

'Is everything all right?' said Mum.

'Everything's fine,' said Beth.

Will looked away, his mind back on Izzy, and on what was to happen next.

The church bells started to ring.

25

The numbers round the church had multiplied considerably and there was now a steady procession of people heading down the path to the entrance. But not all the people in the street were churchgoers. Will quickly spotted Brad and Micky Wetherby hanging around outside the Harbour Café.

Both seemed distracted and kept looking up and down the road. Further down the street Buzz Murley had reappeared on his bike and was now riding towards them. There was no sign of Del. Buzz stopped a short distance away and lounged in the saddle, watching. Brad and Micky had clearly seen him and there was no mistaking their cold glare.

The police were out too. DI Cutler and DC Drake were standing by the railings that ran along the outer edge of the graveyard. DC Griffiths was by the gate with another officer, talking to some of the parishioners as they made their way towards the church entrance. There were more officers up and down the street.

'This looks a bit serious,' said Mum. 'All these police.'

Will felt Beth take his arm again.

'You OK?' she said.

He whispered into her ear.

'I'm glad you're here.'

'I don't like all these police hanging around,' said Dad. 'Will? Do you want to forget the idea?'

'Yes,' said Will. He took a deep breath. 'Only no.'

'Meaning we're still going in?'

'I've got to do it, Dad.'

'OK, then,' said Dad. 'Let's go.'

They walked across the street and stopped by the railings. DI Cutler caught sight of them and nodded.

'Why the police presence?' said Dad.

'We thought it might be best.'

'This can't all be for Will?'

'It's for everybody, sir. Just to make sure things run smoothly this morning.'

The bells went on pealing. Will shuddered. It seemed such an enormous sound, now that they were closer to the church. He looked over at the bell-tower, wishing the noise would stop, but it went on, relentlessly. He turned to DI Cutler.

'You knew I was coming to church this morning.'

'Is that a question?' said the officer.

'No. I'm just telling you.'

The policeman shrugged.

'We were aware that you might turn up.'

'How come?'

'John Shepherd mentioned that you might be attending this morning's service. I think he was worried about your safety. So we thought we'd come and help things along.'

Will stared at the man's impassive face, then turned to the others.

'Let's go in.'

They made their way down the path towards the entrance to the church. The crowd that had been there before had now dispersed and most of the people were either inside the church or in the process of entering. John Shepherd was standing in the open doorway, greeting late arrivals.

'I can't stand that man,' muttered Dad.

Mum looked at him.

'John Shepherd?'

'Not John,' said Dad. 'I mean DI Cutler. There's something cold about him.'

'He's only doing his job. And I'd rather have the police here than not.' Mum looked at Will. 'Are you still sure about this?'

No, he thought, he wasn't sure at all. He was frightened of the church and frightened of the people in it. Dimly he realized that he'd stopped, that Mum, Dad, and Beth had stopped too, that latecomers were edging past, staring. He turned back towards the street and saw two more faces approaching. But these were smiling.

It was Stu and Rose Palmer.

'What happened to you?' Stu said to Beth. 'We were expecting you at the Harbour Café.'

'Got held up,' said Beth. 'I'll have to meet Jack's new girlfriend another time.'

'We'll go on in,' said Rose. 'Will, come and sit with us if you need any moral support. But you look like you've got plenty.'

And she and Stu disappeared inside the church.

'Will?' said Mum.

But Will barely heard. A new feeling was starting to take him over. It wasn't the fear. That was still there, but this was something else. It was something powerful and its source was close. He stared round at the gravestones on this side of the church, then past the belltower to what he could see of the graveyard beyond.

229

No clue there as to what this feeling was—or what it meant.

'Will?' said Mum again.

He looked at her.

'You and Dad go on ahead,' he said.

'We're not leaving you out here.'

'I will come in. I promise. I'm not going to run away.'

Dad took Mum by the arm.

'Come on,' he said. 'Beth'll make sure Will comes in. Right, Beth?'

'Sure,' said Beth.

'OK,' said Mum, and she and Dad made their way into the church.

The bells went on ringing, ringing, ringing. Then suddenly they stopped and silence fell, like a sound itself. Will stood there, Beth holding his arm. John Shepherd had now disappeared from the doorway but still there were a few late arrivals hurrying down the path. Among them another familiar face.

Peter Blanch, with a neat, auburn-haired woman. Nothing like the nurse from Acacia Court. He saw Will and smiled.

'Surprised to see you here, Will.'

'Surprised to see you.'

'This is my wife, Melanie. Melanie, this is Will.'

'The mad boy,' said Will.

'I'm sure that's not true,' said Melanie.

He looked at her. She had nice eyes, like Mum, like Beth.

'I'm the boy who hallucinates,' he said. 'The boy who sees things that aren't there.'

'That's not true,' said Peter.

'No, it isn't true.' Will looked hard at him. 'Some of the things I see are real.'

230

Peter smiled again, nodded to Beth, and walked with Melanie into the church.

'Will,' said Beth. 'I promised your mum and dad I'd bring you in.'

'I know.'

He frowned. She was right. They should go in now. But he still didn't want to. The hostility that he'd sensed beneath the polished piety of the parishioners would be worse inside with all of them gathered together. The presence of his few allies would not be enough to offset that—and there was still this other feeling that he couldn't work out.

It was something to do with the church.

Something to do with the mortal wrong that afflicted Havensmouth.

From the main street came the sound of voices. He turned again and saw Geoff and Sarah Wetherby walking past the gate in the direction of The Sea Chest. Izzy was plodding between them, her head down. None of them looked his way and a moment later they were gone.

'They found her,' said Beth. 'Thank God for that. I was getting really worried about not being able to tell Sarah.' She moved closer to Will. 'Are you ready?'

He pressed his lips together, then nodded.

'Hold my hand,' she said. 'Walk in with me that way.'

'You really want that?'

'Yes,' she said. 'I want them to know whose side I'm on.'

They walked up to the door of the church, stepped inside and stood there at the back. Before them the pews were packed with people, most of them facing towards the altar where John was standing, ready to start the service. In the background the organ was playing a soft, unfamiliar melody.

Four faces turned towards him from halfway down: Mum, Dad, Rose, and Stu, all sitting together. They'd saved two places nearest the aisle. But as these four turned, so other faces started to turn, and before long the whole congregation seemed to be staring towards the back of the church. Will felt Beth's hand tighten in his.

'Don't flinch,' she whispered.

But he wasn't thinking of that, or the faces watching him, or the figure of John Shepherd indicating the places next to Mum and Dad. He was thinking of the light pouring in through the stained-glass windows beyond the altar—a strange, luminous glow, tinged by the colours of the glass but carrying with it something else: that unsettling red he'd seen out on the horizon.

He took a step forward, Beth beside him, her hand still in his. Even without looking at her, he could feel her defiance towards the congregation. The faces stared back. Yes, he thought suddenly, they were frightened of him, some very frightened indeed.

But what frightened him now was not them but this deep red light, and now he could see that it wasn't coming from the stained glass windows at all. The sunlight passing through them was merely a distortion of something that was already here in the church, and that was deepening by the minute.

'The light,' he whispered to Beth, 'can you see it?'

'The sunlight?'

'No.' He stopped in the aisle, still holding Beth by the hand, all eyes now upon them. 'The red light, all around. Can't you see it?'

A voice called out from one of the pews.

'Get out if you're not going to behave properly!'

Beth turned and glared at the speaker. Will took no notice. He could feel that icy touch upon his skin again, starting at the feet and moving up the legs and spine. He saw Beth watching him again, saw Mum and Dad stand up, and Stu and Rose, and the two police officers at the back. He saw John Shepherd stride down the aisle towards him.

The sound of the organ stopped.

John reached him and put a hand on his shoulder.

'What are you seeing, Will?'

Will's whole body now shivered. He stared about him. The red appeared to be seeping from the ceiling but it was most concentrated over in the far corner of the church. Then he realized that a figure was standing there, and that he recognized who it was.

'Crow,' he murmured.

He pointed towards him.

'There!' he shouted. 'Over there!'

The faces of the congregation turned in that direction.

'What?' said John. 'What can you see?'

The tramp was standing there, dripping as if from the sea. But the drops were a deep, sickly red. Will let go of Beth's hand and ran towards the figure.

'Will!' Dad's voice called after him.

It was drowned in the hubbub of noise that broke out all around the church. Will took no notice. Behind him he heard the sound of footsteps but he didn't look back. All he could see was the figure of Crow. More shouts, more movement, many of the congregation standing as he raced past. The police officers were all on their feet and one was speaking into his radio.

'Will!' called Beth.

She was just behind him. It must have been her footsteps he'd heard. But he couldn't stop, even for her. He was close to the corner of the church and the figure was fading before his eyes. But even as it disappeared, he saw what was behind it.

A small door.

He wrenched it open and saw a flight of steps circling upwards.

'It's the bell-tower,' said Beth, still close by.

He didn't answer and simply raced up the steps. Red was now streaming over him in a torrent. Somewhere above him was the source. He knew that for certain; and he was starting to guess what it was.

'Will!'

'Will!'

'Will!'

Voices behind him, footsteps behind him, but still he ran upwards, round and round through the redness, and then at last he was at the top. The church bells hung there: heavy, silent. Sun was breaking in through the windows at the top of the tower. Like the figure of Crow, the redness was fading before his eyes, and as it cleared, he saw the little boy staring up at him from the corner.

26

'Muck,' he murmured.

Muck peered up at him. The child's eyes were so blue and so wide they reminded him of the angel girl's; and as with hers, they seemed to dominate the whole face. With his tiny, dishevelled form crouched in the corner as far back as he could go, the eyes seemed the only part of him that held any life.

And now they were clouding over.

'It's all right,' said Will.

The boy screamed. Will dropped to his knees, keeping as low as he could, but he quickly realized that it wasn't him the child was frightened of. It was the crowd of figures now pushing into the little space from below: John, Mum, Dad, Beth, and DI Cutler. Other faces appeared behind them and a roar of voices sounded all the way down the stairs to meet the clamour rising from the congregation below. Will jumped up and rounded on the figures in the doorway.

'Get back! He's terrified! Get back!'

John held out his arms and stopped any further advance. Will looked at their faces, daring them to move.

'It's all right, Will,' said John. 'No one's going to hurt the boy.'

Will turned back to face the corner and as he did so, Muck darted forward.

'It's OK,' said Will. 'Don't run away.'

But Muck wasn't running away. Instead he threw himself against Will's leg and clung to it. Will looked down, unsure what to do. Below him, the shock of black hair bobbed about as the boy pressed his face into the thigh.

'Stroke his head,' said Beth. 'He wants you to.'

Will looked round at her.

'Go on,' she said. 'Do it.'

He reached down and touched the back of the boy's head, half-expecting him to jump back. But Muck simply pressed his face harder into the thigh. Will let his hand run over the boy's hair. It was messy and smelly and had the trace of cobwebs on it. He went on stroking it even so. He could feel Muck trembling and found to his surprise that he was too.

He glanced over at the corner where the boy had been. There was an empty bottle of mineral water there, lying on its side, and further round behind the bells he could see crumbs and apple cores and a half-eaten sausage roll. He looked round and saw DI Cutler staring at the same things. But the officer quickly turned to John Shepherd.

'How long have you been keeping him up here?'

'I haven't been keeping him up here,' said John. 'I didn't know he was in the bell-tower.'

'So how did he get in?'

'I've no idea, but it wouldn't be difficult. The church is open all day. I only lock it at night. But first thing in the morning it's unlocked again and it stays unlocked. He could have slipped in without anyone noticing and crept up here.'

'And what about the food and drink?'

'I don't know how he got that.'

Will thought of the sound of the bells that had so disturbed him when he was standing outside the church, and tried to imagine what that noise must have sounded like to the little boy hiding in here. It must have been deafening. But that was clearly the least of Muck's problems. The boy was crying now, snivelling into Will's trouser leg. Will went on stroking Muck's head. DI Cutler cleared his throat.

'Well, we'll get the lad to the station and take things from there.' He glanced at John Shepherd. 'You'd better come along as well.'

'I'll come,' said Will.

The officer shook his head.

'Just the little boy and the vicar.'

'But I need to be with him,' said Will.

'Oh?' DI Cutler raised an eyebrow. 'And why's that?'

'Because . . . ' Will hesitated. 'Because I do. He knows things. He's . . . the key to all this.'

'All what?'

'Whatever's wrong in Havensmouth.'

'We'll call you if we need you.' DI Cutler looked round at the others. 'Same applies to all of you. But for now we need to get the child away. He's obviously terrified and the fewer people crowding round him the better.'

'That's why you've got to take Will with you,' said Beth. 'Look at the boy. He trusts Will. Do you think he'll trust anybody else?'

'I'm sure we can manage,' said the policeman stolidly.

'I wouldn't bank on it,' said Beth. 'When he was living in the tent, he wouldn't let anyone near him except Crow. You know that yourself. He doesn't trust many people. That's why you should let Will come with you.'

The officer merely shrugged.

'I'm sure he'll trust DC Griffiths.' He spoke quickly into his radio. 'Drakey, send Joanna up.'

A moment later DC Griffiths was at the top of the stairs, edging her way through the others. She saw Muck clinging to Will's leg and bent down.

'Poor little boy,' she murmured. 'What's been happening to you, eh?'

Muck simply clung on more tightly.

'Easy now,' said DC Griffiths.

Muck didn't look at her. Will went on stroking the thick, dirty hair. DC Griffiths reached out and did the same. The boy screamed at once. She drew her hand back and looked up at DI Cutler.

'We need to get the boy to the station,' she said. 'He's scared out of his mind. He needs a wash and some food and a medical check. And he doesn't need all these faces gawping at him. That'll only make it worse.' She glanced at Will. 'You'd better come with us. He obviously trusts you.'

Will gave DI Cutler a baleful look, but the officer simply turned to the others.

'OK, let's clear this place. Make your way back down to the church, please. John, you'd better cancel the service.'

'No,' said John. 'People have come here to worship and I'm not going to let them down. If you want to ask me any questions, you can do so after the service. Though I have to tell you, I know nothing whatever about this boy being here.'

'We'll come and collect you after the service,' said the officer coldly.

'Please yourself.'

'Can we all go down, please?' said DC Griffiths. 'Everybody else go on ahead and let Will and the boy come down last. Keep well back and give them plenty of room. Remember—the boy's terrified.'

Will watched as the others made their way down the stairs. DI Cutler and DC Griffiths hung around, waiting.

'You two go on ahead,' said Will.

'No,' said DI Cutler. 'We'll come down with you.'

'But he's scared of you,' said Will. 'Can't you see? You've got to go on ahead. Both of you.' He looked down at the boy, still clinging to his leg. 'I don't even know if I'm going to get him to come down at all. But I certainly won't with you two hanging around.'

'It's a fair point, sir,' said DC Griffiths.

Will looked up at DI Cutler, who frowned, then gave a curt nod.

'All right. Come down as soon as you can. And if the worst comes to the worst, we'll just have to carry the boy out of the church.'

'No, you won't,' said Will. 'Whatever happens, I won't let you do that.'

'You won't have a choice, young man. Not if I decide that's going to happen. But let's hope it's not necessary.'

And DI Cutler set off down the stairs. DC Griffiths glanced at Will, gave the briefest of smiles, and then followed. Will waited until they'd disappeared from view, then looked down at Muck again. The boy was still trembling, still clinging on.

'It's all right,' said Will.

He reached down, traced a path with his hands along the thin arms until he found the boy's fingers, then eased their grip from his leg. Then he knelt down. With the boy standing, their faces were almost level. But Muck's head was bowed. Will whispered to him.

'I'm your friend. I promise I'm your friend. Do you understand?'

There was no sign of comprehension in the boy: no word, no expression in the face, no nod of the head. Will looked down at the boy's hands, still held in his own. They seemed so small, so frail. The child couldn't be more than seven years old.

'Are you going to come downstairs with me?' he said softly.

Again no sign of comprehension. Will let go of one of Muck's hands, then reached out and cautiously raised the boy's face. There was no resistance and the blue eyes moved slowly upwards until they were peering into his own. He thought of the girl again.

'Come on,' he whispered.

He stood up, his other hand still holding the boy's, and took a step towards the stairs. The boy followed, his eyes downcast again. They reached the stairs and started to make their way down. A strange silence had fallen below. Will wondered about the congregation. Somehow he had blocked out the sounds from the church while he was focusing on Muck up in the bell-tower. Perhaps the police had made the parishioners file out.

But they were still there, sitting in the pews again, all heads turned towards him. Mum, Dad, Beth, Stu, and Rose were waiting at the bottom of the stairs, together with DI Cutler and DC Griffiths. DC Drake was waiting just outside the church door with several other officers. John was standing in front of the congregation, ready to start the service.

Will looked down at Muck. The boy was clinging to his leg again.

'Let's get him outside,' said DC Griffiths.

'You first,' said Will. 'All of you.'

This time there was no argument. Even DI Cutler made his way towards the church door. Will followed, aware of the congregation watching, aware of Beth looking back at him as she walked ahead with Stu and Rose beside her. The others stepped outside and he saw them turn and wait. He reached the threshold and Muck started to scream.

'It's all right,' said Will. He bent quickly down and put an arm round the boy's shoulders. 'We're going outside but I'll be with you.'

Still the boy showed no signs of comprehension. Will started to stroke Muck's hair again, murmuring as he did so.

'Easy, easy, easy.'

Gradually the screaming stopped and he led the boy out into the sun. Behind him he heard John's voice, resolutely natural, as he started the service.

'Right,' said DI Cutler. 'We need to get the boy to the police station with as little fuss as possible. It's probably best if he goes in the car with DC Griffiths and . . . ' His eye fixed on one of the other female officers. 'WPC Shaw.'

'What about Will?' said DC Griffiths.

'Will's done his bit and done it very well. But you and WPC Shaw can take over from here.'

'This is stupid,' said Rose. 'If you can't see that the boy's traumatized—'

'I can see that perfectly well, Mrs Palmer. I don't need you to point it out. I can also see that what he needs is—'

'What he needs,' said Rose, 'is a wash, some food and drink, some sleep, some kindness and understanding, and above all, Will. It's obvious. He needs Will.'

'I agree,' said Stu.

'So do I,' said Dad.

'I'll go in the car,' said Will. 'I want to be with him. I think I can help.'

As he spoke, he felt the child cling to him again. He looked down, then back at DI Cutler.

'Let me come to the police station. Let me be there with him while you wash him and feed him and everything. I promise not to do anything else. But let me be there. For his sake.'

All around him he saw heads nodding, even among the police officers—apart from DI Cutler. The man stared at him for a while, then at the boy, then suddenly turned towards the main street.

'All right,' he snapped. 'Let's go.'

27

The large room, set back from the main section of the police station, with squashy sofas, mobiles hanging from the ceiling, toys in the corner, a view of the sea from the window. In the centre of the room the tiny boy, newly-washed, newly-clothed, wailing. Will stood in the doorway looking in, DI Cutler at his shoulder.

'I'll concede that you had a point,' muttered the officer. 'But you can't say we didn't get him washed and dressed.'

'You should have let me do all that,' said Will. 'I told you. He's scared of everybody else.'

The policeman shrugged.

'I thought the women would manage it. They're used to handling traumatized people, rape victims and so on. This one's obviously going to take time.' The officer looked at him. 'Do what you can, OK? Only I can't leave you with him on your own. You must have at least two police officers with you.'

'DC Griffiths and WPC Shaw.'

'All right.' DI Cutler glanced round at the two women, standing close behind. 'Probably the best choice. I'll leave him to the three of you.'

Will looked round at them. The women had been good with the boy—all the police officers had—but there was no escaping the fact that Muck was terrified of everyone except him. It was as though he'd taken over from Crow the role of protector. The boy had been quiet during the car journey and had walked into the police station without resistance, but the moment any of the officers had tried to separate him from Will, the wailing had started.

Even with him present things had been hard. They'd managed to wash the boy and get some new clothes on him, but that was all. He hadn't touched the orange juice or any of the food, hadn't spoken a word or given any sign of understanding anything anyone had said to him.

And now he was crying more loudly than ever, his eyes staring bleakly out at them. Will watched. No, he thought suddenly, the eyes were staring at him alone. They were awash with tears but there was no mistaking the direction of their gaze. He looked round at the two women again.

'We'd better go in,' he said.

DC Griffiths nodded.

'OK, but listen.' She leaned forward. 'Best to use first names with us. Everything as casual as possible. He might just pick that up. Forget about the DC Griffiths and WPC Shaw stuff. Joanna and Kate, OK?'

He looked at WPC Shaw.

'I agree,' she said. 'Call me Kate.'

'OK.'

Behind them, at the far end of the corridor, he saw Mum, Dad, and Beth watching. Stu and Rose had gone but John had now arrived at the station and was watching too. DC Drake and another officer stood close by. The wailing went on inside the room.

He looked at Joanna and Kate.

'Come on,' he said.

They entered the room, all three moving slowly. Muck saw them coming and ran, howling, towards the window. Will heard a gasp from Mum down the corridor. He turned to Kate.

'Can you close the door? It's best they don't see us.'

Kate and Joanna exchanged glances, then Kate turned to close the door. Will watched her, thinking. Maybe he was being naive about keeping everything secret. The police outside the room probably had a way of seeing what was going on inside. But that needn't matter, as long as no one burst in.

He looked back at Muck, now cowering in the corner.

'Easy, Muck,' he murmured. 'Easy now.'

The boy was pressed against the far wall by the window, his face clouded with pain, his eyes fixed on Will. Will walked as far as the centre of the room, and then stopped, trying to think what to do. Joanna and Kate joined him but he didn't look at them. He kept his eyes on Muck, then, on an impulse, sat down on the floor.

The boy watched. He had stopped wailing but was clearly still frightened. Will spoke quietly to the women.

'Can you both sit down on the floor?'

They sat down beside him. The boy's face grew dark again.

'No,' said Will. 'Behind me. A good way back.'

He wished he could be left by himself with the boy. Joanna and Kate were kind and understanding but he sensed that if he could just have some time alone with Muck, they might be able to bond; and something of the boy's secret might come out.

But the officers had to be here. DI Cutler had made that clear. So he'd have to work with them. To his relief, they moved back without complaint. The boy was silent now, his face wet with tears, his mouth open, as though ready to sob or scream at any moment. Will closed his eyes and into his mind came an image of the girl.

A strange image, not as clear as it usually was. It reminded him more of the drawing he'd seen in the sand that day. A sniffle from the boy made him open his eyes again. The pain in the boy's face seemed more intense and he sensed it had been the closing of his eyes that had caused the distress.

'It's all right,' he whispered. 'I won't do that again.'

The boy went on staring, his mouth now open—a wide, untidy mouth, gaping like . . .

Will gave a start.

Like one of the shadowfaces. The boy suddenly looked exactly like them: the staring eyes, the gaping mouth. Will frowned. Who was this child? The boy's eyes flickered towards the two women.

Will glanced at them too. They were sitting still, watching quietly, doing nothing wrong. But again he wished he could be alone with Muck. Kate caught his eye, then leaned towards her colleague and whispered something. Joanna nodded.

'Will?' she said quietly. 'We're going to leave you alone with Muck for a bit. We'll be just outside the door if you need us, OK?'

'OK.'

Again he had no doubt they'd be watching pro-ceedings somehow from outside the room, but he said no more and turned back to Muck. From behind him came the sound of the women edging towards the door. He kept his eyes on the boy, who was watching the officers in some alarm, even though they were moving away from him.

'It's all right, Muck,' said Will. 'They're going to leave us for a bit, but everything's OK.'

He heard the click of the door as it opened, and another as it closed; then silence fell. He stayed where he was, sitting on the floor and wondering what to do, but before he could decide, the boy ran towards him. Will opened his arms and Muck threw himself into his embrace.

'Good boy,' said Will.

He was slightly startled by Muck's behaviour but he tried not to show it. The boy was clinging to him more tightly than ever. Will held onto him, stroking the top of his head.

'Good boy, good boy.'

They stayed there for some time, locked together, Will doing nothing more than stroke and murmur and hold. He knew the child wasn't ready for anything else. Gradually he felt Muck start to calm down. The sun broke through the window and brightened the top of the boy's head. Will slowly relaxed his grip and started to ease himself back. The boy tensed at once.

'It's all right, Muck,' he whispered. 'I'm not leaving you.'

The boy seemed to relax again, but not completely. Will tried to think. They couldn't stay like this indefinitely. It was good that Muck was starting to trust him but somehow he had to find out what was wrong. He glanced round the room, searching for ideas.

It was clearly a place designed with children in mind. He ran his eye over the toys and games and fluffy animals. It was hard to imagine Muck getting much from any of these things. Then he saw something on the far table, half-hidden behind the building bricks.

A pad of drawing paper and some coloured crayons.

He looked down at Muck. The boy clearly wanted to be held and was unsettled by the thought of being let go. Will glanced back at the paper and crayons, and made up his mind.

'Easy, Muck,' he said. 'Trust me.'

The boy stiffened the moment he felt Will change his position.

'Trust me. It's OK.'

Muck started to whimper and clutched at him. Will reached under the boy's legs, gathered him up and held him close.

'God, you're heavy,' he joked.

He was glad that wasn't true. Even so, he found it hard to stand up while holding Muck at the same time. Somehow he managed it and carried the boy over to the far table. Muck held on, clearly uneasy. Will hugged him closer and it seemed to help, but the whimpering was still there and tears didn't seem far away.

'Let's do some drawing, Muck. Shall we?'

As before, the boy gave no indication that he'd understood the words. He didn't even glance at the paper and crayons and kept his gaze focused on Will's face. Still holding the boy, Will eased himself down onto his knees, then pulled Muck carefully round so that the child was sitting on his thighs.

'Are you comfortable, Muck?' He kept one hand hooked round the boy's stomach. 'All right sitting on my legs?'

He didn't expect an answer and none came, but the whimpering had stopped and for the moment the boy was silent. Will peered over Muck's shoulder at the table before them. Luckily it was low and they could both reach it easily from where they were.

'Let's do some drawing,' said Will.

Muck stared ahead, his mouth wide open again. Will reached out and pushed the building bricks off the table to clear some space, then drew the paper towards them and took one of the crayons.

'Do you want to draw something?' he said, holding the crayon up.

Muck didn't move. He simply stared at it, gaping as before.

Will started to draw. He'd known the moment he saw the paper and crayons what image he wanted to create. But he wasn't going to draw all of it. He traced the outline slowly, taking his time, checking the boy's face every so often.

It was rapt.

No part of the boy seemed to move. He'd even stopped blinking.

'Do you recognize her?' said Will.

He held the crayon back from the paper and stared at the image before them. Only half a face, the half that would have been the last to go when the tide came in and washed his angel from the sand. Muck reached out and took the crayon from him.

Will watched, tensely.

The boy started to draw, slowly, clumsily. It wasn't a good drawing, but it was a clear drawing—and it was her. Will gave a start. There was no question about it. The girl was gazing back at them in black and white. Muck had even made the eyes bigger. But he wasn't finished yet.

He was stretching across the table. Will watched, trying to work out what the boy was seeking. Then he saw it: the blue crayon. Muck took it and returned to the picture; and a moment later the girl's eyes blazed at them with all their force.

'You know her,' Will whispered.

And still Muck was drawing. The blue crayon was moving again, shading in the background above and below the girl's face. Will thought for a moment, then reached out and stopped the moving hand.

Muck tensed.

'It's all right,' said Will. 'I won't stop you colouring it in if you want to. But let me just . . . '

He took the first crayon and started to draw a new shape in one of the uncoloured white spaces. As before, he felt the rapt attention of the boy as he watched the image appear. Again Will stopped halfway through the picture, and waited.

Muck stared so long at the new image that Will began to wonder whether he should complete the drawing himself. Then he felt the boy tremble. The hand that held the blue crayon was squeezing it tight and Muck looked ready to scream.

'It's all right, Muck,' he said quickly. 'It doesn't matter about this other picture. I was just trying to see if you—'

But then Muck dropped the blue crayon and reached for his, and again started to draw; and the new image appeared, clumsily drawn as before, but as clear as ever.

A shadowface, staring up with the girl's.

And still Muck was drawing: more shadowfaces started to appear, spread around the image of the girl in the uncoloured spaces on the sheet. Will said nothing, but silently counted: three, four, five, six.

'Six,' he murmured.

He remembered the time he'd counted the shadowfaces. There'd been five but Muck had drawn six. Perhaps it didn't matter. Or perhaps . . .

He looked at the shadowfaces again, then turned and studied the wide eyes and gaping mouth of the little boy; and Muck turned from the drawing and looked back at him.

'It's you,' said Will. 'You're the sixth shadowface.'

They stared at each other in silence. From outside the door came the sound of voices. Will stiffened. He wasn't ready to be interrupted. He knew the police would have to come back and that he was going to have to tear himself away from the boy. Muck wouldn't be allowed to come home with him. He also sensed that the boy knew they were about to be separated.

'It'll be all right, Muck,' he said. 'I'll soon be back. I promise I'll soon be back.'

The voices were louder now. He could hear John Shepherd asking questions and DI Cutler saying something about 'Social Services' and 'proper procedures'.

He stroked Muck's hair again.

'They'll want to take you into care,' he said quietly. 'And that'll be best. You'll be fine. They'll try to find out where you've come from. They'll try to find your mummy and daddy. But even if they don't, they'll find some other lovely people to look after you. You'll be fine. I'm not the only person you can trust.'

The eyes went on staring. Will turned from them and looked over the picture again: the girl, the shadowfaces, the blue; and then he remembered something else. He reached for the pencil in Muck's hand. The boy clutched it, as though unwilling to let it go.

'It's OK,' said Will. 'You keep it.'

He scanned the carpet, searching for the blue crayon that Muck had dropped earlier. There it was, by the table-leg.

'I'll use this one,' he said.

He picked up the crayon, looked back at the picture, then slowly started to write the letters he'd seen in the sand. There wasn't much room left for them now. The paper was covered with the images of the girl and the shadowfaces, and much of the rest was coloured in blue, but he found a space and wrote the first of the letters.

D R E

He waited to see whether the boy would complete the word that had appeared in the sand. But Muck merely watched. From outside the room came the sound of DI Cutler's voice.

'All right. We'll go in.'

Will hurriedly added the last two letters.

D R E A M

'Do you recognize that, Muck?' he said quickly. 'Did you write that in the sand?'

And without hesitation Muck leaned forward with the other crayon and in the small space that was left wrote three more letters. They were cramped and knotted but perfectly legible.

W A Y

The door opened and he saw Joanna and Kate standing there, with DI Cutler close behind. Mum, Dad, Beth, and John were watching in the background. Muck dropped the pencil and screamed. Will turned away and stared out of the window towards the sea.

'Dreamway,' he murmured.

28

The walls of his bedroom were almost covered now. He stood back, pencil in hand, and surveyed his work; and the picture of Muck stared back through haunted eyes. There were almost as many pictures of the boy now as there were of the girl, and together with the shadowfaces he'd added in the spaces all around, there was scarcely room left on any of the walls for more pictures.

But there was room for one more thing. He leaned forward and slowly printed the word in the space above Muck's head.

DREAMWAY.

A strange word for a small boy to write, especially one who gave no sign of even understanding English. Perhaps it was a mistake. Yet Muck had added the final letters without hesitation. It seemed to mean something, though Will had no idea what. He stared out of the window at the sun dipping over Breeze Point and thought of the little boy back at the police station.

Crying, no doubt. He frowned. The boy had more to tell, much more. If only they could have had more time together. Will stared at the pictures again. Somewhere amidst these images he could sense the truth. He could sense the girl too. She was close again; unseen but close. He felt he could almost reach out and touch her.

'Where are you?' he whispered. 'I saw you before. Why can't I see you now?'

He looked round the room, searching, but all he saw was her likeness sketched upon the walls. He walked up to the largest of the drawings. A good picture of her, he thought, maybe the best: one of the pictures he'd drawn before the accident.

He stared into the wide eyes. So much strength seemed to come through them. He thought back to the accident and how this girl had pulled him back from death. She'd seemed so scary then. But she was a friend. He knew that now. He heard Mum's voice behind him.

'All right, sweetheart?'

He looked round at her. She was standing in the doorway, a smile struggling to form on her face.

'I've made you sad again,' he said.

She walked slowly up to him.

'My smile didn't fool you?'

'No,' he said. 'But it was still a nice smile.'

She pulled him to her and they held each other.

'I keep thinking of that little boy,' she said.

'So do I.'

'I know.' She gave a sigh. 'All these pictures, Will. What do they mean?'

'I don't know.'

'They're scary.'

He felt her head moving against his shoulder as she peered round the walls.

'That child,' she went on, 'he looked like a frightened tot in the police station. But you've made him look like . . . ' She hesitated. 'Is that meant to be blood streaming from his hands?'

'Yes.'

'And his eyes?'

'Yes.'

'It looks horrible. Is that what you see?'

'Not all the time.'

'But you've seen him like this? In one of your—'

'Yes,' he said, 'in one of my hallucinations.'

'I was going to say visions.'

He pulled her closer.

'In one of my whatevers,' he said.

'And the girl?' she said. 'And those . . . face things? Do you see those too in your whatevers?'

'Yes.'

'She's beautiful, the girl.'

'You've never said that before.'

'Maybe I was a bit scared of her before.'

'It's only a drawing,' he said.

'But it's not, is it?' Mum let go of him and drew back. 'Not to you. It's real to you. She exists to you. She's more than just a drawing. To you.'

'She's an angel,' he said.

Mum said nothing. She was staring at the nearest picture. He studied it too: the girl with the shadow-faces all around, and Muck close by.

'If she's real,' Mum went on, 'then you're lucky if you've seen her. Maybe she really is an angel.'

'Maybe they're all angels,' he said.

He felt Mum look back at him but kept his gaze on the girl's face. He could sense her still, and she was closer than ever, closer even than Mum right now. He stiffened.

'Are you OK?' said Mum.

'Yes.'

He felt the girl draw nearer still. She was like an embrace now, holding him in invisible arms. Mum

256

reached out and pulled him close again; and both seemed to hold him at the same time. He heard footsteps on the stairs, then on the landing outside his room, then silence. He didn't look towards the door. He knew Dad was standing there, watching, waiting for Mum to nod that it was all right to go in.

'Come in, Dad,' he called.

'Are you sure you're—'

'I'm fine. Come in.'

He heard steps behind him, felt Dad's hand on his shoulder.

'I'm all right, Dad. Honestly.'

They stood there in silence for a while. He was glad they weren't forcing him to speak. He held on to Mum and stared towards the balcony door. The last rays of the sun were struggling through it into the room, but the light was draining from them even as he watched. A few moments later it was gone.

So too was the girl's presence.

He drew back from Mum and stared out of the window. There were no figures to be seen walking by the surf or along the dunes or up on Breeze Point. The sea was turning to a dusky grey.

'What does "Dreamway" mean?' said Dad.

Will turned and saw his father studying the word on the wall.

'It's something Muck wrote,' he answered.

'Muck wrote that?'

'I think so. Or he was trying to. I saw the word "Dream" in the sand and Muck running away from it—just before I got attacked on the balcony.'

He waited for some sign of disbelief on Dad's face. But there was none.

'Go on,' said Dad.

257

'So I thought maybe Muck had written the word in the sand.'

'Strange for a little kid to write a word like "Dream". Especially a terrified little kid.'

'But "Dreamway" is even stranger,' said Mum. 'Did he really write that too?'

Will nodded.

'I got him to do some drawing when I was with him at the police station.'

'I didn't know,' said Mum.

Will pulled out the picture that he and Muck had drawn together.

'We both did this,' he said.

'Both of you?' Dad stared at him. 'You mean . . . '

'I started the picture of the girl but left it half-done. And Muck finished it off.'

'I can see his bit.' Dad studied the paper. 'And these horrible . . . shadowy faces . . . did you and he . . . '

'Yes. I started one and he finished it. And the same with the word. I wrote the word "Dream" and—'

'I can see it.' Dad frowned. 'He's added the last three letters.'

He looked round at Mum, who was also staring at the picture.

'Julie? Make any sense to you?'

'No.' She looked at Will. 'I didn't know you and Muck were doing this.'

'Couldn't you see what was going on from outside the room? I mean, didn't they have some kind of . . . spy-screen or whatever they call it?'

She laughed.

'If they did, we weren't allowed to use it. Though DI Cutler and some of the other police officers did disappear for a bit while you were in there.' She looked back at the paper. 'So you smuggled this out, did you?'

'I wanted to have it. Might be all I ever get to keep of the little boy.'

Mum and Dad both looked at him.

'Is that how you feel about him?' said Dad after a moment.

'I miss him,' said Will. 'I know he's nothing to do with us and Social Services will have to look after him. But I care about him. And I care about his . . . ' He stared back at the pictures on the walls. 'His companions.'

'Will,' said Mum softly. 'We've—'

'I know,' he said, still staring at the pictures. 'We've still got to move on.'

She stroked him on the arm.

'Havensmouth isn't a good place for you any more,' she said. 'In spite of what's happened today with Muck, there's still bad feeling in the town towards you.'

'Same old story, then.'

'Yes,' she said. 'But, Will, we can start again somewhere else. We've done it before. We can do it again. And sooner or later we'll find a place we like and where people like us.'

'Where people like me, you mean,' he said. 'They already like you. It's me that's the problem.'

'We'll find somewhere,' said Dad. 'We won't go today like we planned. It's too late now for that. But tomorrow we'll start a new life somewhere else.'

Will stared out over the beach again. The light was fading so quickly that even the surf seemed grey.

'What about Muck?' he said. 'Will he start a new life somewhere else?'

'He'll find somewhere too,' said Dad. 'A lovely family who'll care for him.'

Will thought of the girl and the shadowfaces. It was too late for them to start a new life. He knew that with a desolate certainty. But there was one thing he could do for them: he could care. The doorbell rang.

'It's Beth,' he said.

'Were you expecting her?' said Mum.

'I'm just guessing it's her.'

'I'll get it,' said Dad.

'No,' said Mum. 'I'll go.'

She hurried downstairs and a moment later Will heard Beth's voice in the hall. It was too low to catch the words but the tone was clear.

'Something's wrong,' said Dad. 'Let's go down.'

But Mum and Beth were already hurrying up and a few seconds later they were in the room.

'What's happened?' said Will.

'It's John Shepherd,' said Beth. 'He's been attacked in the town centre.'

'Bloody hell!' said Dad.

'I just heard it from Robbo,' she said. 'I bumped into him in town. He saw it all happen.'

'But I thought John was talking to the police,' said Mum. 'He was still there when we left the station.'

'They'd obviously finished with him and let him go.'

'But who attacked him?' said Will.

'You know Fraser Kenyon?' said Beth. 'I did mention him.'

'I'm not sure if I—'

'You remember Del Kenyon and Buzz Murley? The boys with bikes?'

'Yes.'

'Well, Fraser's Del's father. He runs a chain of betting offices. Nasty piece of work. Dad can't stand him. Anyway, Fraser was in The Sea Chest with some other guys. Andy, Robbo, and Lee were in there too, having a drink. And John comes past with Peter Blanch, you know, the—'

'Guy from Acacia Court, yeah. Go on.'

'Fraser sees them through the window and runs out and starts mouthing off at John. He's obviously heard about the business in church. Calls John a pervert and a child abductor. Says there's no way John didn't know the little boy was in the bell-tower. Says he's as bad as Crow. And Fraser's mates start joining in about John giving Crow bags of food and being friends with him. Two pervs together, another paedo priest, all that kind of stuff.'

'Horrible,' said Mum.

'But is John all right?' said Dad. 'You said this man attacked him.'

'John's OK,' said Beth. 'Fraser swung a bottle at his face but Robbo said John disarmed him quite easily.'

'He's good at judo,' said Will.

'Just as well,' said Mum.

'But it was still nasty,' said Beth. 'Robbo said he ran out with Andy and Lee to help when they saw what was happening and even though nobody got hurt, there was lots of bad feeling towards John from Fraser and his friends. And there were other people in the street shouting abuse as John walked away.'

'Horrible,' said Mum again.

'That's settled things for me,' said Dad. 'I'm even more decided about us leaving. And it's going to be first thing in the morning. First bloody thing.' He turned to Will. 'And you're grounded till then.'

Will looked at Beth and saw her try to smile. Dad spoke again.

'I'm sorry, Beth, I really am. I can imagine what you must be feeling and I'm so grateful—'

'We're both grateful,' said Mum.

'We're both really grateful for all you've done for Will.'

Beth's mobile rang. She glanced down at her pocket, then back at Will. He felt a sudden tension in her gaze.

'Answer it,' he said. 'I think you should.'

She pulled out the phone and checked the screen.

'It's Mum,' she said to them, and took the call. 'Mum, did you get my answerphone message about John Shepherd? OK.' A pause, then, 'I'm at Will's place.'

A long silence, broken only by the murmur of Rose's voice in the earpiece of the phone, too faint for the words to be clear.

'No!' said Beth suddenly.

She glanced round at them, then walked over to the balcony and stared out.

'No!' she said again.

Will watched her as she listened to her mother, her hair bright against the spreading dusk. She did not speak again for some time. She simply listened, rigid; and Will, Mum, and Dad listened to the silence, and waited.

'OK,' she said at last. 'I'll wait here for you to come and get me.'

She rang off and turned to face them.

'It's Davy,' she said. 'Dad's had a call from Mrs Weller. She says he's gone missing. She's phoned Robbo and Andy and Lee and Dad and the Wetherbys and everyone she can think of. Nobody's seen him.'

'But isn't that fairly normal behaviour for Davy?' said Dad.

'He's often out drunk,' said Beth. 'But he's a big kid underneath. He always comes home to his auntie. Only this time he's scrawled her a note to say he's not coming back. He's never done that before. But that's not all. There's something else Mrs Weller told Mum. It's not just Davy who's gone missing.'

Beth's face darkened.

'Izzy's gone missing too.'

29

The long night, sitting on the bed, the walls weeping in the silence. He stared about him. Red streams trickled down from the pictures all around him, not just the image of the boy, but the girl, the shadowfaces, everything. Even the word Dreamway wept, the letters dripping in an unceasing flood yet somehow keeping their shape in the still room.

Outside, through the open balcony door, he saw the night sky, cloudy and intense, just a few stars visible and no moon to be seen. A strangely red sky. He thought of Rose's face when she'd turned up earlier to collect Beth and take her home.

An anxious face, like Mum's face, and Dad's, and Beth's. Probably like his too. He reached out and touched one of the trails running down the nearest wall. It felt moist and cold. He put his finger to his cheek and rubbed the tip against the skin, and still the moisture was there, and the coldness, and the sense of red, unyielding pain.

He wouldn't sleep tonight.

There was no point in trying. His last night in Havensmouth would be a wakeful one, as so many seemed to be. He stood up and walked out onto the balcony. Below him the beach stretched away, the surf a silent fringe of white, the sea uneasily still. Breeze Point reached into it like a long, bony arm.

He turned his gaze upon the town. It too seemed wakeful, though nothing stirred that he could see, and no lights were visible. He wondered what time it was: two, three in the morning. He hadn't checked for a while and didn't much care. He had but a few hours before Mum and Dad came to rouse him, and then they would leave.

That was that.

Except that it wasn't.

He'd said his goodbyes to Beth but there were other goodbyes he wasn't ready for. He looked back into his room at the pictures on the walls. He wasn't ready for these goodbyes. The sickness in Havensmouth was still there and these faces had something to do with it; and surely the disappearances of Davy and Izzy had too.

He sat down on the balcony floor and waited for the dawn.

When it came, it brought a blood-red sky and the song of a bird down in the garden. He sat up, transfixed by the sound. He recognized it at once: a songthrush, the same song he'd heard just after the accident. He stood up and leaned on the balcony rail. The garden stretched away to the right, the dawn already squeezing the darkness from the lawn and hedges.

The song appeared to be coming from the silver birch at the top of the garden. He could make it out clearly from here, but not the bird. Yet in spite of that, the song went on rippling through the dawn.

'Maybe you're the same bird,' he murmured. 'Maybe you've come back to tell me something.'

He didn't suppose either of these thoughts were correct. The likelihood of the selfsame thrush appearing here seemed pretty remote, as did the notion of a bird wanting to communicate with him. It was just a thrush waking up. Yet something else was waking too.

A question.

He pondered it, listening all the while to the bird, then, on an impulse, he stepped back into his room, dressed and slipped out to the landing. From Mum and Dad's room came the sound of heavy breathing. He frowned. With an early start planned and him grounded, or meant to be, he'd have to be extra careful about this. They'd be furious if they caught him sneaking out of the house.

Yet he had to. He knew it. This was his last chance before they left.

He crept downstairs and stopped by the back door. Still no sound from upstairs. He eased open the door, slipped out and closed it again, then stole over the lawn towards the silver birch. To his disappointment, the song had ceased during the time it had taken him to tiptoe out of the house.

The garden was silent and still, though eerily beautiful with the red light spreading across it. He walked up to the tree and stood there at the base, looking up. There was still no sign of the bird.

'Why have you stopped singing?' he said. 'Have you flown away?'

But at that very moment, the song started again, high up in the tree. He stared, searching the branches, and then saw what he'd missed before: the dumpy little bird, chirruping its song.

'You *are* the same bird,' he muttered. 'I'd swear to it.'

266

He studied it from the base of the tree.

'But if you are,' he said, 'then you're a long way from where I first heard you.'

And the question came back.

'Why was I there?' he said aloud. 'Why was I by that sycamore tree in the first place? It's nowhere near where I live, nowhere near anything important. Just a lane and some woodland. Why was I there?'

And now a second question came.

'Why was Izzy there?' he went on. 'It's nowhere near where she lives either. And where is she now?'

He gripped the trunk of the silver birch. He must have been by the sycamore tree for a reason. He must have been doing something, or looking for something; and then there was the accident. Someone else was there, someone who nearly killed him. And then there was Izzy, who rescued him and ran away.

He glanced back at the house. No lights on, no figure on Mum and Dad's balcony, no voice calling him. He made up his mind, slipped out of the garden by the side gate, and set off at a brisk pace down the hill. At the bottom he turned away from the town and took the lane that led towards the junction with the sycamore tree.

This time he took in his surroundings properly. When Mum and Dad had driven him home from the hospital, he'd been too struck by the hostile faces of the passers-by to think of much else. Now, with nobody to distract him, he had a greater sense of where he was over the two-mile walk to the junction.

The woodland to the right of the lane was unremembered country but that to the left was not. Beyond it the dunes were visible in snatches between the trees, and the woodland itself was becoming increasingly familiar. He'd stumbled through it, though from the other direction, when he'd found his way to Stu and Rose's house. He walked on, looking warily about him. The old Will must have come this way, searching.

'What did you see?' he whispered to his other self. 'What were you looking for?'

He saw a track to his left and a signpost saying: 'To Greenheys'.

Beth's house. He remembered the name now. He walked past it and on down the lane, anxious to reach the junction where the sycamore tree was. Then suddenly he stopped. The morning was still, tranquil even, yet for some reason it felt anything but peaceful, and though he hadn't seen anyone, he had the strangest feeling that he was being observed.

He tried to push the thought from his mind. It was surely fanciful. He knew he had enemies but there was nobody on the lane apart from him and the only way someone could keep an eye on him and stay hidden at the same time would be by tracking him from among the trees, and that was no easy task. It would mean flitting from trunk to trunk and he felt sure he'd see anyone trying to do that.

He hurried on, trying to ignore his doubts, yet still the feeling persisted that he was being observed. He tried to think. Perhaps he was confusing this feeling with something else, for here as he walked was a growing sense of the old Will. This whole experience felt familiar: the walk down the lane with the trees on either side. The dawn chorus had broken out and was now filling the silence. He looked about him, listening to a thousand songs, and aware of the clear whispers of memory.

He spoke to the old Will again.

'You walked this way. You came from this direction. But you came at dusk.'

His footsteps sounded light upon the surface of the lane.

'It was dusk,' he said. 'But what were you looking for?'

His eyes moved about from side to side, searching the trees on both sides of the lane. The chorus of birds grew louder. He sensed someone near him again, someone watching, but still he saw no one; and now he could feel other presences. The girl surely. He could not see her but he sensed it was her.

'I've missed you,' he said. 'Where have you been?'

The only answer was a feeling that she was closer.

'I know you're there,' he whispered.

So were her companions. He could sense them too. He stopped in the middle of the lane and closed his eyes. To his surprise he saw no shadowfaces, nor any image of the girl. Instead he saw a deep, red void. He opened his eyes and looked up at the sky. It too was a deep, red void. And still he could feel presences close.

He walked on, growing increasingly disturbed. Everything was starting to feel wrong. He'd thought he could sense the girl and the shadowfaces, and glimmers of the old Will, and memories, but now he wasn't sure what he felt. Nor could he see anyone following him in the trees.

He was not alone—he knew that for certain—but who or what was near, he couldn't tell. He hurried on down the lane, aware of the redness deepening in the sky. Even the tops of the trees were tinged by it: a curious, creeping redness that clashed with the green of the foliage. The chorus of the birds continued.

He walked on, feeling more and more frightened, less and less alone. But at least the walk was coming to an end. He could see the junction down at the bottom of the hill where the lane met the road to Newton Barnet. He slowed down, searching for danger.

Nothing as before, either in the trees or on the lane. Yet all around him he felt presences, too many to number. It wasn't the girl or her companions, or any sense of the little boy, or anyone he had come across before. These were other forms, new forms, ghostly forms. He reached the junction and stopped.

Shadows swirled about him like wind. He stared at the sycamore tree. How familiar it seemed, almost exactly as he remembered it. But memory was moving fast now, the old Will moving with it, and the new Will's eyes were turning, turning, turning away from the sycamore.

To a gate just down from the lane.

And a track beyond, slanting through the woodland.

He had no memory of this gate from the accident. Yet it looked familiar. He walked over and studied it. A nondescript object, rickety and in need of paint with a loop of string hooked over the post to anchor it. The track beyond was narrow and bumpy and overhung with foliage from the trees on either side.

Yet the swirl of shadows felt thickest here.

And the old Will felt close again.

He shivered. The old Will had stood on this very spot. He'd found something out and this gate and this track were part of it. The shadows thickened further. He could see them more clearly now: faint, featureless clouds floating down the track towards him and past into the lane, and then away in the direction of

Newton Barnet. The old Will seemed to float away with them. But the new Will watched and tried to understand.

From somewhere up the lane came the sound of a car.

It was coming from the direction of Havensmouth. He scrambled over the gate and hurried down the track. He had to find out more and this was his only chance. He also had to keep out of sight. He put on speed, keeping as close as possible to the trees at the side of the track. The sound of the engine grew louder but to his relief, the track soon twisted to the right and hid the lane from view.

The engine grew louder still.

He looked about him, searching for a place to hide if there was any danger. The safest option would be to cut through the trees to his left. That would take him into the woodland. The other side of the track had woodland too but it was sparser and there was also a fence he would have to climb over first. Another alternative was to continue down the track itself, but he had no idea where it led.

A few steps later he realized that he was wrong. He did know where it led. He recognized it now. This was the track he'd escaped down when he'd fled from the balaclava gang the night Crow was killed. He'd run along the beach as far as the slipway where the tramp found Muck, and then he'd cut down the first part of this track. He could see the beach now, down at the other end, and the sea beyond.

The sound of the engine stopped.

He heard car doors open and close. He looked around him, unsure what to do. It might be nothing; it might be coincidence. But if his enemies had seen him leave the house, it was just possible they could have mobilized themselves quickly enough to get here by now. Either way, there was nothing to be gained by hanging around.

He heard the groan of the gate as it was opened behind him. He turned and raced down the track. At least the escape route was obvious now: run to the beach, down it to Breeze Point and home. Then a figure appeared at the far end of the track. A figure in a balaclava.

He stopped, breathing hard.

Another figure appeared, also in a balaclava, and the two started down the track towards him. From behind him came the sound of footsteps tramping from the other direction. He tried to calm himself, tried to think. If he ran fast enough, he might just make it through the woodland to Stu and Rose's place. He turned to the left.

And froze.

Two more figures were standing there, blocking his path through the trees. Both were wearing balaclavas and one was speaking into a mobile phone. They watched him for a moment, then started to advance.

30

Will turned to the right, vaulted over the fence and raced off into the woodland on the other side of the track. It seemed a fruitless escape route but there was nothing left to him now with the other ways blocked. Yet already he could see he was being cut off.

The figures from the beach end had also cleared the fence and were tearing towards him on a diagonal run. The pair from the other side of the track were over too. He could hear them thundering behind him. And now from the right, he saw two more figures racing across from the direction of the lane.

Six figures, all in balaclavas.

Dimly he remembered there'd been five on the dunes and on the harbour wall, but that was of no importance now. He looked quickly from side to side, dodging trees as he did so. The two to the left were closer, having moved first, and the figures to the right were still some way back. He glanced over his shoulder at the other pair. Fifty metres behind, maybe a bit more, but gaining.

They all looked powerful, and most of them looked fast.

He pelted on, terror mounting. The sparseness of the woodland helped for running but he yearned for some hiding places now. He tried again to think, to formulate some plan, but it was no good. He could only run and run and run.

He saw the figures to the left draw closer. They were barely thirty metres from him now and overtaking fast. In a few more moments they would cut round in front of him. He veered to the right, putting on speed, but that only pushed him towards the figures running from the lane.

He blundered on even so, desperate to pull away but growing tired now. There were the figures to his left again. They'd made up the ground he'd gained by swerving to the right, and were now moving round ahead of him. The figures behind him were closer too. He could hear their heavy breaths just a few metres behind, a freakish contrast to the birdsong still echoing in the woods.

He veered again to the right, heading towards the figures from the lane, then veered yet again, back towards the fence. If he could just break through to the track, or the lane, or into the trees on the other side . . .

And then he stopped.

It was useless running. There was no point. He was surrounded on all sides. The figures stopped too, all of them. Two in front, two to the right, two to the left. A nod from the tallest one and they drew apart without a word, adjusting their positions until they were evenly spread out in a circle around him.

He clenched his fists, determined not to show his fear.

'So who's the girl with the black hair?' he yelled. 'Eh? Who is she?'

There was no answer from behind the balaclavas.

'And who's Muck?'

Again no answer.

'You know, don't you? Eh? And there's lots more you know. Maybe you're scared to tell me.'

The tall figure gave another nod. The others moved slowly in. Will shouted at them again.

'And what about the track? What do you use that for?'

Still no answer.

'Got no words?' he bellowed. 'What are you worried about? Six of you against one boy? You can't be scared. Or maybe you are.' He remembered the voice that had mocked him on the harbour wall, even the words it had spoken; and he mimicked them back now. 'Maybe I'm the Evil One. Prophet of doom. See stuff, yeah?'

He saw one of the figures stiffen.

'Oh,' said Will, 'it was you, was it?'

'Don't know what you mean, mad boy,' came the answer.

Will mimicked the voice again, and its words.

'Yeah, kooky, and I've got horns in my head.'

'Bastard!' muttered the figure.

Will stared round at them, aware suddenly that he could feel the girl's presence, and that this time there was no mistake. She was close, she was clear, and she was whispering into his mind.

'Fight,' she was saying.

The figures stepped forward.

'Fight,' said the girl.

He glared at them as they closed round. He spat and kicked and punched at them, but they overpowered him easily. Then everything went black.

How long he stayed unconscious he did not know. But when he came to, he found that the blackness was still there. His head was pounding and he could hear a low rumbling sound. He knew at once what it was. He had somehow expected it.

He was on a boat.

A fast boat too, judging from the sound of the engine. More than that he couldn't tell. Blackness still covered him, and for the moment it was pleasant, even with the pain of the blow and the certainty that he was about to die.

'Fight,' whispered the girl inside his head.

Yes, he thought, though there really was no point. He had no hope against so many, and he was weak already. He felt his eyes move. It was hard to tell whether they were open or closed. Blackness filled him, whatever he seemed to do. Yet gradually it was clearing. There was still darkness before him but his eyes were definitely open now and he could see something pressed against them.

Some kind of cloth or cover. A tarpaulin, he decided, that's what it was. But even as he thought this, it was whipped back and he found himself staring up from a bunk inside a small cabin. Four of the figures were standing around him, looking down. A fifth was kneeling to his right, holding a long rope.

The balaclavas were still on.

He thought of the girl again, felt her defiance.

'Still got the masks on, big boys?' he said.

All of them stiffened; none of them moved. He glanced at the figure kneeling to his right. This one at least he knew something of. He squeezed all the contempt he could manage into his voice.

'How are you doing, kooky?'

'Shut it, mad boy.'

'What are you scared of? Showing your face to a kid you're going to kill anyway?'

'I said shut it.' The figure started to wind one end of the rope round Will's right arm. 'Yakking ain't going to make nothing better.'

'Yakking *isn't* going to make *anything* better.'

'You shit!'

The figure dropped the rope and drew back a fist. Will braced himself but one of the others reached out and stopped the blow.

'Easy, Lem,' he muttered. 'No point, OK?'

The figure called Lem moved back and picked up the rope again. But he was breathing hard and the eyes in the slits of the balaclava were small and hard. Will clung to the girl's strength.

'So it's Lem, is it?'

'Shut your mouth.'

'What are you doing with my arm?'

'You'll find out.'

'How old are you, Lemmy?'

No answer.

'Nineteen? Twenty? Come on, Lemmy. How old are you?'

Again no answer. The engine roared on in the background. Will looked round at the other figures. They seemed strangely ill-at-ease and more so since he'd started talking back. He wondered about the sixth member of the group: the tall one, the one in charge.

At the wheel no doubt and presumably not wearing his balaclava for fear of attracting attention. Will looked for a porthole in the cabin that might show the wheelhouse but there was none. He stared back at his right arm.

277

Lem had wound the rope round and round it, starting just below the shoulder with a tight, complicated knot and continuing down with a series of hitches to the wrist, where he'd tied another complicated knot and let the rest of the rope trail free.

There was nothing attached to the end.

Will thought of the girl again. He could feel her so close now, urging him not to show his fear. But it was hard. Acting cocky had helped him a little but now his terror was overwhelming him again. He forced himself to speak.

'I suppose there's some point to all this, Lemmy?'

'Oh, there's a point, mad boy.' The eyes glared at him through the slits. 'Good at untying knots are you? With your weak hand?'

'How do you know I'm not left-handed?'

'I seen you close up, mad boy.'

'Oh, yeah, I forgot. That time you attacked me on the balcony.'

Lem said nothing.

'That was you, wasn't it, Lemmy?'

'Shut your mouth.'

'What's the problem admitting it? I'm not going to tell anyone. I'm going to be dead.'

Again he felt the other figures stiffen. He glanced at them.

'You're not really up for this, are you?'

None of them answered.

'Killing, I mean,' he said. 'You're here for the muscle but Lem's the one who does the real stuff. Only he hasn't got the balls to admit it. He's too much of a coward to—'

'You bastard!' shouted Lem.

Will turned his head away as Lem's fist came down. It smashed into his cheekbone and the hard edge of the bunk thudded against his temple. He heard a scuffle behind him, then a change in the sound of the engine. They were slowing down.

A moment later they had stopped.

He turned his head painfully back and looked at the figures through blurred eyes. Lem was standing over him, the end of the rope in his hand. Two of the others were holding him back. He shook them away, then leaned forward.

'You want to know what happened, mad boy?' His voice was low and hoarse. 'Well, I'll tell you. It was me on the balcony. It was me done the tramp. And when you snuff it, remember: it was me done you too. I want that to be your last thought.'

Will answered, trying not to flinch.

'So what do you look like, kooky? Going to be a big, brave boy and show me? Or are you too scared?'

The eyes peered out at him, glowering, then, with a sudden movement, the figure reached up and tore the balaclava away; and there was the face, a face he'd never seen, but a face that made perfect sense. Nineteen, twenty—just as he'd thought—and features that told him all he needed to know.

'You're the spitting image of your dad, kooky.'

Lem said nothing.

'So where is he?' said Will. 'Going to see him, are we? Now that we've arrived.'

Lem looked down at him with contempt, then turned towards the door of the cabin where a figure had appeared. He had no balaclava on and was carrying an anchor.

'Hi, Robbo,' said Will cheerfully. 'Come to finish me off?'

Robbo didn't answer. His eyes were moving round the cabin, taking in the others: his son with the balaclava removed, the others still masked. Then he looked at Will—and smiled. Will stared back with all the scorn he could muster.

'Didn't see you in church yesterday, Robbo.'

'Couldn't make it.'

The man watched him calmly, weighing the anchor in his hands.

'But you're a churchgoer,' said Will.

'How would you know?'

'You were there that other time. When I had my trance and upset everybody. I remember it.'

'How could you? Your memory's gone.'

'It's coming back, Robbo. Scary, isn't it? And you know what I remember now about that day?'

Robbo fingered the anchor and said nothing.

'Your family,' said Will. 'You were all there, even Lemmy.' He looked at Lem. 'Weren't you, kooky?'

Lem clenched his fists.

'Thought so,' said Will. 'I remember it now. The whole family was there.' He looked back at Robbo. 'Your wife, and Lemmy, and you've got a daughter, haven't you? A little girl, brown hair, cute face. You're one big pillar of the community, Robbo.'

Robbo glanced at the four masked figures.

'Get him.'

They didn't move.

'I said get him!' Robbo glared at them. 'You've been paid enough, for Christ's sake! Earn your keep!'

Still the four hesitated. Will turned quickly towards them.

'Did Robbo tell you about the girl with black hair?'

No answer.

'Did he?' said Will.

'Lem!' shouted Robbo.

Lem threw an arm round Will's neck and forced him towards the doorway. With an effort Will twisted his head round to face the other four.

'Didn't think so,' he breathed. 'He must have forgotten.'

Lem's fist drove into his stomach.

'Ah!' He doubled up, gasping for air, but somehow managed to splutter some more words at the masked figures. 'Shouldn't . . . shouldn't you be doing this? That's what you signed up for, wasn't it? Beating up a teenage kid. Ah!'

Another blow from Lem, this time to the face. Will felt his head spin, but still somehow he managed to speak.

'Missed your chance there, boys,' he muttered. 'But maybe . . . maybe . . . '

His head was pounding, his thoughts swirling.

'Maybe, you can . . . help Robbo and Lem . . . with the murder.'

He felt his legs sag beneath him. Lem yanked him upright and bundled him out on deck where Robbo was already waiting. The other four started to follow but Robbo roared back at them.

'Stay in the cabin!'

'Robbo, listen—' began one.

'Stay in the cabin! And keep out of sight!'

They stayed where they were, watching through the door.

Robbo and Lem forced him across the deck to the stern of the boat. He stared back towards the distant shore. It was barely visible and there were no other vessels in sight. The early morning sun threw down a muted glow.

'Know where we are, boy?' said Robbo.

'Course I do.'

'The very spot you got so worked up about.' He looked Will over. 'You wanted to know what's here. Well, now you can find out.'

'Who was the girl?' said Will hurriedly. 'Who were the others? Who's the little boy?'

Robbo took the rope that Lem had tied to Will's arm and attached the loose end to the anchor.

'Tell me,' said Will.

Robbo gave him a wink.

'Don't much matter now, eh?' he said.

And without another word, he handed Lem the anchor, stepped into the wheelhouse and revved up the engine. The boat started to power off in the direction of the land. Will braced himself as Lem closed upon him, but there was no hope of escape. A kick to his back, a tug on the rope, then the splash of the anchor, and he was plunging after it into the sea.

31

Down into a void he had seen before, into colours he knew and feared: the blue, the black, and then the red, only now they rushed past him in a blur of terror and bursting lungs. Down, down, chasing the misty arrow of the anchor that towed him by the arm to certain death. He kicked and writhed and struggled to break free, scrabbled at the knots with his left hand, and then he gave up. It was no good. He would never untie them in time.

But in that moment time seemed to stop.

Even as his form spun downwards, he felt the end of life, and somehow its beginning too, and all its length. Pictures flashed over him, drowning the sea itself, pictures of a life lived and forgotten, and now vividly back: pictures of himself, of Mum and Dad, of people, places, feelings, fears—things he'd done, seen, known.

The cascade of his life, and then . . .

The lane, the tree, the bird, the gate, the track, the lane again, the car, the face at the wheel; and then that slipped away, and here was the sea again, and more faces, faces he knew: the girl, her blue eyes bright against the red of the sea, and the shadowfaces around her, around him.

They pressed close, mouths gaping. He stared into the girl's eyes, felt the strength in them, the fight. But what was the point of fighting now? It was over. He was already dead. The mouths moved again, widened, as though shrieking at him. He stared at them through the red mist. They were calling to him, he sensed it, yet their voices were silent.

Then a word lodged in his mind.

Knife.

He saw the girl's face change. The mouth closed; the eyes hardened. The word came again.

Knife.

It made no sense at all. But it came again, fiercely now.

KNIFE.

And then suddenly he remembered.

Izzy's penknife. He'd thrust it in his trouser pocket and forgotten about it. It might still be there. He reached out with his left hand and fumbled in his pocket. No knife but the clear feel of his body, wet and streaming and cold. He was alive, he was still alive.

But then time started again.

The faces vanished in a blur of red. The pain closed around his lungs. The ache in his right arm grew. He dug again into his pocket, desperately now. Nothing but a handkerchief, a sodden, messy handkerchief, but then some coins, his door key, and . . .

There it was.

The penknife.

He closed his hand round it, squeezed tight, pulled it out, one thought screaming in his head: he mustn't, mustn't, mustn't drop it; and now he was reaching out with his left hand to the half-disabled right, praying that the fingers of that hand would be loose enough to work the blade free.

They were, just. He plucked, plucked, plucked at the edge and somehow levered it out, and now he was sawing at the rope, the girl's presence close again, her voice more urgent than ever in the tumbling flow of water. Only one word came from her now.

Fight.

He went on sawing as the anchor drew him on into the darkening void.

Fight, fight, fight.

He could feel her hand on his, thrusting the blade with him, harder, harder, harder—and then suddenly the weight left his arm and the anchor fell free. The shock of release jolted his muscles and as the bubbles frothed round his face, he felt his mouth open to breathe.

Yet in that moment she came to him again, her hand over his mouth, stopping the impulse, and he felt her clearly: she was real and close, and she was urging him upwards with her hand—and then he lost her again. But now he was snaking towards the surface.

Fight.

Her voice was all around him now, yet the pressure on his lungs was growing to an extremity of pain. He struggled on, kicking and squirming, his right arm hampered by the rope, but somehow he was climbing, and now a light was growing above him, a faint, distant, unreachable light.

Yet here was the girl again, and the shadowfaces too, and the light was growing brighter; but the pain was growing too, and as he neared the surface, he knew he wouldn't make it.

Fight.

He gave a lunge, another, and with a last, desperate effort, threw himself towards the air. Sunlight broke upon him and a wave splashed against his face. He was floundering on the surface of a smooth, reddened sea. He gulped in the air, thrashing with his arms as he revelled in his freedom, and for a brief moment the joy stayed with him before the reality of his situation returned.

He was still going to die.

There was no way back from this. There were no boats in view, nor even a glimpse of the shore from this low down, and it was certainly too far to swim. He tried to think, to recapture some functioning part of his mind, but nothing worked except his awareness of death.

He had not cheated it after all.

He trod water, drinking in more air and grateful at least that the sea was calm. His right arm ached badly, the knots still tightly in place, the severed end trailing loose. The knife was gone. He reached out with his left hand and tried to pick at the knots, but even this was made difficult by his need of at least one arm to help control him as he trod water. But somehow he managed and one by one, the knots came loose, and the rope slipped away.

He took a deep breath and lay on his front like a corpse, head down, arms out, floating there with his eyes closed; and as he floated, so memories drifted through the chamber of his mind, memories of the recent past, and the distant past, of childhood and growing up, and walks, and visions, and floating like this, in swimming pools and in the sea.

There was no sense of the girl now, nor of the shadowfaces. He opened his eyes and peered down into the gloom. There was no sign of them, but it didn't seem to matter. He would be joining them soon anyway. Yet even as he thought this, the word came back, reaching almost angrily through the sea.

Fight.

What was it about this girl? She just wouldn't let him give up. He raised his head above the surface, gulped in more air, and stared up at the sky. It was still early morning and he was shivering badly now. He studied the sun for a moment. At least its position in the sky showed him the direction of the land. He turned and stared towards the unseen shore.

And without quite knowing why, struck out towards it.

It seemed pointless. He was never going to get there. Yet still the girl's challenge rang through his head. He spoke back to her, muttering into the waves that broke over his face.

'Don't know why you're making me do this. I can't swim two miles or whatever it is.'

The word flew back at him.

Fight.

He said no more and swam on, stroke after stroke, shivering more violently as the minutes passed. The sun rose higher in the sky and still he swam on. At least the redness in the sea was easing. He might be swimming towards oblivion but he was glad to be leaving that hateful patch of water behind. He just hoped he wasn't leaving the girl behind too.

'Don't leave me,' he murmured. 'I want to be with you at the end.'

But she was still there. He could not see her but he sensed her, somewhere near. He thought of Mum and

Dad, and the pain they would feel, the anguish of not knowing what had happened to him. Perhaps his body would be washed ashore; perhaps not. He didn't know which was best for them.

Both would hurt.

He swam on, the sea growing calmer still with only the gentlest of waves to disturb him, but he was weakening now, and growing so cold it seemed useless to continue. He stopped and trod water again. This was foolish. Better to give up, fold up and slip away.

He looked around him at the passionless face of the sea. He had no idea how long he'd been swimming. Time seemed to have stopped again, just as he had. Apart from that, all was the same: the water, the sky, the absence of land, the cold in his body. His mouth chattered; his limbs felt frozen.

He drew a long breath, turned onto his front and floated again, face down, his eyes open this time. Below him the sea was a cloudy grey. No trace of red, blue, or black. Just grey: a familiar grey too. He remembered it now. The first colour he'd seen on coming to after the accident, and strangely comforting. The gold and the blue and the black and the red—all had held some extra meaning for him, but not grey.

It was the politest of colours, demanding nothing. He would be happy to sink into grey. He peered down into the folds of the sea. He was running out of breath now and would have to take another gulp soon if he was to go on floating here. He pondered this for a moment.

Strange how his mind could feel so calm even as the chill immobilized his body. He was losing all control now. His limbs still worked after a fashion, but they wouldn't go on much longer. He went on pondering the question of breath. No, he decided. There was no point in taking any more. No point at all.

Then he saw it.

Down in the grey, so deep it was hard to believe his sight would reach that far, yet there it was, a ghostly form rising towards him. No shape to it at all, just a faint contrast of light, grey against grey, and then brighter, the grey of the sea remaining, the grey of this other thing slipping free as the shape defined itself. But he'd guessed what it was, even before he saw the black and the blue.

She was coming for him at last, and she was not alone. More forms were moving beneath her, following in her wake, and they too were defining themselves. There were the faces he'd seen so many times, but the shadows were leaving them as they rose in the stream of the girl, and as they drew closer, following her trail, he saw them properly for the first time. Five of them, and their faces were clear, and they had bodies too.

They were children. Two boys and three girls, hair swirling about them as they moved through the sea. How old they were he did not know. The three girls looked about ten, the boys about seven, like little Muck. All seemed ancient.

He studied the girl, his girl. She too seemed ancient, though her face was no older than his. She was close now, her eyes still bright against the grey, the forms of the other children tight around her, all six of them peering up at him. He reached out a hand to the girl. She moved closer, her eyes on his.

'You've come to take me,' he whispered, 'and I'm ready.'

He ran a finger over her mouth—and then it moved.

'Breathe,' it said.

He stared into her face. The eyes were fixed and strong, and he could feel her will again, but it was no good. He was finished and he knew it. Even her fire would not save him now. He shook his head and saw her face change. But there was no scorn. The eyes softened and he knew that she understood.

The faces of the children started to recede. He stared at them. One by one they slipped back into the depths, watching him all the while. But the girl remained, just below him, her mouth moving again as though speaking to him. One word, it seemed, but he could not catch it. She was not urging him to fight or breathe. He had stopped fighting, and he had stopped breathing too.

He was simply floating and she was floating beneath him, and still her mouth was moving, moving, moving; and then he caught the word. It was so simple and clear he wondered how he could have missed it. She was murmuring his name.

'Will.'

He smiled at her but she didn't smile back. She was slipping away too now, into the depths, still watching him, her mouth moving as before, and still somehow the word reached him.

'Will.'

And then she was gone, enveloped in gloom, and he could feel his body starting to follow. The sound of his name was gone too. But then, as he slipped below the surface, it came to him again.

'Will.'

Only now it was different. He couldn't work out how. But as he sank, he felt the word again, and the voice that spoke it, and he knew as the sea closed around him that someone else was calling him.

32

Grey light. The absence of pain. A certainty that he was dead. And then a feeling that he'd experienced these things before—and been wrong: about death, about certainty, about everything. The voice still spoke his name; that much he knew. He also knew that he was being moved. He had no idea where he was going and after a while he forgot where he had been.

Something lingered in his mind, something about the sea, but then that slipped away, together with the voice, and all became a blur. Yet it was a restful blur, especially now that he'd realized there was nothing whatever he could do. Then the voice returned.

'Will.'

And he recognized the speaker.

Beth.

An image of her face floated into his mind. He wondered whether he could speak back to her. He wanted to, but he felt so tired, and he still wasn't sure where he was. He wasn't even certain that he was alive. Then he felt something, something cool. A part of him flickered with movement.

His body, surely. Yes, it was his body. He could feel it, and he could feel this other thing, this cool thing, and it was touching some part of his face. His cheek. It was definitely against his cheek. An intake of breath, a gulp of air.

Who was breathing? Was it him? Another gulp of air, and this time he knew it was him. He felt a cough splutter out, felt his body shake, heard a moan from his lips, yet still the cool thing remained on his cheek. A hand, he decided, that's what it was. Beth spoke again.

'Will, open your eyes if you can.'

He did so and found himself staring into the face of Muck. The boy was standing by the bed, his arm stretched out. It was the child's hand that he could feel on his cheek. Behind Muck stood Beth, and Mum and Dad, and John Shepherd, and a policewoman who looked familiar. WPC Somebody . . .

Will tried to remember.

Kate, yes, she was called Kate Shaw. She was holding Muck's other hand. But Muck wasn't looking at her. The boy was looking directly at him. Will spoke, softly.

'She was your sister, wasn't she?'

Muck stared back.

'Your big sister,' said Will. 'Your brave, beautiful sister.'

Mum and Dad edged forward.

'Will,' said Mum.

She reached out, taking care not to push Muck aside, but the boy seemed strangely unconcerned about her, and all these other people crowded nearby. He simply stood there, his hand on Will's cheek, the other in Kate's grasp. Mum stroked Will's hair.

'Sweetheart, we thought we'd lost you again.'

'You've been out for three days,' said Dad.

'Where am I?' he said.

'Don't you recognize this place?' said Mum.

He looked around him. He was lying in a comfortable bed in a bright pleasant room with plants, flowers, and a small indoor water fountain tinkling in the corner. If it hadn't been for the medical instruments beeping around him, he'd have taken this for a high-class guesthouse. But he knew where he was now.

'Acacia Court,' he said.

'Yes,' said Mum. 'The emergency people were going to take you to Newton Barnet Hospital again but once they'd stabilized you, we asked if they could bring you here, and they agreed. The facilities are fantastic and Peter and the staff have been wonderful.'

'Thank you,' he whispered.

He felt Muck take his hand away and turned back to the child. The boy was still holding Kate Shaw's hand but his eyes remained on Will. John Shepherd stepped forward.

'I'm glad you're OK, Will.'

'Are you in trouble with the police?'

John shook his head.

'What about the people in town?' said Will. 'You got attacked.'

'I don't think you should be talking right now, Will. You must be tired out.'

'I'm OK.' Will took a heavy breath. 'I want to talk. I want to know what's happened.'

He took another laboured breath, aware of the eyes of all upon him; and more eyes than ever now, since others had entered the room. Peter was standing there, and three of the nurses from Acacia Court, including the one who'd been with him in the alleyway that night. But Will gave no further thought to that.

'They pushed me over the side,' he said. He glanced at Kate Shaw. 'You know the people I'm talking about?'

'Yes,' said the policewoman. 'They're in custody.'

'They tied an anchor to my arm and pushed me over.'

'Bloody hell,' said Dad.

'I managed to cut myself free and swim to the surface. It was at the place where the children drowned.' He looked at Kate again. 'You know about the children?'

'We do now,' she said.

Three more figures entered the room: DI Cutler, DC Drake, and DC Griffiths. Will saw Muck stiffen, then realized with relief that it was a sign of pleasure at the sight of Joanna. The policewoman was already bending down and smiling at him. Kate let go of Muck's hand and Joanna beckoned.

For a moment Muck seemed unsure which way to go. It was obvious to Will that both policewomen had somehow bonded with the boy, but Muck also seemed reluctant to move away from him. Joanna clearly saw this too and hurried over. Muck relaxed and turned back to the bed.

'Will,' said Peter, 'it's time to rest, not talk.'

Will shook his head.

'I want to know what happened.'

'But, Will, you've only just come round. You need—'

'Please, Peter.'

Peter frowned.

'I'm OK,' said Will. He looked at DI Cutler. 'I want to know about the children.'

He felt a sudden tension in the room. All faces turned towards DI Cutler. The officer walked up to

295

the bed, Muck watching him closely. The man stopped, then, to Will's surprise, he gave the boy a wink and reached out a hand towards his face. There was no scream and Muck let the policeman ruffle his hair without complaint.

'Good boy,' said the officer. 'Well done.'

He took his hand away and looked at Will.

'Obviously you and I will need to have a proper talk when you're feeling better.'

'I want to hear now,' said Will. 'I'm not that tired.'

'You look exhausted.'

'I want to hear.'

DI Cutler glanced at Peter, who gave a brief nod.

'Well,' said the officer, 'I don't see why I shouldn't fill you in on what's publicly known.'

The officer cleared his throat.

'First thing is we don't know who the children are. Or were, since six of them are dead, Muck here being the only survivor. We don't even know where they've come from.' He cleared his throat again. 'We do know where they were going.'

Again Will felt the tension in the room.

'Child trafficking is a very ugly business,' said the policeman. 'It's also a very lucrative one and there are some big players involved. But moving kids from source to destination without getting caught takes a lot of organization, and there are various ways in which it's done.'

DI Cutler paused.

'One way is by a journey of small, innocent-looking stages. In this case the children were brought across from the continent by boat, probably in a series of journeys on small, unobtrusive craft, changing from vessel to vessel somewhere out of sight of land to avoid suspicion, then landing the kids at an isolated place on shore.'

'The track through the woodland,' said Will.

'Yes,' said the officer. 'Robbo's syndicate is run through Newton Barnet and it uses Havensmouth as a landing point. A boat brings the children from the previous stage—we're not sure where that is yet but we're working on it—and this boat then meets up with Robbo's boat offshore. The place where you were thrown overboard.'

'Go on.'

'They bring the children at night, transfer them from the first boat to Robbo's boat, and he brings them ashore on the other side of Breeze Point. Perfect spot. End of the second beach, out of sight of town. There's an old stone slipway, as you know, and it links up with the track through the woodland. A van meets the boat by the slipway, takes the children down the track and out through the gate, and off down the lane to Newton Barnet. And on to their . . . er . . . ' DI Cutler frowned. 'Intended destinations.'

One of the nurses burst into tears and hurried from the room. Will pictured the gate and shuddered.

'I saw their shadows,' he muttered.

'What?' said Dad.

'When I was by the gate. I saw their shadows swirling down the track towards me. And away down the lane.'

There was a long silence. Out in the corridor Will saw the nurse who'd run out standing by one of the windows that looked over the lawn. She was still crying but one of the reception staff was comforting her.

He looked down at Muck. The boy seemed to have changed so much during the time the police had been looking after him. He was still wary of people but he clearly trusted Kate Shaw and Joanna Griffiths. Yet there was something strange about the boy's eyes.

Will stared into them and saw more than one pair of eyes peering back. There was no mistaking it. The girl was watching him too through her brother's gaze. He shivered for a moment and looked back at DI Cutler.

'So what happened?'

'It was a shipment that went wrong,' said the officer. 'It was the girl who spoiled things for them. The oldest of the kids. Like I said earlier, we don't know where these particular children came from. We've got no details about them at all. We don't know what stories they were told to persuade them to go with these men. There might not even have been any persuasion. They might just have been forced. The people who run these rackets do whatever they need to do to get the kids on board.'

'Horrible,' said Mum.

'Yes,' said the officer. 'But this girl wasn't your average kid. She was clearly a very gutsy character. She stood up to the men. It was the early hours of the morning, pitch dark, and they were bringing the kids to the transfer point out there.' DI Cutler nodded towards the horizon. 'The boat bringing them was a fibreglass motor cruiser called *Dreamway*.'

Will bit his lip. Of course. He should have guessed.

'We're trying to trace the owners,' said DI Cutler, 'and work back to who might have been using her at the time. Anyway, whoever it was, they met up with Robbo's boat out there and made ready to transfer the kids. Five of them were locked in the cabin up in the bows. Muck and the older girl—'

'His sister,' said Will.

'We haven't been able to establish who she was.'

'She was his sister. I'm telling you.'

'Whoever she was, she didn't like the look of Robbo's lot—can't say I blame her—and refused to leave the *Dreamway*. So the men crowded round and threatened her. She broke free and ran off round the boat. Muck here screamed and ran after her. The men crowded round again and in a moment of panic—or bravery—she caught hold of a flare pistol that was lying nearby and fired it at them.'

'Christ!' said Peter.

'But she missed and the flare went straight into an open locker down in the stern. It must have had some propane or butane or petrol or something in there. Maybe someone was drawing off some fuel. We don't know. Either way, the flare caught it and there was an explosion. A massive one, too. It blew the back off the boat.'

'My God!' said Mum.

'The boat went down very fast,' said the policeman. 'And, of course, being fibreglass, she left very few traces.'

'Why's that?' said John.

'Because fibreglass has no positive buoyancy. It also burns. So there'd have been no wreckage from the hull floating about.'

'But there'd have been other things, wouldn't there?' said Dad. 'I mean, wooden bottom-boards or lifejackets or oars or other stuff that floated?'

'Yes.' DI Cutler paused, frowning. 'And that's where little Muck comes in.'

33

All eyes turned to the boy. He caught their attention and looked nervously around him. Kate leaned quickly down.

'It's all right, Muck. It's OK.'

He looked at her, his eyes still wary.

'We're talking about what happened,' she whispered. 'We're talking about how brave you were.'

She threw a glance at DI Cutler.

'Can you carry on with the story, sir? And can the rest of you stop looking at him? You're making him edgy.'

They all looked away again and DI Cutler continued.

'The boat started to go down. The men jumped into Robbo's boat and roared off, leaving the kids to drown. We can only guess what happened next. The five in the cabin had no chance. Maybe the girl tried to get them out but she wouldn't have had much time with the boat sinking so fast. I'm guessing she tried to help Muck, maybe tied him to something that might float, stuck a lifejacket on him. Or maybe not. Maybe he was just lucky and found something by himself. Because although the girl didn't make it, or the five in the cabin, Muck obviously did.'

Again all eyes turned to the boy; and then—as though remembering Kate's warning—turned quickly away.

'We don't know how he got back to shore,' said DI Cutler, 'because he hasn't been able to tell us.' He looked down at Muck. 'And maybe you never will, eh? But you got back somehow, didn't you?'

The officer looked back at the others.

'Anyway, he made it to the beach and Crow found him, or he found Crow. And somehow or other, they bonded.'

Will pictured the dark night: the men, the frightened children, the screaming, the explosion, the boat going down. He thought of the five locked in the cabin. No wonder he'd seen them as shadowfaces. He'd been staring at the mouths and eyes of drowning children. Only the girl's face had been clear.

But she had been the strong one.

He reached out and put a hand on Muck's shoulder. The boy looked at him and there again in the wide eyes he saw the girl peering out. He remembered the touch of her in the dark, misty sea. He looked up at DI Cutler.

'How did you find all this out? You're not going to tell me Robbo and Lem admitted it.'

'Davy told us,' said the officer.

'Davy?'

'Davy was part of the child trafficking racket. He was on Robbo's boat that night, with Lem, just the three of them. He'd done several of these transfers before with them but he was starting to feel uncomfortable about it.'

'Why didn't he say something?' said Mum. 'Or stop?'

'Too weak,' said Dad.

'Robbo was always his best mate,' said Peter, 'and the dominant one. They go back years, those two.

301

Robbo probably threatened him or cajoled him or offered him money to keep quiet.'

'Whatever the case,' said DI Cutler, 'it got to him and he started drinking. Everybody in Havensmouth saw that. And when the *Dreamway* incident took place, he went to pieces.'

'He still didn't say anything,' said Will.

'But he did,' said the officer. 'That's the point. He went missing, remember?'

'Yes.'

'And he left a note to Mrs Weller to say he wasn't coming back. And that was probably his plan. To go away. Only being Davy, he couldn't quite manage that. He made it as far as the woodland round Greenheys but then he got drunk and passed out.'

Will was starting to guess the rest. Or some of it.

'He saw what happened to me.'

'That's right,' said the policeman. 'He woke in the early morning to find himself lying in a thicket. And he saw two figures in balaclavas moving past. They didn't see him and carried straight on. He was still pretty far gone with drink but he saw them overpower you and carry you off.'

DI Cutler leaned closer.

'And that was the real moment when you nearly died.'

'What do you mean?'

'That was when Davy had to make his big decision. To shop his friends—because, I mean, he knew who was behind what was happening—or to protect them. He seems to have taken a while making his mind up. If he'd acted quicker, you might never have been thrown in the sea. But in the end he got it right. He blundered through the woods to

Greenheys, woke up the Palmers and blurted the whole thing out.'

Will looked round at Beth.

'I didn't know you were involved.'

'I wasn't really,' she said. 'I wanted to be but Dad wouldn't let me come, or Mum, or Jack. He said it was too dangerous for us. He rang Lee and Andy and told them to meet him at the harbour, and got Mum to ring the police and tell them what was happening, and to ring your mum and dad. I didn't see anything after that until the emergency people brought you back unconscious.'

'But how did they get to me?' said Will.

'They took Andy's dory,' said DI Cutler. 'Nippy little thing. Even so, it was close. By the time they got out there, Robbo's boat was coming back, but they carried on past to look for you and left us to pick up Robbo and his crew, which we did. We also had the medics on the way by then.'

Will stared out over the sea again. It was a rich blue now.

'I can't believe they found me out there,' he murmured.

'They nearly didn't,' said DC Drake. 'They motored about, searching like mad, and then one of them—'

'My dad,' said Beth.

'Spotted your body face down. You were just starting to slip under the water. They powered over, Andy and Lee dived in, and they pulled you out. You were some way down, they said.'

Mum put a hand over her face and Joanna gave the policeman a disapproving look.

'Mum?' said Will.

303

She looked at him.

'I'm all right,' he said. 'I'm OK.'

She didn't speak.

'And I'm starting to remember things,' he said.

'Are you?'

'Yes. I saw pictures of my old life when I was close to dying. And I can still see them. I can remember you, and I can remember Dad. Like I used to know you, I mean. It's coming back again. Or some of it is. And I can remember Beth. And other things.'

He frowned.

Other things.

Yes, he could remember other things, and one of them he would have to sort out very soon. But for now there were still questions to be answered.

'What happened to Davy?' he said.

'He went a bit crazy,' said DC Drake. 'Ran out of Greenheys and into town, yelling at people and telling anyone who'd listen about Robbo and Lem and the *Dreamway* and the kids. Cornered John in the main street and poured it all out again. Then went charging off, bellowing at people. It turned very nasty in the end.'

'What do you mean?'

'There was some violence. Child abuse always stirs up strong emotions—'

'Understandably,' said Mum.

'And there's Davy mouthing off about what's been going on, with his own part in it clear to all. It's not surprising he got knocked about. He's in police hands now.'

'What kind of sentence will he get?' said Peter.

'Hard to say,' said DI Cutler. 'He's obviously got a lot to answer for but one thing in his favour is the fact

304

that he helped save Will's life. Another is that he probably saved Muck's life too.'

'Muck?' said Will.

Yet again all eyes turned to the boy; and, as before, moved swiftly away again.

'Yes,' said the officer. 'When Crow got killed, the boy must have hidden or run off. Lem and his gang certainly didn't find him. But Davy did, on one of his drunken night-time rambles. Found the boy on the beach, he said, drawing something in the sand. And Muck let Davy take him away.'

DI Cutler shook his head.

'You'd think Davy was one person Muck would never want to go off with—a guy he last saw as *Dreamway* was going down. But then he seems to like weird characters. He was drawn to Crow.'

The policeman's eye flickered in Will's direction but he said no more.

'Kids can be strangely intuitive,' said Kate. 'Maybe Muck just sensed Davy wasn't going to hurt him.'

'Anyway,' said DI Cutler, 'Davy borrowed Mrs Weller's key to the church—without telling her, of course—then he let the boy into the bell-tower in the small hours of the morning and gave him some food and drink. I'm not quite sure what prompted all this. Some bizarre form of penance probably. It would have been far more sensible if he'd brought the lad to the police station. But as we all know, Davy's mind doesn't follow logical patterns. Even so, his helping the boy will probably be another point in his favour when the case comes to court.'

'What about Robbo?' said Will.

The policeman shrugged.

'His boat's been torched—we're not sure who by—and his wife and daughter are in a safe house.'

'Have they been attacked too?'

'There's been some stuff.'

'And Lem?'

'Helping us with our enquiries. Like his father.'

'Or not, I imagine,' said Dad.

None of the police officers answered this.

'What about the other four?' said Will. 'The bala-clava boys.'

'Can't say too much about them,' said DI Cutler.

'But you've told me all this other stuff.'

'That's because it's public knowledge. Davy's been shouting it all over Havensmouth. But he hasn't said much about these other four and we're not sure he knows who they are.'

'Then let me have a guess,' said Will.

He thought back to the four figures on the boat.

'They're not part of the child trafficking racket. They're friends of Lem. Robbo told his son to get a gang together to scare off Crow so they could get at Muck, because he's the only person left who wit-nessed what happened with the *Dreamway* and they were worried he might cause them trouble. Only they couldn't get at him because he wouldn't leave Crow.'

Will paused, thinking.

'Then I arrived in Havensmouth and started feeling stuff, and talking about it around the town, and in the church. And suddenly they had three problems. Crow and me and Muck. So I'm guessing Robbo got Lem to put together this gang to scare the tramp and the mad boy away so they could get at Muck. Only it turned to murder and got out of hand.'

He looked back at DI Cutler.

'Any of that make sense?'

'It might do,' said the policeman.

'It was Lem who attacked me on the balcony,' said Will. 'He admitted that on the boat. He also admitted he killed Crow. You need to know that. But those other four were just hired muscle. I know it. Some of them must have been told to watch The Four Winds and that's how they saw me when I left the house to go to the site of the accident.'

'Well,' said DI Cutler, 'that's one of the things we're going to want to talk to you about—exactly what made you go to the track in the first place. And obviously we're going to need to go through everything with you in more detail and get a statement from you. But that's for another time and another place.'

'It certainly is,' said Peter. 'Will's had quite enough for now.'

'There's one last thing,' said John Shepherd, 'before Will has his rest.'

They all looked round at the vicar.

'Will, if you're not too tired, there's something I remembered.'

'I know what you're going to say, John.'

'You do?'

'Yes,' said Will. 'Because I remembered it too. When I was drowning.'

They stared at each other in silence.

'You're going to tell me about the incident in church,' said Will. 'That time just before my accident when I had a trance and started talking about sickness. When you thought I was close to discovering what was wrong in Havensmouth.'

John nodded.

'Will, listen. I always felt that your behaviour wasn't just random, that something triggered it, but I couldn't work out what it was. Then yesterday I remembered what I was talking about that day at the moment when you had your outburst.'

'You'd quoted some passages from St Matthew and St Luke.'

'Yes,' said John, 'and I was talking about—'

'Innocence,' said Will.

There was another silence between them, a longer one. Then John looked away.

'Yes,' he said quietly.

Muck stirred suddenly. He'd been standing rigid for the last few minutes, but now his right arm stretched out—and it was reaching for Kate's bag. She saw what he wanted and opened it. He squeezed his hand in and felt around. Kate looked up at their watching faces.

'I was going to show you this later,' she said, 'but Muck seems to want to show it now.'

The boy drew his hand out of the bag. Clasped in it was a sheet of paper with a coloured drawing on it. He looked round at them, his mouth so wide it reminded Will of the shadowfaces again. Then the boy's eyes fixed on him.

'Is it for me, Muck?' he said.

The eyes stared back at him: the boy's eyes, the girl's eyes, and somehow the eyes of the other five children too. Will reached out and took the picture.

'Thank you,' he said.

'He drew this by himself,' said Kate. 'He was sitting with Jo and me and he just started. We didn't prompt him or anything. I think it tells a story, don't you?'

Will felt the others crowd round to look.

The picture did indeed tell a story: a story of night and sea and boats and men, and a terrifying explosion. But most of all it told a story of children. Will stared at them, breathing hard. For he could feel that familiar chill running over his feet, legs, and spine.

'I need to go into Havensmouth,' he said.

34

B ut it was two days before they let him go: two days of medical checks and a forced rest he had no wish for, the rage still burning inside him to finish this thing off once and for all. Yet even as he fretted through the nights, a more rational part of him was conceding—albeit grudgingly—that this was probably for the best, not just for him, as he was still very weak and short of breath, but for the business itself.

For this was the final unravelling.

And it was complicated. It could go horribly wrong. He needed to think. He needed to do it right. He still wasn't sure of the best way to go about it. All he knew for certain was that he didn't want a crowd of people involved. Just Beth preferably, and maybe Mum and Dad, but nobody else.

No police yet. Later, of course, but right now their presence could ruin everything; and besides, he wanted to do this himself. It was his affair, not theirs. This was personal. So he kept his counsel, and waited, and raged.

But finally it was over. A last medical check, a long talk with Peter, and then the hobble to the car under a bright, morning sun, Beth helping him as Mum and Dad walked on ahead. The drive out of Acacia Court and down the hill, the sea below them a living blue.

Yet for all that he felt strangely detached as he stared out of the window.

'Are you all right?' said Beth, sitting beside him on the back seat.

'Not yet,' he said.

He felt Mum and Dad stiffen in the front of the car. But neither spoke and they drove on, down to the bottom of the hill, left along the link road and on into the main street of Havensmouth. Will watched the houses and shops go by, then called out to Dad.

'Can we stop here?'

Dad pulled over to the side of the road.

'Are you sure, Will?' he said. 'We can drive a bit further if you want. I can see loads of parking spots up there.'

Will reached for his stick.

'No, I want to walk from here.'

He saw anxious looks on their faces. Even Beth seemed worried. But she passed him his stick, climbed out of the car and ran round to help him out his side. He hauled himself to his feet and stood there, balancing himself with a hand on her shoulder. Mum and Dad climbed out too, still looking worried.

'Will,' said Mum, 'I don't think you should walk too much. Especially on your first day out of Acacia Court.'

'I'll be fine,' said Will. 'I'm going to get my strength back, OK?'

'I know you are,' said Dad, 'but Peter said it'll take time. Which is one reason why I'm not too happy about you wandering about so soon. Can't we just drive round the town? What's to do here anyway that can't wait for a few more days?'

Mum shook her head.

'I wish you'd tell us what this is all about, Will,' she said.

'There's a place I want to go,' he said. 'And something I've got to do. Only I need to think how to go about it. I need to get my head straight before I get there. And the walk'll help me.'

'OK, Will,' said Dad. 'If you really don't want to tell us.'

He didn't. He felt certain they'd stop him if they found out what he was planning, and he couldn't bear that. This thing had to be resolved and he was determined to do it today. If he could just summon up the courage.

'Let's go,' he said.

'You walk, we'll follow,' said Mum. 'Since you know where you're going and we don't.'

So they walked, or rather Mum, Dad, and Beth walked, and Will struggled with his stick, and gradually they made their way along the main street, faces turning to look at him as he passed. Will stared back, matching gaze for gaze. He felt Beth take his free hand and glanced at her. She flicked her hair back, caught his eye, and smiled. He nodded across the road.

'Can we go that way?'

'To the church?'

'Yes.'

She squeezed his hand and leaned closer.

'I knew you'd want to go there,' she whispered.

He glanced over his shoulder at Mum and Dad.

'We're just going to the church for a minute.'

'Is that the place you were talking about just now?' said Dad.

'Chris,' said Mum. 'Don't push him.'

'Just asking,' said Dad. 'Will? Do you want us to come with you?'

'They don't,' said Mum, with a look.

Dad shrugged.

'OK.'

'You two go on ahead,' said Mum. 'We'll wait for you here. No rush.'

Will walked with Beth to the church entrance and waited while she opened the door for him, then they stepped in. The cool of the church felt pleasant after the heat of the sun. There was no one inside but the silence seemed to resound through the empty space.

Will shuffled down to the altar and turned slowly round. The last time he'd seen this space it had been red. Now the stained-glass windows were bright with a multiplicity of colours. He looked at Beth. She hadn't followed and was standing at the far end of the aisle. John Shepherd had appeared and was standing next to her. He called out.

'So has it gone, Will? The thing you didn't like.'

Will hobbled back down the aisle and stopped before them.

'It's almost gone,' he said.

'Only almost?' said John.

'There's one thing that's still not right. One thing I've got to sort.'

John narrowed his eyes.

'This is a good church, Will.'

'I know.'

'And the people who come here are good too.'

'I know.'

'You mustn't judge them harshly just because of Robbo and Lem.'

'I don't.'

'Or because they're wary of you. You can be frightening sometimes.'

'I know. I freak people out. Beth told me.'

He felt Beth take his hand again. John watched him for a moment, then spoke again.

'So are you still leaving Havensmouth?'

'I don't know. Mum and Dad want to talk about it later today.'

'I hope you stay,' said John. 'And I hope you sort out this . . . other thing that's still not right.'

'Thanks.'

Will leaned on his stick and made his way to the door of the church, John and Beth close behind. Out in the sunlight he turned and gazed over the graveyard. A hand squeezed his shoulder from behind and he looked round to see it was John's.

'Take care of yourself, Will.'

'You too, John.'

And John stepped back into the church. Will watched him go, then turned to Beth. She was standing nearby, her lips tight together. He walked up to her, dropped his stick, and pulled her close. She was crying softly.

'It's all right,' he said.

'I don't want you to leave Havensmouth.'

He stroked her hair.

'It's Mum and Dad's decision.'

'But it's yours too, isn't it?'

'I guess.'

'So are you not sure what you want to do?'

'I'm sure about you,' he said. 'I'm just not sure about . . . what's going to happen next.'

'This thing you've got to sort out?'

314

'Yes.'

They stood there, still holding each other, and gradually Beth stopped crying.

'I'm glad you're sure about me anyway,' she said. 'You weren't at first.'

He kissed her on the cheek, the mouth, the other cheek.

'Your skin's wet,' he said.

'I know. It's tears.'

She pulled out a handkerchief.

'No, let me,' he said, and he kissed both cheeks again.

They went on holding each other for a while, then Beth stirred.

'That's one noisy bird,' she said.

He stiffened, his arms still round her. She was right. He hadn't noticed until now but there was a bird singing somewhere nearby: a very familiar bird.

'It's a song-thrush,' she said.

'I know.'

He eased his arms from her and looked round. There was no sign of the bird but it didn't matter. He knew what the song meant. It was time. He couldn't put this thing off any longer. He looked back at Beth.

'She's alive, isn't she?' he said.

'Who?'

'No one's mentioned her but I know she's alive. I've been feeling her pain ever since I came round at Acacia Court.'

'Who?' said Beth. 'Not the girl with black hair?'

Will shook his head.

'Izzy Wetherby.'

'Izzy?' Beth stared at him. 'What's she got to do with all this?'

315

'Just tell me what happened to her.'

Beth picked up his stick and handed it to him.

'She went missing,' she said.

'I know.'

'But it was nothing to do with you. That's why I forgot to mention it. It was to do with Del Kenyon. You remember him? Friend of Buzz Murley?'

'Yeah, yeah, the bike boys.'

'And his dad's the guy who attacked John Shepherd.'

'I know all that. Tell me about Izzy.'

'OK, OK.' Beth frowned. 'I told you Del had a thing for me. But I wasn't interested and he went after Izzy. Only she didn't want him either. But he kept on with her. And there was that business with the penknife, remember?'

Will thought of the rope round his arm, the water racing past.

'I remember the penknife,' he said quietly.

'Well, Izzy took herself off because she wanted to try again,' said Beth. 'Only this time she used a kitchen knife with a serrated edge.'

Will shuddered. Somehow he'd guessed it was something like this.

'But Brad and Micky found her,' said Beth. 'She was in the cave under Breeze Point and they got to her just in time. Jack heard about it from Micky. Izzy's back home from hospital now and Geoff and Sarah Wetherby are keeping a close eye on her. And Del's keeping his head down.'

'Come on,' said Will. 'It's time.'

And he hurried back to the main street, Beth close beside him. Mum and Dad were standing in the same place as before but their attention was directed towards the harbour end of the street. Will and Beth joined them.

'It's that man,' said Mum, nodding down the road. 'The one who attacked John.'

'Fraser Kenyon,' said Dad.

Will stared down the street. There was no mistaking Del's father. There was a resemblance in both the face and the air of aggression. He was standing outside The Sea Chest and he had a bottle in each hand. He saw them watching and started to blunder down in their direction.

'Oh, God,' said Dad. 'Come on, about turn.'

'No,' said Will. 'We've got to go that way.'

'Not now, Will.'

'Sorry, Dad. We've got to go that way.'

And without another word, Will set off towards the harbour. Beth caught him up and he soon heard Mum and Dad hurrying behind. Fraser Kenyon slowed down at the sight of them approaching and seemed for a moment about to move aside. But then he sloped back to the centre of the pavement and blocked their way.

'Not right, is it?' he muttered. 'Eh?'

'What's not right, Fraser?' said Beth.

'My boy. Done nothing wrong. And that bonehead . . . ' He jerked a thumb in the direction of The Sea Chest. 'That . . . Wetherby . . . he tells me to keep Del away from his daughter or . . . '

The man spat at their feet.

'Or . . . he's coming for me. Well, I'll soon . . . if he tries anything . . . '

Fraser glowered at them for a few moments, then lurched past and stumbled off down the street.

'Nasty,' said Mum under her breath.

'Come on,' said Will, walking on.

'But, Will,' said Dad.

'Come on!'

And Will pushed on towards the harbour. He was desperate now to get this thing over with and he knew at last how he wanted to go about it. But now there was another unexpected figure approaching: Buzz Murley on his bike. The boy rode straight towards them, speeding up as he drew close.

'Look out, Will!' said Beth.

Will stopped and stood his ground. Buzz braked and let his bike spin to a halt not two metres away. Dad bellowed at the boy.

'You stupid idiot! Can't you see Will's got a walking stick?'

'It's all right, Dad,' said Will quietly. He kept his eyes on the other boy's face. 'Buzz wasn't trying to scare me. He always rides fast. It's just his way.'

Buzz looked him over and said nothing.

'Buzz?' said Beth. 'Where is he?'

Buzz chewed his tongue for a few moments, then nodded to the left; and there, slumped on the ground, halfway down one of the alleyways, was Del. Like his father, he'd clearly been drinking. His face looked haggard and as he caught sight of them, the bottle he'd been holding rolled from his hand along the ground.

Will started towards him.

'Will,' said Mum. 'Please don't.'

'It's all right, Mum. This is important.'

He hurried on towards the alleyway, aware of the others close behind. Buzz rode on ahead and jumped off his bike. Will reached Del and bent down. From inside the alleyway came a smell of whisky, urine, and vomit.

'Del,' said Will.

'Get lost, mad boy.'

'Del, listen—'

'What do you care?' Del scowled at him, then threw an even angrier look at Beth. 'Or you? You're just a . . . ' He took some jerky breaths. 'Like that other . . . bloody . . . '

'It's not your fault, Del,' said Will.

'What do you know about anything?'

'Izzy cutting her wrist. It wasn't because of you.'

The boy's eyes darkened and whirled.

'It was something else,' said Will. 'Nothing to do with you. Nothing at all, OK? Don't blame yourself.'

He felt Mum, Dad, and Beth stiffen behind him. He straightened up and turned to Buzz.

'Get him home,' he said. 'OK? Just get him home.' And to the others, 'Come on.'

'Will,' said Beth, 'what's going on?'

'It's time to finish this thing.'

'What's happening?'

'Just come with me.' He looked round at them. 'All of you. I need you there.'

And he didn't speak again until he'd reached The Sea Chest.

The pub was a strangely silent place. It was open for business but there was nobody at the bar and only two elderly men drinking coffee at a table in the far corner. Will walked slowly in, the others close behind. Geoff Wetherby appeared.

'Will!' he said. 'Good to see you, boy. Have they finally let you out of Acacia Court?'

'Yes, thanks.'

'Horrible business.' Geoff looked round at them, shaking his head. 'Couldn't believe what I heard about Robbo and Davy. You think you know people and then you find out something like that. And Robbo's son, too. Lem used to come in here with his mates. Good lads, I used to think.'

'Can I see Izzy, please?' said Will.

Geoff frowned.

'I'm afraid not, Will. It's just that . . . you probably heard . . . there's been a bit of trouble with Del Kenyon and—'

'I really need to see her. It's important.'

Geoff stared at him.

'Look, Will, I mean . . . I don't want to be rude or anything but—'

'It's really, really important.'

'What's really, really important?' said a voice.

Will turned towards the nearest door and saw Sarah Wetherby standing there. She walked slowly forward, glancing round at them.

'What's really, really important?' she said.

'I need to see Izzy.'

'I'm afraid you can't, Will. I don't know if Geoff's told you, but there's been—'

'Yes, I know. There's been some trouble with Del. But this is something else. Something I need to talk to her about. It's really urgent.'

Sarah shook her head.

'I'm sorry, Will, but she's in a terrible state at the moment. Not really up to seeing anybody. Give it a few days and I promise—'

'It's either us or the police.'

A heavy silence fell. The two old men at the corner table stood quietly up and left the pub. Sarah and Geoff exchanged glances but neither spoke.

'It's either us or the police,' Will said again.

'Will, what's this about?' said Geoff.

'Just let me see Izzy.'

The door nearby opened again and Brad's face appeared.

'What's going on?' he said.

'I need to see Izzy,' said Will.

'I know,' said the boy. 'I was listening. What's going on?'

'Just let me see her.'

And to Will's surprise, Brad pushed the door wider and beckoned him through.

'Brad!' said Geoff. 'What the hell are you doing?'

Will didn't wait for Brad to answer and stepped straight through. Beth followed, and Mum and Dad. From behind came the sound of Geoff and Sarah hurrying after them. He followed Brad down a corridor and up some stairs to a small living room. Izzy was sitting on the sofa, wearing her gold T-shirt. Her mousy-grey hair looked dishevelled and her left arm was being held by Micky, who was re-bandaging her wrist.

She stiffened at the sight of Will.

'It's OK, Izzy,' he said.

They all crowded into the room, Beth and Mum and Dad close by Will, Geoff and Sarah in the doorway. Brad sat down on the sofa next to Izzy.

'Brad,' said Geoff, 'you shouldn't have let them through like this. It's not fair on Izzy.'

Brad didn't answer this. He simply reached into his pocket, pulled out his bandana and tied it round his head. Then he put an arm round Izzy and fixed his gaze on Will.

'Too many secrets, eh, Brad?' said Will.

'Talk,' said the boy.

321

Will shook his head and turned to Izzy.

'You talk,' he said. 'Go on. Tell everyone what you saw.'

Izzy didn't speak. She simply stared back at him.

'Izzy,' said Geoff, 'listen, you don't have to—'

'Dad,' said Micky. 'There's stuff happened. And we need to know what it is.'

'Look, Micky—'

'We need to know,' said Micky. 'Izzy won't tell us. She's too scared. But she might tell . . . ' Micky threw a glance at Will. 'Him.'

Will knelt down and looked into Izzy's face.

'Let me help you,' he said. 'Let me tell you some of what happened. And you tell me if I'm wrong.'

'Don't you dare put words in her mouth,' said Geoff.

'I'm not going to,' said Will. 'I'm just—'

But at that moment, Izzy screamed.

It was the shrillest sound Will had ever heard, so loud it was painful to him. Brad pulled his sister close and she screamed again, and went on screaming. Geoff and Sarah hurried forward and knelt down, but Izzy motioned them away and dug her face into Brad's neck. It was some minutes before she quietened down. Will watched, unsure whether or not to prompt her.

'Izzy,' he said eventually.

'Will,' said Geoff, 'I'm not going to allow—'

'Leave it, Dad,' said Brad.

'But—'

'I said leave it, Dad, OK?' Brad turned to his sister and kissed the side of her head. 'Go on, baby.'

'Izzy,' said Will, 'why were you in the woodland that day?'

She peered round at him, her mouth trembling.

'Seeing Del,' she mumbled. 'We were . . . you know . . . '

Will felt the others tense around him. He opened his mouth to prompt Izzy again but to his surprise she went on.

'Only he . . . ' She hesitated. 'He wanted to go further and I didn't and . . . and I told him to go away and . . . '

'You see?' said Geoff, glaring at Will. 'I told you about this business with Del. I think you'd better just leave.'

'She hasn't finished yet,' said Will.

'Do I have to repeat myself?' said Geoff. 'As I just said—'

'Dad.' Izzy spoke again, her eyes on her father. 'Dad.'

'What is it, love?' he said.

She didn't answer and simply turned back to Will.

'What happened next, Izzy?' he said.

'I told Del to go away and . . . '

'Did he do something to you?' said Brad. 'Something you didn't want?'

'He . . . he . . . '

'What did he do, baby?'

'Nothing, he . . . ' Izzy shook her head. 'He just went away. And I hung around in the trees for a bit. I was crying. I was really upset. And then I saw . . . ' She swallowed hard. 'I saw Will walking along the lane. Wandering about like he was looking for something.'

She looked straight at Will again.

'You walked up to the gate by the track and looked at it, then you started to wander up and

323

down, like you were trying to find something or work something out. You kept going up and down.'

Will nodded. He remembered it so well now.

'Then I heard a car,' said Izzy.

Again Will felt the others tense. He looked at Izzy, urging her with his eyes to continue; and she did.

'It was coming from the direction of Newton Barnet. I saw it come up the lane. Will saw it too and stepped to the side to let it pass. But it didn't pass. It swerved towards Will. He started to run up towards the sycamore tree at the corner by the junction. And the car followed.'

'No!' said Mum.

Izzy looked at her.

'It chased him up the lane. He was desperately trying to escape. He even jumped off the lane to the side. And the car followed up the verge and went after him.'

Izzy broke off, crying.

'It knocked him against the sycamore tree,' she said. 'He fell down and didn't move. And . . . and . . . the car pulled up and the driver looked out of the window like to . . . check that he was dead, and then . . . and then drove off.'

Izzy buried her face in Brad's neck again.

There was a long silence. After a while Geoff reached out and stroked Izzy on the shoulder, then he turned to Will.

'Well, I'm sorry, Will. I guess you had every right to want to know about that. Though I'm not quite sure how you worked it out. Izzy certainly hasn't told any of us, not even her mother. We'll have to get her to speak to the police—when she's able to face it. They might be able to trace the driver.'

'They can trace the driver,' said Will.

He felt all faces turn towards him. All except Izzy's.

'Tell them, Izzy,' he said. 'Tell them who was driving.'

Izzy looked slowly round.

And her eyes fell on Sarah.

35

Sleep, a long sleep, longer than he could have believed possible—and a kind of journey: through dream, through memory, through himself. The still room, the voices of wind and surf beyond the open balcony door; the rhythms of afternoon, evening, night. He lay in his bed, sleeping and waking, aware at times of Mum and Dad looking in, but mostly lost in the shadows of a past that was slowly reaching back to him.

Part of him sensed that it would never all come back, that he would never meet the old Will face to face. But the new Will was becoming less bothered about this. The Will that he was now could still move and think and remember and love. One day perhaps he might even be happy.

Though it probably still meant leaving Havensmouth.

He opened his eyes and saw the night heavy around him. The clock on the desk said half past midnight. He sat up in bed and saw moonlight bathing the balcony floor. At the far end of the beach the outline of Breeze Point was dark against the sky. He threw off the bedclothes, stood up and walked out onto the balcony.

A breath of cool air whispered over him. He breathed it in, then leaned on the rail and thought back over the day: Brad and Micky and Geoff yelling;

Izzy's tears, Sarah's silence; Mum, Dad, and Beth hurrying him away from The Sea Chest. The drive to the police station; the drive home. Exhaustion, bed, sleep.

What had happened to the Wetherbys since he did not know.

He stepped back into his bedroom and stared at the walls. Even in the darkness the pictures were clear, yet something seemed different about them. He switched the light on and studied the images of the girl and the shadowfaces; and still there was a difference. Something was missing from them. Then he understood.

They were missing; they themselves. The girl and the five children. They were gone and they would never come back. All he had left of them was drawings on a wall; and it felt right that way. He wanted them to move on. They had lingered here long enough. Yet one image had not moved on. He switched off the light, climbed back into bed and watched it in his mind.

The boy.

Somewhere close he could feel Muck's eyes searching the darkness, searching for him. Right this moment the boy was thinking of him. He knew it. He closed his eyes and found the image of Muck's face still there; and so it remained as he fell asleep yet again.

The next time he woke, sun was streaming through the balcony door.

And he could hear voices downstairs.

He checked the clock again. Quarter past nine. He sat up, listening. Mum's voice was clear, and Dad's, and he was sure he caught Beth's, but there were others too. The tone of the conversation was notice-ably grave. He hurried out of bed, showered, dressed and made his way downstairs. The voices were com-ing from the conservatory and he'd worked out all the people by the time he saw them.

Mum, Dad, Beth, Rose, John Shepherd.

They were sitting in easy chairs by the big window overlooking the garden. Talk ceased as he entered but five faces smiled up at him. He smiled back, feeling slightly awkward. Mum stood up and kissed him.

'Come and join us, Will.'

'Thanks.'

He sat down between Rose and Beth as Mum poured him some tea.

'You've slept for hours, Will,' she said.

'Yeah, I know. Sorry.'

'No, no. It's good. It's great.'

Beth leaned across and kissed him on the cheek.

'I'm glad you've slept,' she said. 'You needed it.'

'I did,' he said.

He looked round at them, aware of the tension beneath the smiles.

'Things have happened since I turned in,' he said.

'Yes,' said Dad.

'Quite a few things,' said Rose.

There was a silence. Then John Shepherd spoke.

'There's a bigger story that's come to light and it's leaked out all over Havensmouth.' He frowned. 'First thing you need to know is that the police have arrested Sarah Wetherby. The second thing is that Davy's hanged himself.'

'Bloody hell,' said Will.

'It should never have happened,' said the vicar. 'He was in custody and somebody should have kept an eye on him. Maybe they didn't think he was a suicide risk. But he clearly was. It seems to have been guilt over the child trafficking, and the *Dreamway* incident in particular.'

'How do you know?' said Will.

'Because he told me.'

'He told you?'

'Yes. I was called to the police station yesterday afternoon. Davy had said he wanted to make a confession but he'd only speak if I was there. For some reason.'

'He obviously trusted you,' said Will.

'More a conscience thing, I think,' said John. 'Anyway, he was in a terrible state. Looked really haggard. They'd obviously told him about Sarah being arrested for your attempted murder and it seemed to have prompted this desire to talk. I don't think he knew she'd tried to kill you.'

'But he wouldn't care about that, would he?'

'Not normally perhaps,' said John, 'but I think it was the final straw for a man already struggling with guilt. Because although he'd shopped Robbo and Lem to the whole town, and revealed his own part in the child trafficking, he'd covered Sarah's back. Until the police told him she'd been arrested for your attempted murder. And out came this story.'

Will felt the tension again in the others.

'Go on, John,' he said.

John continued.

'Sarah Wetherby was the organizer of the child trafficking racket. Geoff knew nothing about it. Davy was adamant about that. It was Sarah's thing and it was about money and power. She arranged everything. She was also the friendly face who reassured the children when they first reached the shore. Told them it was OK to get in the van.'

Mum shook her head.

'I still can't believe it. A woman doing such a thing.'

'I know,' said Rose. 'And when you think of the kind of person we thought she was. I've known her for years. Or I thought I did. I hope she rots in hell. Sorry, John.'

John shrugged.

'She fooled me too. She came to my church and I liked her, thought she was OK. I felt the same way about Robbo. But I guess they won't be the first people to hide their true natures behind a show of faith. And talking of Robbo . . . ' John looked back at Will. 'Sarah was having an affair with him. Davy says it had been going on for some time. I think it hurt him to talk about this. I'm not sure why.'

'That's easy,' said Beth. 'Davy's been drippy over Sarah since forever. That's no secret to anyone. If she told him to eat cement, he'd do it. He'd have had to be in some state to shop Sarah.'

'He was in a state by the end,' said John. 'And like I say, I think it was the revelation about her trying to kill Will that forced the confession out of him. I just wish the police had kept a better watch on him. Anybody could see he was unstable.'

Will stared out over the garden and down to the beach below. The sand looked smooth and golden. Yet no one was walking along the shore today, and no figures were moving on the dunes or on the headland.

He thought of Muck again, felt the boy's searching eyes.

'What else has happened?' he said.

'Lots,' said Rose.

He looked round at her.

'There's been trouble in Havensmouth,' she said.

'What kind of trouble?'

'Brad and Micky have gone wild. Ran off round the town last night, shouting and bawling about Sarah trying to kill you and stuff. Geoff rang us asking for help bringing the boys back. When we got there, it turned out Izzy had run off too. Stu and Andy found her shivering at the end of the harbour wall. First thing she said was that she'd seen Sarah and Robbo kissing one time but never said anything.'

'No wonder she was getting stroppy with Sarah,' said Beth. 'First seeing her mum kissing Robbo, then trying to murder Will.'

'Is Izzy all right?' said Will.

'She's alive,' said Beth. 'But that's about all you can say.'

'What about the others?'

'We couldn't find Brad and Micky,' said Rose, 'but Lee did. They were running riot, he said, but he got them back somehow. Geoff's taken them all away now and The Sea Chest's closed. But some of the windows have been smashed. The story's got out about Sarah being behind the child trafficking racket.'

Will looked at John, but the vicar shook his head.

'I didn't put it around,' he said.

'Then how did it—'

'Everyone's suddenly speaking,' said John. 'Before Sarah's arrest, I gather Robbo and Lem were denying everything. But since her arrest, and Davy's death, they've all started talking. To reduce their sentences, I suppose. And it's not just Robbo and Lem who've been talking. From what I've heard, a couple of the balaclava thugs who Lem hired knew a bit more about what was going on than was originally supposed. So one way or another the story's got out.'

'And Havensmouth is an angry place,' said Rose.

John looked at her.

'More of a . . . hurt place, I think I'd say.'

Will looked over the beach again: the beautiful empty beach.

'It's still a dangerous place right now,' said Rose.

There was a long, heavy silence. Not even the surf could break it. Beth spoke.

'So what are you going to do?'

Will went on staring over the sand. He knew what this question meant. And who it was for. Mum answered.

'We're still planning to leave Havensmouth.'

'I can understand that,' said Rose.

'Especially after what's happened,' said Dad. 'Not just to Will but . . . all this anger and breaking windows. And . . . I mean . . . Will's not been . . . '

'Popular,' said Will.

He looked round at them again. Dad shrugged.

'Well, you haven't been. That's the blunt truth. And a new start somewhere else . . . '

Another silence. Will saw Beth watching him. He reached out and took her hand. Mum spoke.

'It's only because of the bad feeling towards Will. Not because we want to leave you all. You've been so kind and supportive. But we've got to think of Will and his safety.'

'And yet,' said John Shepherd, 'I think you might find a change in Havensmouth after today. It may take time and I can't answer for other people obviously, can't predict what they'll do, but . . . I think you might find a little more understanding towards Will. He did after all pick up that something was wrong in Havensmouth, and he helped to find out what it was, and nearly lost his life in the process.'

John turned to Will.

'You might still have a few problems getting people to like you as much as we all do, but I think you've earned some respect in Havensmouth.'

Will looked down, and yet again found an image of the boy in his mind.

'What about Muck?' he said. 'Has he earned people's respect too?'

He felt Beth squeeze his hand.

'You think about him a lot, don't you?' she said.

'Yes, I do.'

Rose spoke.

'I heard that the police have been trying really hard to get the boy to speak. They've used lots of different interpreters to try and find out if he comes from another country. But he won't say a thing. I don't know how they're ever going to find his parents.'

'His parents are dead,' said Will.

The others stared at him.

'How do you know?' said Dad after a moment.

'I just . . . ' Will frowned, the boy's face still clear in his mind. 'I just . . . see it in his eyes. I don't know where he's come from. Somewhere abroad. All the children on the boat . . . ' He stopped, peering again into Muck's eyes. 'All seven of them came from the same village. Muck and his sister, they . . . they saw their parents killed. And the people who did it took them away, and the other five, and . . . '

He stopped again.

'You don't believe me,' he said.

Mum leaned forward.

'Maybe we do this time,' she said.

The phone rang.

'I'll get it,' said Dad, and he disappeared.

Will stood up and turned towards the beach again. Still the golden sand, still the deserted shore. He narrowed his eyes. John was wrong about Havensmouth. The town wasn't hurt. It was in shock. He heard Rose speak.

'I suppose if the police can't trace Muck's family, then they'll have to find a foster home for him somewhere.'

'No!'

Will whirled round, glaring.

'Will,' said Mum. 'Easy.'

'No!'

He went on scowling at them, unable to stop. He could feel his body starting to tense, and the shiver he knew so well running up along his skin. The boy's eyes were now peering straight into his. He felt Beth stand up, put her arms round him.

'Will,' she said. 'It's OK.'

He held on to her.

'He must live with us,' he murmured.

'Who?' said Mum.

'Muck. He must live with us. You, me, and Dad.'

'I'm not sure the authorities will allow that, Will,' said Mum. 'Even if we wanted to.'

'But Muck wants to.' Will pulled Beth closer. 'And he won't cope anywhere else.'

'How do you know?' whispered Beth.

'Because he's like me.'

He heard the sound of Dad returning. He let go of Beth and turned to the door.

'It's about Muck, isn't it?' he said.

'How did you know?' said Dad.

'They're coming round. That policewoman's bringing him. Because he's got to be here. With me. With us.'

Dad watched him, warily. Will shook his head.

'You've got to make it happen. Whatever it takes.'

He turned back to face the beach.

'I want to go down there.'

'But, Will,' said Dad, 'they're—'

'Bring them to the beach. I've got to be down there. I don't know why.' Will turned quickly to Beth. 'Will you come with me?'

'Of course,' she said.

'Bring them down,' Will said to the others. 'I'll see you.'

And without waiting for an answer, he took Beth's hand and started towards the door.

'Do you want your stick, Will?' called Mum.

He stopped for a moment, looked at Beth.

'No,' she said. 'He won't need it.'

They set off out of the house and down the hill, moving slowly.

'Is it still painful?' said Beth.

'Yes.'

They reached the beach path and made their way down it to where the sand started. Still there was no sign of anyone moving upon it. The dunes and the headland were as empty as before. Beth steadied him as he stepped across the beach. He reached out and put an arm round her waist.

'Does that help you keep your balance?' she said.

'Yes, but that's not why I'm doing it.'

He saw her smile. They walked on across the sand towards the middle of the beach.

'Can we stop here?' he said suddenly.

'Sure. Do you want to sit down?'

'Yeah.'

'Why this particular spot?'

'It's the place where I saw Muck's drawing of his sister.'

They sat down, facing the water. It was a deep blue all the way to the horizon. He ran his eye over it, then turned to scan the town. Figures were moving about the harbour wall, and around some of the streets that were visible from here, but not many. There was something dreamlike about them, and about the place.

'Will it get better?' said Beth. 'Now that the sickness has gone?'

He turned and saw her watching the town too.

'Depends,' he said, looking back.

'On what?'

'On the people who still live here.'

'And will that be you?' she said.

Before he could answer, he saw more figures appear, and these were coming down the beach path: Mum, Dad, Rose, John, and two more: Kate Shaw and Muck. The boy saw him and at once let go of the policewoman's hand and started to race across the sand. Will stood up and struggled towards him.

They met in the middle and Will lifted the boy off the ground. Muck felt so light, so fragile, so strong. The boy was crying and Will could feel his own tears starting. He rested Muck back on the sand and the boy clutched him round the legs.

'It's OK,' said Will, stroking the thick black hair. 'I know you've been looking for me.'

The others joined them and crowded round, but Muck took no notice of them and went on clinging to Will. Kate knelt down and put a hand on Muck's shoulder.

'Is that better now?' she whispered to him.

She looked up at Will.

'He's been—'

'I know,' said Will. 'I know what he's been doing.'

Kate stood up, watching his face.

'Yes,' she said slowly. 'I think you probably do know.'

'We don't,' said Dad.

She looked round at the others.

'Muck's been drawing pictures,' she said. 'He's covered sheets and sheets of paper. He's drawn pictures of the girl—'

'His sister,' said Will.

'OK, well, he's drawn pictures of her, and then he did pictures of those shadowy faces, and pictures of Crow, and a few of me, and Joanna Griffiths, and a funny one of DI Cutler. But that was all on the first day. Since then, everything's changed. He's now taken to—'

'Drawing on the walls,' said Mum.

'Yes.' Kate frowned. 'And it's only one picture now.'

All faces turned to Will.

'I know,' he said. 'He's been drawing me.'

'And he's been in a terrible state,' said Kate.

'I know that too.'

From the direction of the harbour came the sound of an engine. Will stared towards it and a few moments later saw the bow of a fishing boat nudging its way out into the sea.

'*Spindrift,*' he said.

'Dad wants to get back to work,' said Beth.

He could see Stu Palmer in the wheelhouse, and three figures down in the waist. Andy and Lee were easy to recognize but the third was harder to make out. Yet he seemed familiar.

'It's Jack,' said Beth.

Will went on staring at the figure.

'Dad thinks it's time he did a day's work,' said Beth.

'I'll second that,' said Rose.

'And he's short of crew anyway now.'

Spindrift had now cleared the harbour mouth and was heading down parallel to the beach in the direction of Breeze Point. Will glanced down at Muck, still clinging to his legs, and reached down to stroke the boy's head again.

'Will?' said Dad.

Will looked up and saw his father watching intently.

'Your call, Will,' he said.

'Your call,' said Mum.

He stared at them.

'About . . . '

'Yes,' said Dad. 'About where we live. About . . . all this.'

Mum reached down and rested a hand on Muck's shoulder.

'All this,' she murmured.

'If you want it,' said Dad, 'and if it's possible, we'll make it happen.'

Will looked down again. Muck was clinging to him more tightly than ever. He glanced up at Kate. She answered his question before he could speak.

'I'll make enquiries. You'll certainly have my support. But right now, I guess your parents are right. It's your call.'

He knelt down and gently prised the boy's hands from him, then took one of those hands in his and straightened up. With his other hand, he took one of Beth's. Then, with Muck on his left and Beth on his right, he stepped from the group and headed for the water.

Strange, he thought, how different their hands felt. Muck's was cool and frail, Beth's was warm and strong. Yet both spoke to his and took away the need for words. They reached the water's edge and stopped there, just above the line of the surf, all three gazing out.

Ahead of them *Spindrift* was ploughing on towards the point. Stu Palmer raised a hand from inside the wheelhouse. Will felt Beth raise her free hand to wave back. She spoke at last.

'If leaving's best, then you must go.'

He stared over the sea. No trace of the darkness lingered there now, though the eerie quiet still hovered over the town. Only the engine of *Spindrift* broke the silence. He looked round at Mum and Dad and the others, watching from further up the beach, then down at Muck. The boy's eyes were fixed not on the horizon but on him. He felt Beth squeeze his hand. He squeezed hers back, and turned to the sea again.

'We'll stay,' he said.

© Disney